# DA
# IN THE
# MIRROR

# DARKNESS IN THE MIRROR

ERICA LEWIS

Urban soul

URBAN BOOKS

http://www.urbanbooks.net

This is a work of fiction. Any references or similarities to actual events, real people, living or dead, or to real locales are intended to give the novel a sense of reality. Any similarity in other names, characters, places, and incidents is entirely coincidental.

URBAN SOUL is published by

Urban Books
1199 Straight Path
West Babylon, NY 11704



ISBN-13: 978-1-59983-078-0
ISBN-10: 1-59983-078-7

First Printing: February 2009

10 9 8 7 6 5 4 3 2

Printed in the United States of America

*I dedicate this work and all my other works*
*to my mother with love.*

*And*

*I am ever thankful to God for the gift of words.*

# Acknowledgments

My heartfelt thanks and appreciation to the "real" Robert Lewis Mathis, Licensed Clinical Social Worker/ Certified Imago Relationship Therapist, for his insight and sensitivity.

Also, to Dr. Paul William Miller, M.D., B.Ch., BAO, DMH (Belfast), MRCPsych, EMDR Consultant (Europe), EMDR Facilitator (U.S.A.), for his indulgence and guidance.

I would also like to give a very special THANK-YOU to . . .

My agent, Misherald *Missy* Brown

Rhonda J. Brunner, R.N., B.S.N.
Angelia Crawl
Eric and Patricia Barros
Dianne Hamilton
A. F. Scott
Monica Diggs
Kim Sims
Michelle DeLeon
Mr. Pleas Butts

*Jamaican Translated by Jamaicans.com
(David Shire and Carol Connor)

# PREFACE

*For now we see through a mirror, dimly, but then face to face. Now I know in part; but then shall I know just as I also am known.*

*1 Corinthians 13:12 (NKJ)*

Ondie Reid couldn't recall where she'd heard that before, but it was a mantra that replayed itself over and over in her head. She'd spent her entire life looking for some sign of light at the end of a long dark tunnel that was just beyond her reach.

Seemingly doomed to perpetuate wrong turns, she found her choice was either to buckle under the insanity or be strengthened by it. In her pursuit for *ordinary*, the lines were often blurred and the consequences were damaging, but you've got to know the whole story.

# 1

The trek up to North Georgia was beautiful this time of year, but there was an ominous darkness just beyond the mountains that Ruth Reid had been reluctant to share with her husband. Fear of ridicule caused the comely twenty-five-year old, honey-skinned woman to hide her family infamy away from prying eyes for most of her life. A little over an hour's drive away from the city of Atlanta, just outside Bartow County, hidden away by majestic oak trees, was the place that held her secret captive.

"Good afternoon, Ms. Reid."

"How is she today?"

"Just gettin' over a cold, but other than that she's fine."

It was Tuesday. Ruth had a standing appointment on Tuesdays. It was the one day of the week she could slip away for a time and not be missed. She walked up the fluorescently lit corridor and knocked at the door. There was no response; she didn't expect there to be. She opened the door slowly and stepped inside.

"Hi, Mama, how are you feeling today?"

The fifty-four-year-old woman with premature silver-gray hair appeared older and more fragile because of the ravages of arthritis. She stared blankly at the television. It was mostly on for noise. In the three years Naomi Wheeler had come to this place, after a nine-year confinement in an institution in South Carolina, she hardly uttered a word.

Ruth was devastated when her father, John D., had her mother committed to keep her from hurting herself or anyone else. Her sickness had been difficult for the whole family, especially him. They all came to realize it was for the best. Ruth had not been allowed to see her mother until she was eighteen years old. When she finally saw her, she realized that this was not the woman she remembered. It was as if her brain and the memory of her family had been wiped away. Electroshock therapy, the doctors called it; torture was a more appropriate word. The treatment her mother received was grossly negligible. Ruth recalled the asylum being a cold almost decaying place with half-cleaned windows and dingy floors. She'd awakened many nights remembering the wailing and moaning that seemed lodged within the walls when she visited her mother, who just sat there rocking back and forth, removed from it all—much like she was now. Naomi Wheeler's beauty had long faded from Ruth's memory; all that remained were the cobwebs and ghosts of the past.

John D. died in the spring of 1979 from injuries he had sustained in an explosion at the paper mill where he worked. Ruth and her older brother, Frank, received a sizable settlement from an insurance policy after it was proven that the company had violated safety codes that put its workers in jeopardy.

Shortly after her father's death, Ruth had her mother moved to the more agreeable surroundings of the Blue Mountain Sanitarium. (She had come to Atlanta just a year prior to pursue a degree in nursing.) But not even a new facility seemed to awaken Naomi. Frank had visited his mother only a few times since her transfer, and primarily at holidays, or on her birthday. "It doesn't matter," he told Ruth. "It's not as if she knows I'm here." Frank couldn't take seeing his mother in that state. No one really knew if she was cognizant of them or not, but Ruth liked to think so. But it was their shame that swore them to secrecy.

Whenever Ruth visited she always carried on a conversation as if her mother would someday talk back. She believed that similar to some coma patients, her mother was in there somewhere listening to every word she said.

"Mama, you should see Ondie. She's getting so big. Kenny just loves her. We've started adoption proceedings. He's such a good man; a good husband, like Daddy. I told you he worked for the post office, right? Now that I'm finished with nursing school we're starting to look at houses. I've already seen the one I want. Can you believe it, Mama? I'm going to have my own house. And it's going to be a lot better than that shack we had in Greenville." Ruth paused as if she'd said something offensive. "Listen to me going on. We had a nice house, Mama. And you did a really good job keeping it up; turns out, though, that the land is worth a lot more than the house ever was. Frank wants to build on it. I told him he can have the land, I don't want it. My life is here now with Kenny and Ondie."

Ruth sat brushing the woman's silky gray hair wishing she'd respond in some way, grunt, smile, or even blink an acknowledgment, but there was nothing. Her mother just sat there childlike—indifferent. When Ruth finished braiding the woman's hair she offered her a mirror.

"See, Mama, look how pretty you are."

The woman traced her face with her fingers, but her eyes were still empty. They had been so for twelve years, and that didn't seem likely to change.

Ruth stayed with her mother through dinner. Despite her encouragement to try something else, candied yams and meat loaf were all the woman would eat. When *Wheel of Fortune* flashed across the television screen, Ruth thought there was a gleam of recognition in her eyes, but she was mistaken. After cleaning her up and helping her into bed, Ruth glanced at her watch and knew that it was past time for her to leave.

"I've got to go now, Mama. I need to pick Ondie up from the sitter and get Kenny's dinner started."

Ruth kissed her mother's cheek and left the room.

The woman's brittle hand shook as she reached over to the nightstand and picked up the picture of her daughter and her family. She ran her fingers over it, her eyes misted, and she whispered, "John D."

It was nearly nine thirty when Ruth pulled up outside her apartment with her daughter, Ondie. The lights inside the apartment were on and she knew that her husband was home. This was the night that he usually worked late. Afterward he could be counted on to go have a couple of beers with his pals, and when he got home she would have dinner waiting, but not this night.

"Hey, baby." She kissed the man when she entered and went to put Ondie in her crib. He was watching a basketball game, which she took as a sign that he wasn't paying her much attention.

"You hungry? I can fix you something to eat."

"I got some chicken on my way in. I wanted to surprise you and give you the night off from cookin'."

"Thank you, that was nice."

Ruth sat in the man's lap, being careful not to block his view.

"Where have you been? I called Maxine and she said that you hadn't come to pick Ondie up yet. That was over an hour ago."

"I'm sorry. I had some errands to run. Time just got away from me."

He nudged her off his lap and went to the kitchen for a beer. Kenny Reid was Ruth's second husband. Her first marriage, to the inscrutable Lee Earl Samuels, ended in annulment. The brawny young man presented himself well enough for an impressionable twenty-year-old, who'd just arrived in Atlanta, to be attracted to. However, Lee Earl was an unscrupulous con, and couldn't steer clear of a fast buck. In the summer of 1980, after being convicted of killing a man over a bad debt, he became a permanent resident of the South Carolina penal system. Ruth met Kenny the following spring.

Kenny was nothing like Lee Earl. He put you in

the mind of a young virile Harry Belafonte. Ruth sometimes fancied herself the enigmatic Carmen Jones to his Joe.

He leaned against the wall in the living room and took a swig of beer. "Let me ask you somethin', Ruthie. What's goin' on?"

"I don't know what you're talking about."

"What errands did you have to run?"

"I—uh . . . I . . ."

"Cat got your tongue? Can't think up a lie fast enough?"

Ruth had skirted quite a few close calls as they related to keeping her mother's existence hidden, but it was exhausting lying to cover up surreptitious phone calls to the sanitarium, spending a little more time at the "beauty salon" on Saturdays than needed. She'd been with this man for two years. He was the only one she'd gotten close to before or after her previous relationship ended. Surely she could unburden herself now, especially in light of another secret she was harboring. She went to her room, came back out with a small framed picture, and handed it to him.

Kenny shrugged. "This is your mother and father. Is this supposed to mean somethin'?"

"Can you sit down, please?"

Kenny's eyes registered confusion; he hesitated a few seconds before complying.

Ruth sat beside him. "My father died four years ago. I told you my mother was dead, but she's not. She's . . . she's in a mental institution here in Georgia."

"What?"

"My father had her committed when I was thirteen years old. She was . . . she is schizophrenic."

"Ruthie."

"There's a slight chance that Ondie could develop her condition."

Kenny fell back in his seat, trying to digest what he'd been told. Several minutes passed before he spoke again. "What about you?"

"I'm fine. This is a disorder that seems to show up in your teens, and I don't have any of the traits."

"So you've been visitin' your mother in a sanitarium?"

"Yes, I had her moved here after my father died. I've been going twice a week, but the sad thing is I don't think she knows I'm there. She just sits like she's in a trance and doesn't speak. Both Frank and I agreed not to tell anyone."

"But why?"

"We used to make up stories about our mother because we didn't want anybody to know the truth. We didn't know what was wrong with her then, and as bad as it sounds we were too embarrassed. Our friends couldn't come over because of how my mother might be feeling or acting on any given day. The slightest thing would set her off. If she thought you were talking about her behind her back, or out to get her, she could be violent."

"Was she ever that way with you?"

"Once, when I was ten, a couple of my cousins came over for a sleepover. We were in my room laughing about boys or something and she yelled at us to shut up. She kept to herself a lot. She was always in her room. Anyway, we started whispering and giggling like silly little girls tend to do. The next thing I knew my mother had come into the room with one of my father's leather belts. She started beating us and screaming that we were evil children and that we were going to hell. My father came out of nowhere and pulled her off of us and locked her in her room. His sister never let my cousins come over again after that."

Ruth started to tear up and Kenny swept her up in his arms.

"Oh, baby, I'm so sorry."

"She wasn't always like that. I remember how much fun she used to be. She sang a lot. Frank and I used to laugh all the time—Daddy, too. She taught me how cook and sew when I was very young. I can't pinpoint when things started to change. It was like she went to bed one night and woke up a different person. I couldn't let her stay in that place in South Carolina. No matter what she did she's still my mother."

Ruth wiped her eyes and went to check to make sure that Ondie was still asleep. When she came back into the living room, Kenny had turned off the television and was sitting quietly staring at the floor. Ruth went to him and caressed his face. He pulled her back down onto his lap.

"Kenny, are you all right?"

"Yeah, I'm fine. I didn't have to live with what you went through. I don't know how you did it."

"I did it because I had to. I thought it would be easier just to keep up the pretense that she was dead. I should have told you the truth a long time ago, but I'm glad you know now."

He laid his head on her chest. "You're a strong

woman, Ruthie, but you can't bear everybody's burden by yourself."

"I need to tell you something else and I don't know how you're going to feel about it."

He rose and looked at her.

"I found out yesterday that I'm pregnant."

Kenny's expression was a mixture of excitement and shock. "Oh my God."

He embraced her again and they kissed.

"You're okay with this?"

"Why wouldn't I be?"

"Because of what I just told you about my mother."

"I love you, and I want to take care of my family. Whatever we have to face, we'll do it together."

Two weeks later Kenny and Ruth had a Realtor busy securing their dream house in a cozy cul-de-sac in the Atlanta suburb of Sandy Springs. It was a thirty-five-hundred-square-foot, two-story, three-bedroom, brick Colonial, with a full-service kitchen and dining room and a good-sized backyard for all the entertaining that the Reids planned to do.

Although she never wanted Kenny to go with her, Ruth was now free to visit her mother as often, and for as long as, she wanted. In her second trimester Ruth and her brother, Frank, drove up to Blue Mountain to have breakfast with their mother for her fifty-fifth birthday. Frank had forgotten that he'd promised Ruth he would go. He tried to get out of it by telling her he'd made plans to spend the day with his fiancée.

"Frank, you hardly see her as it is. You could at least come for a couple of hours."

"Ruth Anne, she ain't gon' know the difference. I may as well be a plant in the room."

"Come on, brother. Do this for me."

Frank was a tough nut to crack when it came to doing things he didn't want to do, but when it came to Ruth, most of their lives he'd let her have her way. Still, he sulked all the way up to the sanitarium. "I don't know why you went to all this trouble to buy cake and balloons."

"I just want to make it nice for her, that's all."

The woman at the front desk greeted them when they entered and pressed a buzzer releasing a door that opened to the main part of the hospital. Ruth and Frank were met by a dour floor nurse as they walked toward their mother's room. Ruth looked over the woman's shoulder to see the stripped bed. "Where's my mother?" came out of her mouth simultaneous to the awareness that there wasn't a need to ask.

"I'm sorry, Ms. Reid. We tried to contact you, but your husband said you were already on your way. Miss Naomi passed away in the night."

Ruth closed her eyes and wobbled. She absently let go of the balloon bouquet she held, and they floated to the ceiling. Frank reached out to steady her, while trying to balance the cake. The nurse assisted by freeing his hands up to care for his sister. He then eased Ruth down onto a bench in the hallway.

"Are you all right, Ms. Reid?"

"Just a little light-headed."

The nurse set the cake down beside her and dashed off for a glass of water.

"What happened?" Ruth asked, sipping slowly.

The nurse glanced at Frank, then back to Ruth. "She had a stroke."

The warm summer day suddenly felt bleak. Ruth was clearly more affected by Naomi's death than her brother was. How much like his father he could be at times like this. Frank was three years older than Ruth, and had always seemed isolated by his mother's illness. He had watched her deteriorate just like the rest of the family, but somewhere inside him he disconnected himself, much like one might do if one had become desensitized to death and sorrow. The tall, lean twenty-eight-year-old offered his sister a shoulder to lean on like he did when they were growing up and observed their mother's increasing outbursts firsthand, but his tears, like Naomi's life, had dried up years ago.

"We need to make arrangements," Ruth said. "I have to go to Greenville. Frank, will you go with me?"

Frank assured her that he would be by her side through the entire ordeal. He was glad that it was coming to its final end.

"Do you remember when Mama used to make us go to church?" Frank's voice was hushed—almost reverent. "I prayed that God would either cure her or take her. It took a while, but it looks like he finally answered."

"Frank."

"I'm sorry, Ruth Anne, that's how I feel."

With the past behind them, there was much to look to the future for. Frank was engaged to be married to Maxine, a woman he'd been dating for almost a year.

She already had two children: a six-year-old girl and a three-year-old boy. Frank adored her children, and unlike Ruth, he made sure that the family's scourge would not be passed on through his lineage, by having a vasectomy.

Ruth, on the other hand, wanted her own. Selfish or not, she would not deprive herself of the joy of motherhood. She prayed that her children would never know such pain. However, if Ondie, or the child she now carried, was to be plagued with this disorder she hoped to be strong enough to bear the burden with them.

# 2

Twelve years passed since the birth of Ruth's second daughter, Serita. Ondie loved having a little sister to play with, but the onset of puberty began to ruffle the fabric of their seemingly close relationship.

Adolescent girls love to play dress-up; Serita Reid was no exception. She preened in front of the mirror of the bathroom she shared with her sister in her parents' Sandy Springs home. Applying a coat of Ruth's favorite shade of lipstick, she smacked her lips together as she'd seen her mother do many times before. She followed by applying eyeliner, to her big doe eyes. The sting of residue caused her to drop the tube of eyeliner, and the applicator splattered on the silky sheer material of the vibrant blue dress she wore.

"Uh-oh!"

She grabbed a towel from the rack and wet it. Frantically, she rubbed it over the stain, but was only making it worse. The moisture from the towel seeped through the dress and wet her T-shirt. Serita heard Ondie bounding up the stairs and panicked. She closed the bathroom door and scurried out of the dress.

"Serita, hurry up. I have to go."

"Can you use the one downstairs?"

"Daddy's in there. C'mon!"

"Uh, okay. I'll be out in a minute." Serita searched for a place to hide the damaged garment. She threw open the shower curtain, but thought better of it.

"Serita!"

"I'm comin'."

With no other choice, Serita opened the hamper and buried it, along with the sopping towel, under a pile of dirty linen; she hadn't noticed that the sleeve of the dress stuck out as evidence to her crime. She then grabbed her mother's makeup from the counter, stuffed it into the pockets of the blue jean shorts she wore under the dress, and opened the door.

"It's about time," Ondie said, sneering. The gangling teenager rushed past her sister, pushed her aside, and slammed the door.

Serita dashed into Ruth's bedroom and returned the makeup to her bureau. As she took off for the stairs, she heard her sister's scream. She froze and shrank back.

The bathroom door opened and Ondie flew out holding the dress in her hand. "What did you do?"

"I—I just wanted to try it on. I'm sorry. I wasn't trying to mess it up."

"It's ruined," Ondie shrieked. "It's ruined!" *She did it on purpose, and you know why. You should teach her a lesson.* Ondie's eyes narrowed and she darted back into the bathroom, removed a pair of scissors from the drawer, and tore into Serita's bedroom. She threw open her sister's closet door, pulled clothes from hangers, and proceeded to cut them up.

"Ondie, stop it! What are you doing?"

"You messed up my dress. I'm gonna show you what it feels like."

Serita grabbed Ondie's arm, and Ondie pushed her back, causing her to tumble to the floor and bump her head on her desk.

"You're crazy. I'm tellin' Daddy," Serita cried.

Ondie spun around wildly. "What did you say?"

"I said I'm tellin'."

Ondie stared at the scissors in her hand and gripped them tighter. She looked at Serita and then back to the scissors and started toward her. Serita shrieked and wedged herself between the bed and her desk.

"What in the hell is going on?" Kenny yelled as he entered the room. Quickly surveying the scene, he grabbed Ondie's arm and wrested the scissors away from her.

Ondie picked up her dress and showed him the violation. "Look what she did!"

"I didn't do it on purpose," Serita defended.

"Yes, you did. I heard them."

"You heard who?" Kenny asked warily.

"She shouldn't have been in my dress at all. She shouldn't have been in my room."

Serita started crying and pulled herself out of hiding. Kenny sat down on the bed and lifted her up into his lap to comfort her. "Look at your face. You been in your mother's room again, haven't you?"

Serita nodded sheepishly.

"What have we told you about that?"

Ondie reached out and viciously yanked one of Serita's thick pigtails.

"Ondie, let her go!" Kenny smacked her wrist and she released her hold. "Go to your room."

"But, Daddy!"

"Go on. Right now!"

Ondie's soft russet curls fell into her face and she teared up. "You can't tell me what to do."

Kenny set Serita down and stood up. His imposing six-foot frame towered over the insolent teenager, and she ran up the hall to her bedroom and slammed the door.

Kenny tried never to purposely show any difference in the way he treated either of his daughters. He did everything he could to show Ondie as much love and attention as he did Serita. It didn't matter that she was adopted, but her rebellious age was making it more difficult to be impartial.

When Ruth came in and settled from work, he informed her of the incident.

"She said 'they' told her. I don't even wanna think about what might have happened if I didn't come in and take those scissors away from her when I did."

Ruth felt in her heart what had become too obvious to ignore. Two weeks before, Ondie had experienced a delusion that caused her to believe that Serita had locked her into the bathroom. She screamed bloody murder until Kenny talked her out. He showed her that the door could only be locked from the inside. But there was no placating her, even given the fact that Serita had spent the night with a friend up the street. Ruth knew something had to be done. Ondie's behavior couldn't be dismissed as simple teenage angst.

"What can I do?" Kenny asked.

"Nothing. I'll take care of it."

"Ruthie, Ondie is my responsibility, too. I care what happens to her. I'm not just a figurehead. I'm her father. I want to help."

"You don't understand what's going on."

"Then clue me in. This is what you told me about, isn't it? The same thing that happened with your mother."

"Yes," Ruth cried.

"Then, baby, I need to be a part of it. You don't have to handle this on your own."

In spite of Kenny's appeal, Ruth felt that she was exclusively responsible for Ondie. In her zeal to ensure that Ondie would not bear the same doom as her mother, she had unintentionally created a wall that slowly began to undermine Kenny's role as husband and father.

Ruth needed to find a doctor for Ondie that she not only trusted, but one that Ondie could rely on. The disruptions that were triggered by the most benign offenses not only scared those around her, but they also frightened Ondie. Ruth tried to explain the abnormality in her brain that consumed her mother's life, and appeared to be taking over her daughter's. A doctor at the hospital where Ruth worked recommended a therapist he knew who had made great strides in adolescent behavioral disorders. Ondie took to him instantly.

Dr. Lewis Mathis had an easy, nonthreatening

manner. He didn't talk down to her and treat her as if she was an idiot who couldn't grasp what might be happening to her. He spoke at length with Ruth about her family's history, and the incidents that led her to believe that Ondie might be suffering the same psychosis.

He spent a good deal of time talking with Ondie about her interests, her hobbies, if she liked any boy in particular. They bonded over basketball and her admission that she had a crush on Michael Jordan.

Her demeanor shifted when the conversation went from basketball to her relationship with Serita. She wouldn't look directly at the doctor. She squirmed in her chair and furiously rubbed her temple.

"Tell me about your sister."

Ondie sat still and tears streamed down her face. "She hates me."

"Why would you think she hates you?"

"She's jealous of me. She always has been."

"Your mother tells me that you and your sister were once very close. What would make you think she hates you?"

"She changed."

"*She* changed?"

Ondie cut her eyes toward the doctor. "Yes."

"Do you hate her?"

"She turned my father against me."

"Kenneth?"

"Yes."

It took a few sessions for Dr. Mathis's evaluation to identify Ondie's symptoms as schizoaffective disorder. He explained to both her and Ruth that with medication and the proper treatment her condition was treatable, and as long as she remained compliant, there was no reason to believe that she wouldn't be able to function well.

Ondie's temperament was managed by a combination of pharmaceuticals, but their adverse effects caused Ruth to spend more time caring for her than she did tending to anything else in her life, especially her husband.

"Kenny, I'm sorry I didn't have time to cook dinner. I had to leave work early and go pick Ondie up from school. She had another episode."

"Ruthie, how long is this gonna go on? I thought you said she was doing better."

"I thought she was, but the meds make her nauseated, so she stops taking them, and as soon as she does she has a flare-up."

"You can't keep up with this pace."

"What do you suggest I do, Kenny? Lock her away? I won't do that. She's my daughter."

"She's my daughter, too!"

"I know. I just need to do this my way. Can't you understand? We just need to find medication that will work without making her sick so she can sleep through the night."

"What about you, baby? Look at yourself. This is wearing you out."

"Ondie needs me right now."

"What about Serita? What about me?"

"It's not going to be this way forever. Dr. Mathis says as soon as her system adjusts she's going to be fine, you'll see."

The process was slow and initially ineffective.

Ondie's illness was not only affecting her, but it had begun to change the dynamic of the entire family.

"Hey, it's me. How are the girls? Yeah, I'm here. Dad looks good, but I think I'm just gonna stay up here overnight, so you don't need to wait up. I'll see you tomorrow."

Driving to Macon, Georgia, was an effortless and, at the same time, complicated ruse. Six months earlier Kenneth Reid Sr., who had a two-pack-a-day cigarette habit over a twenty-year span, was diagnosed with emphysema, but he wasn't the sole reason for Kenny's continued visits. On one of his trips he'd run into a woman he'd known before he met Ruth; a woman that he'd been intimate with. This same woman offered him an ear, a shoulder, and a bed.

The voluptuous Vernice Jenkins was only too happy to accommodate Kenny's needs. There was a time she knew exactly what it took to please him; she hadn't lost her touch. Being with her, there were no barriers, no drama. A man needed to be made to feel like a man, not like he was in the way, or had nothing to contribute. This was the way he felt, and she knew how to pacify him.

Reid Sr.'s death brought an end to his son's illicit assignations. There was no longer a reason for him to go back to Macon. Despite his justification, Kenny recognized that what he'd done was wrong. His repentance caused him to confess. Ruth accepted her part in his betrayal, but the fact that a child had been sired because of the adultery was rewarded with divorce.

# 3

It was an unusually chilly day for mid-April. Heavy dark clouds blanketed the Atlanta skyline accompanied by a cold, steady rain. Ondie Reid stood staring out the window at the traffic tie-up on the interstate overpass off in the distance. Another careless driver. Another senseless accident. That was pretty much how she felt about her life most days: careless and senseless. All she wanted in the world was to live a normal life, free of constant chaos. The confusion was arduous. Why did she still have to keep coming here? Why couldn't she be happy without dependency on exterior stimuli? Why couldn't she be like everyone else?

Ondie caressed her cheek and traced her delicate features. Despite her sometimes crippling malaise, she'd been able to accomplish quite a bit over the years. Perhaps her daughter, Maya, was her greatest achievement, but even she wasn't enough.

The questions that kept asking themselves went unanswered, as the connection to a man that knew her just about as well as anyone continued.

"You've been here nearly ten minutes already and we haven't really talked about anything."

Ondie saw the man's reflection in the glass as he sat there examining her. She could read the expression in his eyes. Most men looked at her the same way, despite the turmoil in her head. Her curvaceous five-foot-nine-inch Nubian frame could always mask the woman few bothered to get to know. Even though this man was a skilled and trained clinician, he was still a full-blooded African-American man. Capable of not only having but acting on carnal desires if he allowed himself to traverse those waters. Her involvement with him was one of the longest and most stable of those she'd had with any other man, with the exception of her father.

There had been occasions when Ondie tested the limits of the invisible boundaries that existed. She'd called him Lewis, instead of Dr. Mathis, and even dared to question his sexuality. He frowned on her overtures and hid safely behind a wall of ethics. That naturally made him all the more intriguing. His tone and his easy manner always allowed her to speak freely with him. In his presence she felt what she had to say mattered; never mind that she was paying him to listen. His concern was obvious. He'd been with her almost from the very beginning, helping her navigate through the shadows. Ondie respected the limits, and made a conscious decision to keep their association strictly professional; anything less could spell disaster.

She anxiously toyed with the open collar of her silk blouse and rubbed her hands together. "I'm a little cold."

"Do you want me to adjust the temperature?"

"No. I'll be okay in a minute. I appreciate you seeing me on such short notice."

"I'm glad I had a cancelation. I assume there is something going on that you needed to talk about. How are you doing with the new meds?"

Ondie sighed and turned away from the window. She combed her fingers through her mop of Afrocentric curls and sat down on the sofa facing him. "They make me sicker than the others."

"Your body just needs time to adjust."

"The cannabis was better."

The doctor chuckled. "I've told you that there is no adequate scientific study to substantiate its long-term benefits."

"To hell with that, I'd settle for the here and now. Give me a joint and a glass of merlot and we got a party."

"You haven't been drinking, have you?"

"Not unless you count thinking about it."

"You are sticking to the prescribed dosage, right?"

"And suffering with the side effects."

"Would you rather hear the voices?"

"I got news for you, Doc. I still hear the voices despite your tasty cocktail of mood stabilizers and antidepressants."

Dr. Mathis crossed his legs, scratched his bald pate, and pulled at the hairs of his salt-and-pepper beard in a Sigmund Freud, *I see* sort of way. "Have you had any other episodes?"

"I couldn't get out of bed yesterday. I didn't go to work. I was terrified."

"What were you afraid of?"

"Fire."

"Like when you were in college?"

Ondie scanned the contemporarily decorated office trying to find something to focus on. Her eyes rested on a multicolored clown fish appearing to be listening in from its large walled-in aquarium across the room. She tugged nervously at the pillow she held on to for security. "Yeah, something like that. I was remembering waking up screaming for my roommates to get out. I could smell it then. I smelled it last night in my dreams. Only there was no fire, but I can still hear them laughing at me."

The second hand on the clock on the wall ticked loudly, echoing through the room as her voice trailed.

Ondie had nearly failed her first attempt at emancipation. Although she wanted to attend a college out of state, she settled on Spelman College, where she allowed herself the liberty of choice. She met and roomed with two other girls in an apartment near the campus, but in her angst she soon sought Dr. Mathis's counsel.

"Was Maya in the house?"

Ondie shook her head. "She's with her father this week."

"So your arrangement with Dexter is working for you?"

The mention of her ex's name caused her face to light up and brought a smile to her lips.

"Is there a new development between the two of you?"

"Maya turned four last week. Dexter came over and we had birthday cake and ice cream together. It was really nice. We were like a family. I know he still cares about me."

"Of course he cares about you, Ondie."

"I think he wants to get back together."

Dr. Mathis's brow furrowed. He uncrossed his legs and leaned forward. "Has he expressly told you that, or is this something you're hoping will happen?"

Ondie stood up and moved back to the window. Several seconds passed before she spoke again. "The rain stopped."

"Ondie."

"What?"

"You didn't answer the question."

"It's a stupid question."

"Do you remember last Thanksgiving when you told me that Dexter had been spending more time with you and Maya?"

"Yes, of course I do."

"Do you remember how you felt when you discovered you misinterpreted his intentions?"

"This is different."

"How so?"

"He sees how much I've changed."

"Ondie, remember how you felt when Dexter confessed that he was afraid that you would hurt Maya."

Ondie's eyes welled with tears at the recollection. "I would never hurt her. In his heart he knew that. He was just being an ass."

"He was looking out for Maya's well-being."

"He loves her."

"Yes, he does."

"He could learn to love me again, too."

"Ondie."

"You think I'm being silly, don't you?"

"I think you're being human. You're lonely. Dexter is familiar."

"So, what do you think I should do?"

"Have you thought any more about what we discussed last time?"

"I'm too old to play the dating game."

"You're only twenty-six."

"I'm twenty-seven."

"Well, in that case maybe we should be looking at retirement homes."

"Sarcasm. I like it."

"Look, Ondie, all I'm saying is you're an attractive woman. You've already proven that there's no reason you can't thrive and live your life as normally as anyone else."

"Right. And as soon as I start to take interest in another man and he finds out about my little problem he'll run, too."

"Like Dexter?"

Ondie turned to face him and leaned against the window. "He said he would do any- and everything to support Maya, but he couldn't deal with my issues. But that was five years ago. We're both different now."

"Do you love him?"

"I almost married him. If it wasn't for my mother we'd be together today."

"You can't know that for sure."

"I didn't get the chance to find out, either."

"We've talked about this before. Do you still blame Ruth for Dexter's decision?"

"If she hadn't told him . . ."

"He would eventually have seen for himself."

Ondie was silent as the truth of the doctor's statements sliced through her delusions. "Maybe I just love the idea of him. I just want someone to come home to that I can have a grown-up conversation with. A man that can hold me in bed at night and make me feel like I'm not so lost."

"That's a perfectly natural desire. Ondie, if Dexter is not the one for you, you can't be afraid to open yourself up to the man that will be."

"I suppose I could always go online. Everyone is anonymous and you can be whoever you need to be."

"Yes, but if you find someone you like, eventually the pretense has to stop; unless you intend to have no more between you than a keyboard."

"Well, it is hard enough," she laughed.

"Ondie."

"Sorry, just keepin' it real."

Ondie's sessions with Dr. Mathis always seemed to be able to lift the fog and allow her to see situations more clearly. As she drove away from the midtown clinic and headed home, she contemplated his advice and wondered if she could afford the luxury of optimism.

It was after noon. She quickly accelerated into a steady stream of cars jockeying for position on the five-lane highway. She passed the Equitable Building where she'd been working as an accountant for the past three and a half years. Her attendance was becoming problematic, but she didn't feel compelled to disclose her condition to her supervisor. Thank God for HIPAA laws that protected medical privacy. She kept a safe distance from most of the others in the office in an effort to keep her business private, but that still didn't stop the speculation and gossip that is rampant among corporate cubical monkeys.

Ondie's cell phone rang and she reached over to fish it from her purse, being careful to keep one eye on the road.

"Hello."

"Why aren't you at work? Are you okay?"

"Hello to you, too, Mama. And yes, I'm fine. I just had some things I needed to do today."

"Something's wrong. I can hear it in your voice."

"Then you need to get your supersonic-mother hearing checked out. Nothing is wrong."

"Where are you?"

"I'm on 75, just about to get off the exit."

"Can you stop by?"

"Mama, I really—"

"You're not working. You don't have Maya. What else do you have to do?"

Ondie continued on without responding. The assumption that she had nothing else to do with her day off was unnerving.

"Ondie?"

"All right, I'll come by."

She was deliberate with the information she dispensed to her overprotective mother. She'd come a long way in therapy just to be able to share anything with Ruth again. It took a great deal of time and effort for her to understand, or even forgive her alleged betrayal. If she'd told her about reliving the incident in the dorm room at college, or having an unscheduled visit with Dr. Mathis, the hovering would have begun immediately. Instead, Ondie felt it best not to bring it up for now.

She pulled into the cul-de-sac of the Sandy Springs subdivision, just as a sporty black Honda Civic barreled up behind her blasting hip-hop at a decibel that was loud enough to be heard all the way to Kennesaw Mountain.

"Oh Lord." Ondie glanced up into the rearview mirror and simultaneously pushed open her door. The passage of time and therapy helped Ondie to realize that Serita was not the foe she once thought her to be, but the adversarial voices still lingered.

The other woman jumped out of her car and grabbed a large bag from the backseat.

"Serita, when did you get back?"

"Two o'clock this morning."

"So, how was it?"

"All I needed was a sexy-ass man and the mile-high club could've inducted another member."

"What about that pilot you were so crazy about?"

"Over before it started. You know me, girl, I need to keep my options open."

"Don't let Mama hear you talk like that, or you're going to get the *settle down* speech again."

"I'll settle down someday. But until then a girl's gotta do what a girl's gotta do."

Serita had grown into more of a firebrand than her sister. She stood an inch shorter; she was three years younger, and a shade lighter. Her short-cropped asymmetrical bob cut framed her face and her big brown eyes sparkled when she smiled. Like Ondie she had no trouble getting the attention of most any man, but she didn't share Ondie's disorder, which caused her to be more gregarious. Her personality suited her well as a flight attendant.

"Are you two just gonna stand out there yappin' in this damp weather?"

They both turned to see Ruth standing in the door and continued into the house.

One look at the now forty-nine-year-old woman and it was easy to see the visible beauty that she'd passed on to her daughters. Her even-toned complexion and the soft highlights in her auburn tresses told very little of her hardships. Age embraced her like a dazzling sunset painted across a crimson sky.

"I just fixed some chicken salad. You girls go wash your hands."

"None for me, Mama. I'm on a diet," Serita said.

"You're on a what?" Ruth snapped. "You ain't big as a minute now. A little chicken salad is not going to hurt you."

"It ain't the chicken. It's all that mayonnaise you put in it." Serita sat down on the sofa and fell into Ondie laughing.

"You've never had a problem with my chicken salad before, girl."

"C'mon, Serita," Ondie encouraged as she stood up. "You know you can't argue with Mama's chicken salad."

"Don't you all want to know what I got you from Thailand?" Serita beamed as she opened her bag and proudly handed each of them a gift.

Ruth ripped open her box like a kid at Christmas to find a stunning handcrafted tea set. "Oh, baby this is beautiful." She reached out and pulled Serita into her ample bosom.

Ondie marveled at the handbag she was given, made from a coconut shell. "Does this come with a date with Gilligan or the Skipper?"

Serita sneered. "Ha-ha, very funny."

"How about a mai tai, or a piña colada?"

Serita reached for the bag. "If you don't want it, I'll keep it."

"Girl, I'm just kidding. It's really a cute purse. I just need to go out and buy some bamboo shoes to go with it."

"All right, y'all," Ruth injected. "Enough of that; let's go eat."

"Is Daddy coming over? I got something for him, too."

"Your father went to Macon. I don't know when he'll be back," Ruth said, sneering.

Ondie and Serita gave each other a look. They knew what Macon symbolized and they didn't think talking about it was going to do anybody any good. After washing up, the women adjourned to the kitchen and huddled around the table. This was nice, carrying on with her mother and sister as if she didn't have a care in the world. Many meals, laughs, and tears had been shared around this table. There was something reassuring about returning to it from time to time.

Ruth spread crackers on a plate and sat down to join her girls. "Serita, are you just getting back? You must be exhausted. You want to go up to your room and lie down?"

"We got in really early this morning. I stayed with a friend who flew out with me. She lives closer to the airport, and I was too tired to drive back here."

"Are you sure it was a *she* and not a *he*?" Ondie cracked.

"It was definitely a she. I'm not a lesbian, so there was nothing going on."

"Now, is all that necessary?" Ruth chided. "Nobody said anything about you being a lesbian."

"Well, good, because the only carpet I like is on the floor."

Ruth gasped and Ondie's mouth flew open. Hilarity ensued once the realization of Serita's offhanded remark sank in.

Ruth laughed so hard there were tears in her eyes. She wiped them away and calmed down. "So, how was your trip?"

"Thailand is beautiful, as much of it as I saw. You guys should get one of my buddy passes and go with me the next time."

"I don't know," Ondie responded, wiping her fingers on a napkin. "The year's not even started good and I've already used up a lot of my accrued time at work."

"So, accrue some more. When was the last time you actually went more than a hundred miles outside Georgia? What about you, Mama? Don't you have some vacation time coming?"

"You can save your breath. You know I don't fly standby. All that waiting around to get on an available flight, and I could still get bumped. No, thank you."

Serita continued smothering crackers with chicken salad and stuffing them into her mouth as Ruth and Ondie eyed each other, amused.

"I thought you said you were on a diet." Ondie chuckled.

"I am," Serita responded, chewing at the same time. "But there's only so much lettuce you can eat in a week."

"Slow down, girl," Ruth quipped. "There's more."

They all laughed again as a beeping alarm sounded from Ondie's watch, a sobering reminder that she occupied a space slightly to the left of center.

"Time for my happy pills." Ondie reached into her purse for the meds that were as much a part of her being as her arms or her legs. She caught Ruth's pinched expression and reassured her, "I'm doing okay, Mama."

Serita got up from the table and busied herself in the refrigerator looking for a soda she really didn't need or want, trying to appear unfazed, but knowing all too well the necessity for her sister's medication. "So, where's the little munchkin?"

"You know Dexter took her to Florida to see his family," Ondie replied. "They all were supposed to go to Disney World. That was his birthday present to her."

"Lord, I know that little girl is running him ragged," Ruth added.

Serita lit up. "You know what, Ondie, since Maya is gone this week you and me ought to go out and have some fun. There's this club downtown that I've been dying to get to."

"It's Tuesday night. Who goes out on a Tuesday night?"

"C'mon, sis. We haven't been out together in forever. It'll be fun. We can get all dressed up and get our flirt on."

"I don't know about you, but my flirt is broken."

"Okay, how about we go out Friday night, then?"

Ondie looked into her sister's sheepish brown eyes realizing that surrender was imminent. "Well . . ."

"If you don't go out with me I'm going to pick up a couple of men and bring the party to your house."

Ruth weighed in. "It might do you a world of good to go out and be around people for a while, Ondie. I'll even go with you." She stood up and danced around the table. "You know Mama still remembers how to drop it like it's hot, too. How do you think the two of you got here?"

They erupted into laughter once more.

Ondie acquiesced. "All right, fine. Friday night."

Serita blissfully threw her arms around her sister and thanked her.

Normal, what did it mean? Despite her reluctance to act on it, Ondie wanted to know what it was like to be just like everyone else. Perhaps this was just the thing she needed. They all knew the agony she lived with. Their grandmother's misunderstood demons were met with humiliation. The so-called cure left her nearly incapacitated in the last few years of her life. Ruth was determined not to let Ondie fade away as her mother had. She was determined to keep this insidious scourge from overshadowing her family no matter what she had to do to stop it.

Dr. Mathis had encouraged Ondie to get out more, even to date. If the evening turned out to be a train wreck, she would have at least broken free of her self-imposed cocoon. Besides, it would give her much to talk about in their next session.

# 4

Ondie awoke just before the radio alarm sounded. She lay there listening to the quiet; that's all there was. She smiled and threw back the comforter; today was a good day. This was the time of morning she went about not only preparing for work, but also getting her four-year-old ready for day care. With Maya away, she could enjoy an extra hour of leisure.

She flipped on the television to catch the morning news and became amused by the puff-piece touting the upcoming observance of National Marijuana Appreciation Day. "Well, it looks like somebody recognizes the medicinal benefit."

A hot shower and a cup of coffee later, Ondie was ready for her ride into midtown. The first thing she noticed after arriving at the office was that things were out of place on her desk; personal pictures were moved, and her favorite pen was missing. She scanned the area looking for the culprit. Two of her coworkers were huddled together munching on muffins and chatting. They acknowledged her and returned to their scintillating exchange without skipping a beat. Ondie then discovered the missing pen in the hand of another of her quad-mates. The young woman was on the phone and focused on the display of her computer. Ondie stood over her and waited. Annoyed, the woman asked her caller to hold, huffed, and shot Ondie the *can I help you?* look.

"I want my pen back."

"Excuse me?"

Ondie snatched it from the woman and showed her the offense. "Whose name is on this?"

The woman rolled her eyes and scoffed.

"Look, I would appreciate it if all of you would stay the hell away from my desk, and keep your hands off my things!"

With that, Ondie returned to her work area and booted up her computer."Damn it! My account is locked. Who in the hell has been using my computer? I asked you bitches to stay off my desk."

The woman she had found with her pen piped up. "Wait a minute. Who you callin' a bitch?"

Ondie did not back down. "You, if you were sitting at my desk. And by the looks of it you were. You logged on to my computer."

The woman stood, put her hands on her hips, and cocked her neck. "Well, maybe if you brought your ass to work once in a while you could log on to your own damn computer and none of us would have to pick up your slack!"

The other two women moved away and prepared for a fight.

"Slack?"

"Did I stutter?"

"You just want to start some shit. Takin' my stuff. Movin' my pictures. And I know it was you that put the wrong account number on that invoice last week. You're trying to get me fired. You've been after me since I walked in the door."

"Don't blame me 'cause you can't do your damned job!"

One of the other women, more lamb than lion, stepped forward, as others on the floor drew closer. "C'mon, y'all, stop this. We have to work together. Don't say anything now that you can't take back."

"Shut up, Anne," Ondie snapped. "I know you're in on this, too! You all are!"

"What?"

"Don't none of y'all like me, and I don't give a damn. Just keep your hands off my stuff."

"What's going on over here?"

The crowd that had gathered separated as the department manager stepped through. She was a stern, brittle, no-nonsense type with a blond, almost white, pageboy haircut that made her facial features appear more severe than they might have otherwise. She turned to address the small mob.

"You all need to go back to your own areas." She waited until they had dispersed, and then turned back to the other women. "I asked a question."

"Sally, Ondie came in here freakin' out and accusin' me of some kind of sabotage, just 'cause I borrowed her stupid pen."

"You didn't 'borrow' a damned thing. You took it. And that's not all you did," Ondie defended. "I can't even log on to my computer."

"That's no reason to go off the deep end, Ondie,"

the manager injected. “I had your password changed. We needed to get to some time-sensitive information. Just call IT and have them reset it.”

Ondie felt the familiar sensation of walking a tightrope without a net. Her eyes watered. She rubbed her temples to keep an approaching headache at bay. “Anne, I’m sorry I snapped at you.”

“It’s okay.” The heavyset woman fussed with a stack of papers coming off a nearby printer.

“Pat, I’m sorry I accused you and overreacted.”

“Yeah, whatever,” the confrontational woman spat, returning to her desk.

“Ondie, can I see you in my office?” The short blond-haired woman pushed her glasses up on her nose and walked out of the pod. Ondie followed.

A verbal warning put Ondie on alert that she was on her way to an HR censure. Fully aware that her employment was in jeopardy, she felt the need to confide in the woman. “Sally, I’m under a great deal of stress. My husband and I are going through a really bad breakup, and I’m having a tough time dealing with it. My doctor has even prescribed sedatives just so I can sleep at night.”

A necessary lie, accompanied by the proper amount of contrition. She couldn’t risk becoming the object of pity or ridicule, nor did she wish to be branded a lunatic. What woman doesn’t understand the emotional upheaval that a pending divorce might cause? Even someone as matronly as Sally Camden should be able to appreciate the havoc that is left in the wake of a man walking out on you. If indeed she’d ever been with a man at all. Ondie didn’t wear a ring, but figured the framed photo on her desk of Dexter and Maya would suffice.

"Ondie, I do sympathize with your plight, but this wasn't the first time. I can't have you going off on your coworkers over every little slight. And your attendance?"

"I know what you're going to say, Sally. I'll do better, I swear. I need this job. I have a little girl to support. I think Pat and I are just not suited to work together. We're like gasoline and fire. Maybe if I could work in another area?"

The woman sighed and turned to pull up something on her computer. "Jack's division needs help with month-end close. Do you think you could do any better there?"

"I'm sure I can."

Sally was surprisingly kind. By the end of the next day, Ondie was securely tucked away in another cubical on another floor. She'd known many of her new comrades only in passing. They were linked together mostly by e-mail correspondence. She would be friendly, but not overly so. She needed to concentrate on keeping her head on straight and not letting her emotions run amok.

Traveling on any interstate in Atlanta is a nightmare virtually any time of the day or night. Construction delays, orange barrels, and big monster cranes hovering over and lying in wait to remind you of their power to destroy your sense of reason continually assault commuters. Should that be accompanied with bad weather, getting to your destination is a traumatic proposition at best.

Radio reports overstating the obvious didn't help. On the heels of stop-and-go traffic from her midtown office to her Cobb County home, Ondie teetered on the brink of an anxiety attack. Her cell phone rang as she pulled up in her driveway.

"Yes, Serita."

"Dang, why you gotta sound like that?"

"Sorry, it's been one of those days."

"Are you all right?"

"Yeah, I'm fine. I just got home."

The conversation continued as Ondie got out of the car and headed into the house.

"So, you're still going tonight, right?"

"I don't know, Serita. I think I just want to take a hot bath and watch a movie."

"Are you serious? You promised."

Ondie dropped her purse on the breakfast nook, went on to her bedroom, and kicked off her shoes.

"Are you there?"

"Yes, I'm still here."

"C'mon, Ondie. Look, we could go grab something to eat before we go out, wherever you want, my treat. I'll even pick you up."

"You're paying? That's a first."

"Hey."

"So, what time do I need to be ready for this outing?"

"I'll be by there at seven thirty."

"That only gives me an hour and a half."

"Then I suggest you get a move on. Wear something sexy, although I doubt if you'll be able to keep up with me."

"Bye, Serita. See you later."

"You better be ready."

Ondie tossed the phone on the bed and went to her

closet to find something appropriate. "That girl, I swear. Wear something sexy."

Nothing was right. Over an hour later Ondie stood confused, with no more on than her bra and panties, in the middle of a pile of skirts, dresses, and slacks. "What was I thinking? What the hell do I look like trying to go out to a club?" She picked up a handful of clothes, screamed, and flung them across the room. "Damn it!"

She was startled by the doorbell ringing. "Who is it?"

"It's Serita."

"Serita?"

"Let me in, silly."

Ondie didn't move.

"Hello. Will you open the door? I have to pee."

Ondie shook herself from her dazed state and finally opened up. Serita sashayed in past her with the scent of Angel perfume trailing behind, dressed for action in a teal silk tunic mini, showcasing lots of leg and plenty of sex appeal. "You're not ready."

"I—I can't go."

One look at her sister and Serita knew. She cautiously moved toward her. "Ondie, if you're really not feeling up to this, I understand."

"I want to go, but I couldn't find anything to wear."

"Ondie, have you taken your pills?"

"Of course I took my damn pills. What the hell kind of question is that? Don't treat me like I'm an idiot, Serita."

"I'm sorry."

Ondie rubbed her hand over her face. "No, I'm

sorry. I just got a little frazzled after I got out of the shower. I didn't know what to put on."

"Do you want me to help you find something?"

Ondie smiled. "Yeah, that would be nice."

"Okay, let me go to the bathroom first and then I'll give you a hand. By the time we're through with you, you'll have to beat the men off with a stick."

Serita stepped around Ondie and proceeded up the hallway to the bathroom. When she was done, she came into the bedroom and was taken aback by the garment explosion. "Well, you've got a lot to chose from," she cracked. "We just need to sort it all out."

Serita milled through the clothes as Ondie set about doing her makeup.

"Oooh, how about this? This is cute. I could wear this myself."

Ondie stuck her head out of the bathroom to see what she was holding up. "No, I haven't been able to get into that dress since before I had Maya."

"Well, can I have it?"

"You really want that old thing?"

"You've been holding on to some of this stuff for a long time. I may as well take it off your hands."

"There's a pair of scissors on the dresser if you want to fix that problem for me."

"Oh, you got jokes, huh?"

"Gotta laugh to keep from cryin'."

"I hear that."

"I really need to go shopping, but I haven't been in the mood."

"You don't need to be in the mood to shop, you just need the money."

"Well, maybe I'll consider it when Dexter's next support check comes."

"I'll go with you if you need any help spending it."

"On me or you?"

"Well, I wouldn't mind a little sumpin' sumpin'."

"Why doesn't that surprise me?"

Serita held up another garment. "How about this one?"

"Do you really think so? Isn't it too cold outside for something like that?"

"Girl, please, it's sixty degrees. Besides, you need to show off your body, not cover it up."

"I think you're showing enough skin for the both of us."

"You know it's not too late for me to call Mama and invite her to go with us."

"No, thank you. Somehow the sight of seeing my mother shaking her groove *thang* is not what I'd call a good time."

They laughed.

Ondie was starting to feel even again. She squeezed into the black stretch dress that Serita picked out, and completed her look by pulling her hair up away from her face to accentuate her regal cheekbones. Serita scoured her jewelry box for the right accessories.

"Hold up. What is this?" Serita asked, holding a joint in her hand.

"Oh, I forgot I had that. We should smoke it."

"Ondie."

"C'mon, it's a holiday."

"What holiday?"

"National Marijuana Appreciation Day."

"What about your meds?"

"A couple of tokes won't hurt."

"Well, I can't. Delta does random drug screens, and I'm not interested in unemployment. So I'll just put this back where I found it, and you can save it for a rainy day."

"Buzz killer."

"Whatever."

Ondie touched up her lipstick and spritzed Dolce & Gabbana's Light Blue on her erogenous zones. "There, how do I look?"

"You look good, girl. But it's all about that scent!"

"Ah-ah-ah; this is for mature audiences only."

"Sexy bitch!"

"Don't sleep on it!"

"Let's get out of here. I'm starving."

After a quick meal of sushi, the vivacious duo headed out to party.

The M Bar was one of the hottest spots just south of downtown Atlanta. There was a definite air of sophistication. Fresh flowers were the centerpiece of mod artwork and museum-style displays. Patrons lounged on cozy white leather sofas, or snuggled together at secluded candlelit tables.

As Ondie absorbed the ambiance, she was struck by the fact that there was very little, if any, dancing. "I thought you said we were going out."

"We are out," Serita responded. She stepped up to the bar and ordered a drink.

"Dancing? You said we were going dancing."

"I said we were going out. We're out. C'mon, soak it all in. Give it a minute. If you still want to go dancing, we'll do that. You want something to drink?"

"Sprite."

The bartender handed Serita an apple martini and fixed a Sprite for Ondie.

"Ondie, I'll be right back. There's someone over there I need to talk to."

"Wait a minute. Don't leave me standing here by myself."

"You act like you've never been to a bar before. Relax, it's just like riding a bike."

With that Serita was gone, leaving Ondie perched on a bar stool trying to look inconspicuous. She took a sip of the Sprite and grimaced. "Excuse me, miss, this is flat."

"Do you want me to get you another?" the perky brunette chirped.

"Yes, uh . . . I mean . . . no. Can I have an apple martini?"

"Coming right up."

Within seconds, the vodka-laden beverage was sitting in front of her. "One drink won't hurt," Ondie rationalized. She put the glass to her lips, closed her eyes, and savored its taste. When she opened them, she spotted an attractive well-dressed man staring at her from across the room. She swallowed hard and smiled. That seemed all the invitation he needed. She checked him out as he sauntered toward her: tall, broad shouldered, chiseled jawline, smoldering eyes, close-cropped coal-black curls, no facial hair (his smooth dark chocolate skin seemed perfect without it). His swagger in his well-fitting suit was confident, sensual. He looked like a big jungle cat sizing up its prey.

"I couldn't help but enjoy watching you enjoy your drink." He extended his hand. "My name is Paul St. James."

She returned the gesture. "Ondie Reid."

"Ondie?"

"Short for Ondrea, spelled with an *O*."

"That's different."

"You can thank my mother for that one. The name comes from a story she read in college. According to German mythology, *Ondine* was supposed to be a beautiful and immortal water nymph. Her curse was falling in love with a mortal and bearing his child, which caused her to lose her immortality."

"Are you making that up?"

"No. There've been operas and plays written about her."

"How does the story end?"

"Not very well."

"So, how will *this* story end?"

Ondie smiled. "It hasn't been written yet."

"Well, let's see what we can do about that." He held on to her hand. "Perhaps like this mythical nymph of yours, I could easily fall under your spell."

"How corny is that?"

"Give me some credit. I'm just warming up."

She blushed. It was a line, but he delivered it with such magnetism she didn't care. "I detect an accent, so I'm guessing you're not from Atlanta."

"Jamaica."

"Really?"

"Have you ever been?"

"No, but maybe I should."

"Well, why don't I buy you another drink and tell you all about it?"

Ondie knew that she shouldn't have been drinking,

but the allure of this handsome Jamaican was much more than she could say no to. They found a spot on one of the leather sofas in the back.

"You look like an island girl," Paul whispered.

Ondie couldn't stop smiling. It had been a long time since she felt so appreciated. She caught the glint of a sliver chain that hung around the man's neck. "Is there significance to the ring?"

"It belonged to my mother. I told her that I would wear it until the day I found someone special to give it to."

"You're still wearing it, so I'm guessing you haven't found anyone."

"Not yet."

Minutes later Serita interrupted them. "Here you are." She gasped when she saw the drink in her sister's hand. "Ondie."

"What?"

"Are you sure you should be . . ." She cut her eyes toward Paul. "Can I talk to you for a minute, please?"

Ondie excused herself. Serita took her by the arm and pulled her into a corner.

"What are you doing?"

"I'm having a good time. What does it look like?"

"You're drinking."

"So are you."

"You know what I mean."

"I'm a grown woman, Serita. I appreciate your concern, but I can take care of myself."

"But—"

"This is my disease. I'll handle it my way. You wanted me to come out with you. Now, leave me alone and let me enjoy myself. I'm fine. I promise. Cross my heart and hope to die."

Serita shook her head and sighed. "All right."

"Now, why don't you go back over there to that guy, or whoever you were talking to? If I need you, I'll call." Ondie turned and sashayed back to the sofa.

"Is there a problem?" Paul inquired.

"Nothing I can't deal with." She removed an ink pen from the clutch she carried, scribbled her cell number on the back of a bar napkin, and passed it to him. "I'd better be a good girl and stay close to my sister."

"She doesn't look like she needs a babysitter, and neither do you."

"I don't."

"So why not relax and be an adult?"

One more drink was all it took to further alter Ondie's perspective. The mixture of drugs and alcohol made a reckless and dangerous combination, wreaking havoc on her psyche. Without so much as a good-bye to Serita, she slipped away with Paul.

Ondie was enamored with the décor of Paul's Atlantic Station loft. Modern and impressionist art by Jamaican-born artists Bernard Hoyes and Leopold Barnes adorned the walls, complementing the big overstuffed sofa, love seat, and chaise.

Ondie kicked off her shoes and sat. "So, what is it you said you did for a living?"

Paul joined her with two glasses of chardonnay. "I'm a corporate attorney. And yes, it pays very well."

"I can see that."

He handed her a glass.

"No, I don't think I should have anything else to drink."

"Are you intoxicated?"

"Not by the alcohol."

"Are you afraid I'll take advantage of you?"

"No, I'm afraid of what I might do to you."

"Is that right?"

Paul moved in for a kiss. Ondie's cell phone rang.

"Hi, Serita . . . I'm sorry I left you at the bar. . . . I'll make it up to you. . . . Yes, I'm fine. No . . . No, Paul will bring me home. . . . Nothing at the moment, but that's about to change. Good night, little sister. Get home safe."

Ondie turned her phone off and dropped it back in her purse. She took Paul's wine glass, gulped down a mouthful, and kissed him. They shared the nectar as their tongues danced together. She then pulled at his shirt, nearly ripping the buttons off, and yanked at the belt on his pants. It didn't take long for him to discover that there wasn't much else one could wear under a body-hugging black dress. He laid her back on the sofa and buried his face in her breasts. Ondie gasped with pleasure and ran her hands through his thick lush curls. He kissed a trail down her stomach, entwined his fingers in the straps of her thong, and slid them over her hips. He then gently separated her legs and began his exploration.

"No," Ondie shrieked. "Stop." She pushed at him.

He didn't budge. She shoved more forcefully. "I said stop!"

"What's the matter?"

"I can't do this."

"What?"

"I can't." She jumped up and grabbed her dress from the floor. "Take me home."

"Are you kidding me?"

"You're trying to hurt me," she screamed.

"This is bullshit," Paul spat, pulling his pants back up. "I thought this is what we both wanted. I'm not going to hurt you."

"Liar! I want to go home. Take me home."

"I can't believe this. What the hell is wrong with you?"

Ondie's hand swung out and slapped Paul in the mouth. She then grabbed her shoes and purse and bolted toward the door. "Fuck you! I'll call a cab!"

Given the circumstances, it wasn't hard to believe that she let things get so out of hand. It could have been worse. She was in the middle of a potentially dangerous situation in a stranger's apartment, and he might not have stopped just because she wanted him to. She cried all the way home. Liquor sloshed around and churned inside her stomach. Her body convulsed.

"Stop the cab!"

The driver looked up at her in his rearview mirror. "Are you crazy, lady? We're about to get on the interstate."

"If you don't pull over I'm going to get sick all over your backseat."

Without haste, the cabdriver signaled and pulled off the side of the street. Ondie threw the door open, jutted her head out, and heaved.

Whether a foregone conclusion, or simply the result of bad judgment, Ondie learned yet another valuable life lesson. Would there ever really be *normal* for her? Meds or no meds, would the best she could expect equate to just getting by?

# 5

The acrid smoke of burning rubber and wires seeped into the room like a fog. It was a horrifying odor to be awakened by. Ondie sprang straight up out of bed, panicked. She covered her nose with her hand and breathed in through her mouth, as she stumbled through a sea of clothes left strewn about the previous night, and made her way to her bedroom door. She ran up the hall toward her daughter's room. "Maya!" Fear consumed her when she flung the door open to discover that the little girl wasn't there. The bed was made. Her toys were in place. Everything was as it had been. There was no fire. Ondie fell into the wall, shook off the delirium, and took deep cleansing breaths to calm down. "Chicken Little, the sky is not falling." The telephone rang and she hustled back to her room to answer.

"Ondie?"

"Hello, Serita."

"Girl, what in the hell?"

"Serita, I'm really not in the mood for this right now."

"You scared me to death last night. Why did you run

off with that man? You didn't know him from Adam's house cat. He could have raped you or something."

"Serita, nothing happened. I came home. I slept in my own bed—alone. I've gotta go now."

"Ondie, wait."

"I'm hanging up. Good-bye."

Ondie went to the kitchen to take her meds. She followed with a cup of yogurt and a piece of dried toast as a pot of coffee brewed. She went back to her bedroom, put her closet back together, and made her bed. After showering and dressing, she discovered two missed calls and a message on her voice mail.

"Hi, Ondrea. It's Paul. I know I'm the last person you expected to hear from after last night. I called to apologize for my insensitivity. I am so sorry, and I hope you can forgive me. I know we got off to a terrible start, but I'd like to make it up to you if I could. I really want to see you again. If you're interested, call me. Let me prove to you that I'm not the total *rassclat* that you may think I am."

Ondie sat and stared at Paul's number on the phone display contemplating whether to call back. She knew she shared a good deal of the responsibility regarding how badly things ended between them. Despite her manic behavior, she had led him on. She should apologize as well; he was owed that much at least. The doorbell rang when she hit Redial. Ondie peeped through the sheers and spotted Ruth's car in the driveway.

"Mama, what are you doing here?"

"I tried to call, but you didn't answer."

"I didn't get a message."

"I didn't leave one. I was worried when I didn't hear from you, so I thought I'd stop by to make sure everything was all right."

"You've been talking to Serita, haven't you?"

"Serita? Why? What happened?"

"Nothing. I just thought she might have told you . . ."

"Told me what?"

"Never mind. Forget it."

"Well, are you going to invite me in, or are you going to make me stand out here like a Jehovah's Witness?"

Ondie moved back from the door.

Ruth stepped inside and continued to the kitchen. "Mmmm, I smell coffee."

Ruth opened the cupboard and helped herself. "So, what exactly is it that you think Serita was supposed to have told me?"

"Huh?"

"You heard me. I know you two went out last night. Did something happen?"

"We went to dinner. We went to this bar. End of story."

Ondie picked up her cup of coffee from the counter, moved into the living room, and perched on the sofa.

Ruth followed. "That was the short story. I want the details."

"I'm not sixteen, Mama. I wasn't out on a prom date."

"Ondie, I know you're not a child, and I'm not trying to treat you like one. But I think you know what I'm talking about."

Ondie rubbed her eyes and flashed on the abrupt exit she made from Paul's loft. "I met a man."

"You did?"

"Nothing happened. He was interesting. We talked. Had a few laughs. That was it."

"What's his name? What's he look like? What's he do for living? Are you going to see each other again?"

"Why? Do you want to tell him about my mental problems and scare him off, too?"

Ruth's countenance fell. She stood up and took her coffee cup back to the kitchen.

"I'm sorry, Mama. I really thought I had worked through that."

"You know, Ondie, I've only wanted the best for you. I just wasn't sure you were ready to handle the responsibilities of being a wife and a mother. That's an awful lot of stress to deal with all at one time."

"It wasn't your decision to make."

"By keeping the truth from Dexter you would have been taking his choices away from him."

"He chose to leave, didn't he?"

"He's not your husband, but he's still a part of your life; yours and Maya's. Have you ever considered what would have happened if he had decided to take Maya away from you? How would that have made you feel? I've seen firsthand what this can do to a family. My father was never the same after he had my mother committed. I didn't want that for you. I still don't."

Tears flowed from Ondie's eyes. If it was up to her she would have kept from telling Dexter anything about her condition for as long as she could have. Ruth was right; as painful as that time was, he had to know the truth.

Ruth took Ondie in her arms and held her. "I love you."

"I love you, too, Mama."

"I never want you to know what it's like to live a life like my mother had to."

Ondie fell asleep on the sofa after Ruth left, and flashed back on the first time she met the man she wanted to marry.

"Hey, what's your name?"

"Ondie."

"Ondie?"

"Short for Ondrea; spelled with an *O*."

"That's cool. I didn't catch your last name."

"I didn't throw it."

"Okay, so it's like that, huh?"

"Yeah, it's like that."

"You're new here, aren't you?"

"I'm a sophomore."

"I haven't seen you at a game before."

"That's because I haven't been. I don't really like basketball."

"People that don't like basketball just don't understand it, but I'd be happy to teach you the fundamentals. You wanna go out for coffee or something sometime?"

"I have a boyfriend, Mr. . . ."

"*Mr.*? The name's Dexter. Dexter Campbell."

"So, when do you want to have coffee? I'll need to check with my boyfriend to see if he's free."

"I don't think you understand. The invitation is just for you."

"Oh, I understand a lot more than you think."

It took a while for Dexter to wear her down, but Ondie finally agreed to go out with him. Once she cut through his bravado, she found him to be a lot more than he let on to others. Within weeks of breaking it off with her boyfriend, the striking finance major and the senior class Maroon Tigers point guard were dating exclusively.

Some believed that being seen on the arm of a Morehouse jock boosted their social standing around the CAU campus. Dexter was not only a star athlete, but he was a KAPPA, which made his stock more of a commodity.

Ondie was more impressed with who he was than what he was, and she was a little more familiar with the game of basketball than she let on. Kenny played, and he taught her and Serita an appreciation for the sport. However, Ruth had taught her the sport of baiting a man.

Things between them sizzled, as she kept her disorder tightly under wraps. Knee surgery caused Dexter to realize that he would never turn pro. After graduation, he settled into a job working for UPS. He and Ondie decided to get married long before she discovered she was pregnant. After Dexter witnessed what was to be the first of Ondie's episodes he got skittish; fate and timing had another agenda.

Ondie awoke and decided that maybe now would be a good time to move on with her life. As she dialed Paul's number, she heard another car pull up in the drive. She looked out. Maya was back. She excitedly abandoned her call and ran out to greet her.

The chubby-cheeked cherub wriggled to be free of her car seat. "Mommy," she screamed with glee.

Ondie pushed up the front seat of the Jeep and quickly undid Maya's constraints, as Dexter retrieved her luggage and the bags of toys his family had purchased.

Liberated from toddler-torture, the four-year-old wrapped her little arms tightly around her mother's neck and kissed her. "I missed you, Mommy."

"I missed you, too, baby. Grandma Ruth was just here. She's going to want to see you."

"Can we go see her now?

"We'll go see her later, okay?"

A large box split and its contents tumbled to the ground, which drew Ondie's attention to the back of the Jeep. Dexter looked up at her and laughed. His light brown eyes danced in the glow of the sun. His scruffy look caused Ondie to flash on the many nights they had shared; steaming up windows in the Mustang he used to own, or keeping his dorm-mate at bay while tripping over each other getting dressed after "cramming for an exam."

"My mom and dad went a little overboard," he replied.

"A little?"

Some of the packages proved too much for the strapping six-foot-two, cocoa-skinned brother, as he struggled to maintain his balance.

"Don't break 'em, Daddy," Maya squealed.

"I got 'em, baby. Y'all go on in the house. I'm comin'."

Maya chattered on insistently about the bounty that Dexter's parents bestowed on her, and about her adventures with Mickey and Minnie and all the real-life Disney princesses. "You know my favorite one, Mommy?"

"No. Who's your favorite?"

"Princess Jasmine."

"Really?"

"I got a talking parrot, just like hers."

"So Grandma Vivian and Bumper spoiled you. Now you're just a rotten little stinker."

"No, I'm not."

"Yes, you are. Now the tickle monster is going to have to eat you."

Maya started laughing way before Ondie laid a finger on her. To the girl's delight, Ondie made funny gurgling noises and nibbled her neck.

"Well, that's the last of it," Dexter announced. "That should take care of Christmas, Kwanzaa, and her next birthday."

"Her next two or three at least," Ondie cracked.

Dexter reached down, picked Maya up, and tossed her in the air. "I'm hungry. What do you say we go get some pizza?"

"Yay, Chuck E. Cheese," Maya clapped. "Can Mommy come, too?"

Dexter looked into Ondie's eyes. "I don't know; does Mommy want to come?"

"Sure." Ondie smiled. "I'd like some pizza, too."

Was he trying to reconnect? *Don't make too much of this,* Ondie told herself. *It's just pizza. He's not asking to move in. Just take it one step at a time and see what happens.*

Spending a Saturday afternoon surrounded by dozens of screaming kids, her own among them, was not exactly first choice on Ondie's list. But when your child asks you to do something, if it's within your power to do, you do it. Any headache seems worth it just to hear her exuberant laughter. Innocent, untouched, that is how you pray she will always be, but you know the fact is Princess Jasmine won't survive in the real world.

When Ondie had discovered she was pregnant, it was both exciting and terrifying. Given her family history, she had cause to worry. She was assured that her particular affliction would not be visited on Maya, that same speculation that was passed on Ruth when she was born.

It was bittersweet, watching Dexter and Maya play together. Despite their differences, he was a good father. There had been nothing romantic between them for years, but she had been more fragile then. With the new medication, would he see a new Ondie?

The long drive up from Jacksonville and all the excitement of the afternoon finally took its toll on Maya. By the time they got back to Ondie's house, she was down for the count. As Dexter put her to bed, Ondie went to the kitchen to get him a beer. She didn't drink it; she just liked keeping it in the refrigerator for his visits.

"I don't think that pizza set too well with me," Dexter admitted.

"Honestly, Chuck E. Cheese wasn't what I had in mind, either."

"What can I say? The girl's got a thing for big animated mice."

"As long as she doesn't start playing with the real thing, I'm cool with that."

Dexter pulled up to a bar stool around the breakfast nook and took a swig from the bottle. "So, how are you doin'?

"I'm good now. It's quiet."

"You look good, really good. I didn't get a chance to say that to you earlier."

"Things are coming together."

"Glad to hear it."

"Thank you for taking such good care of Maya."

"Please. We had a blast. I hated to come back. But I gotta go back to work Monday."

"You must be exhausted."

He yawned and finished the beer. "You know, I really am. I need to get some sleep."

"You could stay here tonight instead of driving all the way to Stone Mountain."

"Thanks, but I've been away from my own bed for over a week. I should probably just go home."

"Okay, I understand." Ondie wanted to kick herself for sounding so desperate.

They walked silently to the door together. It felt awkward. He turned to her and for a split second she thought she saw longing in his eyes. She wanted to reach out and caress the shadow beard on his face. Her mind wouldn't release her hand.

"Good night, Ondie."

"You be careful going home. Don't fall asleep at the wheel."

"Never that."

She watched him ride off, yearning for him. Why didn't she have the courage to tell him how she felt? Because it would crush her if he didn't feel the same way. Still, there was something in his eyes. Something that reminded her of the man she had fallen in love with. Maybe it was time to find out just how much of her was still in his heart. If there was nothing there, she needed to know that, too.

# 6

"So, how are things going?"

Ondie had looked forward to this session for days. There was so much that she wanted to talk to Dr. Mathis about. Things she needed to confess. He was, after all, friend, confidant, and Father Confessor. There was no judgment here, only revelation. She could trust him. No matter how many times she threatened to end her sessions, she knew this was her safe place.

"A couple of really huge things happened after I last saw you."

The doctor nodded and smiled. "You seem anxious."

"Do I?"

"Not in a bad way. More excited."

Ondie was a bit fidgety. She couldn't sit still. She got up and found a perch at the window. The late afternoon sun was still bright and warming on her face. She stretched up toward it and ran her fingers through her curls. "I almost got fired last week. I went to work and found some of my things had been moved. I hate it when people touch my stuff."

"What did you do?"

"I confronted the bitch, and my manager called me on it. I told her that I was going through a messy breakup, and my nerves were on edge."

"What happened after that?"

"She transferred me to a different department, just like that."

"Are you doing any better there?"

"So far so good. But that's not all that happened. I took your advice. I went out with my sister and I met someone."

"A man?"

Ondie turned to him, pursed her lips, and scowled.

The doctor cleared his throat and smirked. "Sorry."

"His name is Paul. We met at this bar downtown and one thing led to another and I went back to his place." Ondie's mood changed. She moved away from the window and gravitated to the aquarium. She tapped lightly on the glass to get the fishes' attention. "I thought I wanted to have sex with him. Instead, I freaked out and ran away."

"Had you been drinking?"

"I had some wine."

"Wine?"

Ondie spun around sharply. "All right, fine. I had a couple of drinks. They went to my head, and I thought I wanted to go to his place. I was wrong."

"Do I have to warn you again about the dangers of mixing alcohol with your medication?"

"Yes, Dr. Mathis, tell me again how dangerous it is. In fact, why don't you just do one big fat fucking public service announcement!"

The doctor backed down and scribbled some things on a notepad.

"What are you writing? Ondie's been a bad little girl. I just wanted to have some fun. Aren't I allowed a mistake? I'm all right. Isn't that the important thing?"

"This time."

Ondie sighed. "I know I did a stupid thing. But I just needed to feel like my life was my own, like I had some control."

"But you can't control yourself when you're not following your treatment."

"Don't you think I know that? Don't you think I live every damn day thinking about it?"

"Then why would you do something so foolish?"

"Because I wanted to, all right! I wanted to have a drink—and you know what? I enjoyed it!"

"If you think you can cope with this on your own, why are you here?"

"Because I need you."

"Why?"

"Why what?"

"Look, Ondie, I've got patients who really need my help, patients that want my help. It's obvious that you don't, so maybe we should just stop wasting each other's time."

"So that's it, then. You're gonna be like everybody else and walk away."

"I don't want to walk away, Ondie. But you're showing me through your actions that you really don't need me."

"Stop saying that! You have to help me."

"Help you what?"

"Get my shit together. You're the only one I can talk to."

Ondie closed her eyes, fell against the wall, and

rubbed her hands over her face. "Dexter's back. We still have a bond, I know it. I'm going to tell him how I feel, and show him the woman I've become."

"And what about this other fellow?"

"There is no 'other fellow'; it's just some random guy I picked up at a bar."

"You wanted to have sex with him."

"I was horny, sue me!"

"Is he the reason you seem so agitated, or is it something else?"

"I don't know. This guy kind of surprised me. He called me, and he wants to see me again."

"So wouldn't you rather start dating a man that could get to know you as you are now, instead of a man who remembers the woman you were?"

"I know Dexter. I don't know Paul."

"Isn't that the point? You could get to know him as he gets to know you."

"I'm afraid if I open up to him I'll scare him off."

"You're afraid of getting hurt."

"Of course I am. Who isn't?"

"Ondie, what do you see when you look in the mirror?"

"Sometimes I see myself, or at least the woman I wish I was. And sometimes all I see is darkness. There's this vortex of mind-numbing drugs that I feel trapped in, and there's no way to get out."

"You've come a long way from that girl you were at seventeen. You're a woman, a mother with responsibilities. You have a little girl that is counting on you to take care of yourself. You have to find out who that woman is and make peace with her."

"How do I do that? I don't know who I am unless Mr. Depakote, or Mr. Lamotrigine, is whispering in my ear."

"I know it's difficult, but it's really important for you to make sure to continue with the meds. When you're not balanced you have some real challenges and struggles. However, like a diabetic needs insulin, you have to accept that you're going to need these drugs to remain stable. If the medication that you're currently on isn't agreeable, we can adjust it again. Maybe we should even consider some group therapy."

"No, I don't want to be around a bunch of strangers, whining about my life."

"Then you need to manage yourself and your stress better. Stay connected to your family. Stay busy. You have to find a way to coexist with the woman in the mirror. There is no escaping her."

On her way to pick Maya up from Ruth's, Ondie decided to call Paul; she got his voice mail.

"Hi, Paul, it's Ondie. I got your message the other day. Sorry I'm just now getting back to you. I really wanted to apologize for my behavior. It was completely my fault. I don't know what got into me. This is really awkward. I hate apologizing to a machine. I'm sorry for . . . I would like to see you again, too. Feel free to call me sometime." Ondie tossed her phone into the passenger seat. "Well, that was stupid."

She continued along replaying Dr. Mathis's words in her head and repeating them aloud as if chanting a mantra. "You have to find a way to coexist with the woman in the mirror." Lost in thought, she was barely paying attention to her surroundings. A truck was stalled in the center lane of the interstate several feet ahead. Congestion was building up on both sides of her as drivers in her lane abruptly negotiated around it. A rattling hoopty blasting earsplitting bass from oversized stereo speakers stopped short in front of her Maxima, and she slammed on her brakes to avoid a collision. Screeching tires sounded like an alarm as a mammoth SUV in back of her quickly swerved into another lane, forcing others to adjust. Horns blared in concert; their interpretation was obvious.

"Stupid bitch!" the driver of the SUV yelled as he passed.

Ondie's adrenaline surged. Her hands and knees shook; she panted. The cell phone rang and she looked over to discover that it was on the floor under the dash covered by everything that had fallen out of her purse. She didn't dare take her hands off the wheel. She would gather her things as soon as she came to a stop.

Balance was restored by the time she reached the exit to her mother's house. At the first traffic light she came to, she picked her things up and scooped them back into her purse. She checked the phone to see that there was a message from Paul; he would have to wait.

Ondie spotted her father's truck parked in the driveway of Ruth's house when she drove into the cul-de-sac, which brought a smile to her face. She opened the front door to find him sitting on the living room floor playing with Maya and her dolls. The little girl jumped up, ran to her, and wrapped herself around Ondie's leg.

"Whoa, hold up there," Kenny cautioned as he got up

from the floor. "Give your mama time to get in the door." He limped over to them and hugged Ondie. "Hey, baby."

"Daddy, are you all right?"

"My leg went to sleep," he laughed. "You know I'm too old to be sitting down that low for too long."

Ondie picked Maya up. "Where's Mama?"

"In the kitchen makin' chili. I told her that I wanted to take her to a restaurant, but you know how funny she is about eatin' out."

Although Kenny's marriage to Ruth didn't last, his relationship with his daughters flourished. In spite of one seemingly unforgivable indiscretion, Ruth carried a special place in her heart and her bed for him. Older and grayer, they both dealt with the issues that kept them apart, and through his absolution, they found the comfort of a love that had been tarnished, but not destroyed.

"How've you been feelin'?"

"I'm good, Daddy."

"You look good."

"Why does everybody keep saying that? What did I look like before, a raging psychopath?"

"No, baby. I'm just saying that you look like you're coping better."

"I'm trying."

Kenny pulled at the waistband of his pants as he adjusted on the sofa.

"What is that you're wearing?" Ondie chuckled.

"It's some belt your sister brought me from Thailand."

"It looks a little tight."

He sucked in his gut. "I'd like to see you try putting a size-thirty-six belt around a thirty-eight-inch waist."

"When did you see Serita?"

"Yesterday, just before she took off for Chicago. I'm only wearing this thing to make her feel good."

"Daddy, she's not here. You can take it off."

"I like it."

"You're gonna pass out or something, holding your stomach in like that."

"That's exactly what I told him," Ruth agreed as she walked in. "Kenny, you haven't been able to fit into a thirty-six in a long time."

"Ruthie, you know I've been workin' out."

"At the table," she cracked.

"That's all right, woman. You still want all this."

"Yes, Lord, help me."

Kenny got up and chased Ruth around the living room. She laughed girlishly, pretending to fight him off.

Ondie looked at her parents and smiled sadly. They ran after each other like love-struck teenagers. Maya jumped down from her lap and joined their fun. That's what Ondie so desperately wanted, a man that couldn't keep his hands off her. She wanted a man that could love her despite her flaws, and the few extra pounds that might come over time. It didn't matter that Ruth and Kenny had been divorced for the last ten years. This was the relationship they had carved out for themselves and they were making it work.

The more Ondie thought about it, the more she yearned for Dexter. She reached for her cell phone. "Hi, Dexter, it's me. I was wondering if you'd like to get together for dinner sometime next week. Call me."

If her parents could make it work, there was no reason she and Dexter couldn't try.

# 7

The soulful voice of D'Angelo's "How Does It Feel" drifted from the CD player. The glow of burning candles bathed the room with haunting silhouettes. Dexter was propped up on the pillows of his bed with a sheet covering his naked body from the waist down. He slowly sipped a beer, leaned his head back, closed his eyes, and sang along softly. He heard the toilet flush and the water running in the bathroom, and minutes later Serita emerged.

He smiled. His eyes beckoned her. He threw back the sheet and she climbed on top of him. She took the bottle from his hand and set it on the nightstand. The heat of their kiss caused his nature to rise again. Taking the necessary precaution, she mounted him. He threw his head back and gasped as the warmth of her enveloped all there was of him. The rhythm of the music dictated the pace of each thrust. Dexter wrapped his arms around her waist and she leaned back to offer up her breasts. His tongue lovingly caressed her nipples, sending a sensation through her that caused her to jerk and shudder as her vaginal walls tightened around his unyielding manhood. The intensity was exhilarating. Beads of sweat gathered on Dexter's forehead. Their mouths found each other, sharing hot, wet, desperate kisses. Serita grabbed the headboard and her body hungrily accepted more. Song after song after song continued to underscore their passion as they dizzily spun into orgasm.

Breathlessly, Serita rolled off and lay next to him. She gently clawed her manicured nails through the fine hairs on his chest.

Dexter ran his hand over his close-cropped fade and scratched his beard. "Damn."

"You okay?"

"Yeah. You?"

"This is wrong on so many levels."

"How long are we gonna keep this up? Sneaking around. Lying to everybody."

"I don't know."

Dexter stood up and walked into the bathroom to clean up. When he returned he flipped off the CD player and finished the rest of his beer. He then slipped back into his boxers and went to the kitchen for another. On his way back into the room, he picked up his cell phone and retrieved Ondie's message. The sound of her voice made him feel worse.

"Ondie wants to get together for dinner."

"Are you gonna go?"

"I don't know."

"Are you gonna tell her about us?"

"We both agreed not to, right? You know as well as I do what could happen."

"I feel like shit." Serita climbed out of bed and went back into the bathroom. A short time later she came out and dressed. "Maybe we should just end this now before anybody gets hurt."

"It's a little too late for that, don't you think?"

"We can just walk away as if nothing ever happened."

"Is that what you really want to do? We can't undo this." Dexter reached out and smoothed down Serita's tousled hair and caressed her cheek. "I love you, girl. I tried not to, but it is what it is. You said you loved me, too."

"I don't want Ondie to suffer." Serita grabbed her shoes and bolted from the bedroom.

Dexter went after her. He grabbed her arm to keep her from going out the door. "I don't want her to suffer, either, but we can't put the genie back in the bottle."

She yanked her arm from his grasp. "What the hell does that even mean?"

"I thought about you practically the whole time I was in Florida. We tried to stay away from each other once before, remember?"

"We didn't try hard enough, Dexter."

"There's nothing between me and Ondie. There hasn't been for years."

"You have Maya. And I think you know how Ondie still feels about you; we both do."

"But she knows I don't feel the same way about her."

"Does she?"

"I've never led her to believe otherwise."

"So what are you suggesting we do, Dexter? Go public? Hurt my sister? I can't do that. I won't."

"Serita, not being with you isn't going to make me feel any different about your sister."

"If I have to take on more flights and do more layovers to stay away from you, then that's what I'll do, but this has to end. It should never have started in the first place."

Serita pushed past him, grabbed her purse and keys, and ran out.

Serita sat in the parking lot behind Dexter's apartment building unable to move. She thought about the ramifications of what they'd done. Even though things seemed better between her and Ondie since the medication and the understanding of her disease, Serita knew that the discovery of her affair with Dexter could potentially set her off.

There had been times since that New Year's Eve party, a year ago, that she thought of little else. Her date was passed out drunk long before the stroke of midnight. Dexter was there at the invitation of one of his boys. He'd told him how many fine single women would be there and convinced him that he wouldn't be alone for long. Serita recalled watching him from across the room as women, one after the other, practically threw themselves at him.

By midnight, she and Dexter had somehow gravitated into the same space, and each other. Everybody yelled "Happy New Year." He looked into her eyes and smiled. It was so unexpected. His kiss stirred her. It happened so naturally. They'd known each other for years.

One quick peck. One brief innocent kiss unlocked Pandora's box.

Their clandestine liaisons were intense and exhilarating. The guilt she felt behind each tryst was an unforgiving aphrodisiac, but it lessened over time. It was all she could do to force the affair to the back of her mind whenever she was around Ondie. She'd lied about trips she never made, and even the ones she made with him. It was easier to worry less about what the discovery of their involvement would do to the family when it was just about sex. Somehow love found its way into the equation and changed the entire canvas.

She started her car and drove off. She pulled out of the parking lot on to the main street, but before driving a block away she made a U-turn and headed back to Dexter's apartment.

How do you put the genie back in the bottle unless he's willing to go?

# 8

It was a productive morning. There was much more work for Ondie to do in her new position, but the privacy she enjoyed while doing it was well worth the move. She'd not had any conflicts. Everyone pretty much stayed huddled in their own little areas, only coming up for air to take breaks and for meetings. Piles of paper had accumulated in Ondie's cubical in a very short time, accounts that needed a good deal of personal attention in order to ensure that everything balanced. Balance was the key, and a lot easier to maintain at work than anywhere else it seemed.

"I'm headed out for lunch. Would you like to come?"

Ondie looked up from her computer to see one of her coworkers peeping over the wall. It was the first time in almost two weeks that anyone said anything more to her than good morning, good night, or have you finished that report?

"No, thanks, Linda. I'm meeting someone."

"Okay, see you later."

Ondie almost felt guilty for lying about something

so benign. Why couldn't she just have said no, thanks and left it at that? There was no *someone* waiting for her. She would go to the cafeteria like she did almost every day for a sandwich or soup, salad, and a cookie, then come back to her desk to peruse MSN or SOAPnet on the computer. She stood and looked out the window. It was a beautiful sunny day. She inhaled deeply and thought that perhaps she would do something different. "Steve, I'm going to lunch." She grabbed her purse and headed to the elevator. When the doors opened she was stunned to see Paul standing there. He looked very handsome and businesslike in his Brooks Brothers suit.

He smiled; his white teeth dazzled against his dark skin. "Going my way?"

Ondie stepped onto the elevator; a few more people got on behind her. She shot a side glance in Paul's direction, and they rode ten stories without a word.

As is customary, the ladies were allowed to exit the elevator first. Ondie lingered in the vestibule for Paul. Given this chance encounter, she was glad that she'd put a little extra effort into her appearance. She checked herself in the mirrored wall, brushed a piece of lint from her skirt, and ensured that her blouse was neatly tucked.

"You look fine," he said as he approached.

"Do you work in this building?"

"No, I'm just here on business. I take it you work here?"

"Yes. I'm an accountant."

"Well, after two weeks looks like our game of phone tag has ended."

"Yes, it does."

"Are you on your way somewhere?"

"Just to get lunch."

"Do you mind if I join you?"

"It's just the cafeteria."

"That sounds fine to me."

Ondie smiled and led the way. They milled through the line like cattle. She selected her chef salad, and he asked the cook for a sub sandwich and fries.

He noted her diet choice. "Is that all you're eating?"

"Yes."

"Somehow the cookie doesn't seem to go with the salad."

"Chocolate chip is my weakness."

"You're not one of those women that's afraid to eat in front of a man, are you?"

"Given what happened last time, I don't think I should be afraid to do much of anything around you," she cracked.

He insisted on paying, and they then found a table amid the masses.

Ondie's former nemesis saw her sitting with Paul and leaned in to whisper to her companion. *She's probably saying something asinine,* Ondie thought. *It's a good thing I'm medicated.*

"Just so you know, this isn't what I had in mind when I said I wanted to see you again," Paul quipped.

"I would hope not," Ondie replied. "And for the record, I want to apologize again for my behavior the last time we were together, although I can't imagine why you'd still want to see me."

"Believe it or not, I don't make a habit of sleeping

with women when I first meet them. We'd both had too much to drink. And I was willing to step out of my box, so to speak. I would never have forced myself on you."

"Tell me this; what does *rassclat* mean?"

He reared back in his seat and chucked. "I don't want to ruin your lunch."

"Is it that bad?"

"Yes."

"Tell me."

Paul hesitated.

"C'mon, tell me."

He cleared his throat. "It is patois. It is what one might use in the bathroom to clean themselves after—"

"Oh . . . okay, I get it."

"So we're good now?"

"We're good."

"Excellent. Now, can we put that unfortunate business behind us and start again?"

"I'd like that."

He extended his hand. "Paul St. James."

"Ondrea Reid. Nice to meet you."

Lunch was an unexpected pleasure. Ondie didn't even care that she was asked to work overtime. She called Ruth to pick up Maya, but she was working, too. She didn't want to have to call Dexter, but she didn't have another choice. After he declined her invitation to dinner in lieu of a basketball game, she felt a bit put out.

"I have to work until six thirty tonight. Can you pick Maya up from day care?"

"Sure. What time will you be home?"

"No later than seven thirty."

"Okay, I'll bring her home then."

Maybe Dr. Mathis was right. But she didn't want to make the same mistakes with Paul as she had with Dexter. She needed to be up front with him, and if he couldn't handle it, then he wouldn't be the man for her, either. Who was she kidding? She wasn't nearly ready to be that forthright.

As promised, Dexter dropped Maya off just like one of his UPS deliveries. With no fanfare, he kissed her good night and told her that he would see her for the weekend. Ondie watched him drive off as she had done countless other times, but the desire to run after him was not as strong.

"Okay, squirt, are you hungry? Or did you eat at Daddy's?"

"Can I have some ice cream?"

"For dinner? I don't think so."

"But I ate already."

"Really, what did Daddy cook?"

"He didn't. Auntie 'Rita came over and made splaghettis."

"Serita?"

Maya dragged her book bag over to the sofa, opened it, and pulled out a picture she'd drawn in day care. She presented it to Ondie.

"See, Mommy? This is you, and this is me, and this is Daddy."

Ondie examined the stick figures and smiled. "It's beautiful, baby."

"Can I have some ice cream now, please?"

"So this picture is bribery."

Maya looked confused.

"One scoop, all right?"

Maya grinned and held up two fingers.

"One," Ondie repeated.

Maya pouted and pretended to tear up.

"Okay, two small ones. Now, c'mon, you little faker, so I can get you ready for bed."

Ondie went into the kitchen and Maya squealed and ran behind, her stout legs going as fast as they could. After her indulgence, she had a bath and went to bed. Ondie then returned to the kitchen and tacked her daughter's latest masterpiece to the refrigerator along with a dozen others. Something Maya had said earlier began to gnaw at her. She needed to allay her suspicions.

"Hello."

"Serita, it's me."

"Hey, is everything all right?"

"Yeah, I called because Maya told me you were at Dexter's earlier."

"Yeah, I was there. He wanted a buddy pass for one of his friends."

"I thought all you needed was the person's name that was flying. Why didn't you just call?"

"I was on my way home from gettin' my hair done. So since my stylist's shop was close I just stopped by."

"You cooked dinner for them, too?"

"Well, I was already there, so I figured what the hell? Ondie, is something wrong?"

"No, I was . . . Nothing's wrong. Don't worry about it."

Ondie sat in the quiet noise of the room and tried not to think about something that was too absurd to consider. There'd only been one other time when she felt how she'd begun to feel now. It was at the beginning of 2006, just after New Year's. She was having a particularly hard time with a new drug. The festive season was rolling on without her participation. She was sick for nearly a week. When she went to her mother's house to pick Maya up, she thought she'd seen something between Dexter and Serita. In her postdelusional state, she shrugged it off as an overactive imagination. But something wasn't sitting right now. She went to the bathroom, flipped on the light, and jumped with a start. She turned quickly, thinking she'd seen something, or someone, behind her.

"You're being silly," she said, staring into the mirror. "You're seeing things that just aren't there."

Her reflection appeared to smirk. There was mischief in her eyes. *Are you really seeing things that aren't there?*

She needed the phantom to disappear. Ondie closed her eyes, pressed her hands to her ears, and shook her head in an attempt to silence her doubt. "There's nothing going on!" She opened her eyes and the woman she saw staring back at her still wasn't sure.

"Ondie just called. Maya told her that I was at your apartment."

"Shit. What did you tell her?"

"I told her I was there because you wanted a buddy pass for one of your boys."

"Did she believe you?"

"I guess. It's not like she has any reason not to."

"I told you that you can't come by here without calling first. You never know when I might have Maya."

"I didn't know she'd be there. This is insane. I can't keep lying like this."

"Then maybe we should tell her."

"No. We can't."

"Then should we tell Ruth and Kenny and see what they think we should do?"

"Mama would pitch a fit, and there's no telling what Daddy would do."

"All this creepin' is just makin' things worse."

"I wish there was another way."

"Where are you now?"

"I'm at the house. I've got to cover a flight out to L.A. in the morning."

"How long will you be gone?"

"A few days. I'm deadheading from there to Hawaii."

"Can I see you when you come back?"

"I don't know, Dexter."

Serita jumped when she heard a knock on her bedroom door. "I gotta go. I'll call you later." She rolled off the bed and went to answer. "Hey, Mama, how was work?"

"Same as always." Ruth yawned. "I was just checking in on you before I turned in." She noted the clothes strewn on the bed and the opened suitcase. "You got another flight?"

"Yeah, I'm gonna have to leave here at four o'clock in the morning."

"Where to this time?"

"Los Angeles and then Hawaii."

"Oooh, I wish I had your job. Much more glamorous than changing bed pans and being a slave to a call button all day."

"You love nursing. You know you wouldn't be happy doing anything else."

"That's because I've hardly had a chance to be anything else." Ruth reached out and embraced Serita. "You be careful, hear?"

"I will, Mama."

"Will you be back for Memorial Day weekend? You know how much food we'll have. And you know how much your father loves to barbecue."

"I'll be back in time. I wouldn't want to pass up the chance to have some of Kenny's Special Cajun Sauce."

Serita finished packing after Ruth retired. She then got into bed and tried to rest. Dexter was all she could think about. She could almost smell his scent and feel his breath on her neck. Her tongue sensually slid over her lips as her hands caressed her breasts; she felt his hands. She imagined him between her thighs rubbing and kissing and kneading her flesh. She moaned and gently stroked her clitoris, pretending they were his fingers: thick, long, and probing. Several minutes later a muffled cry of ecstasy accompanied a sensation that made her body quiver. Sleep washed over her and she whispered his name as she drifted off, "Dexter."

# 9

"To wi new fucha. To wan new start. To discoovery. It means to our future. To a new start. To discovery."

"To discoovery." Ondie knew she shouldn't have, but a toast just isn't the same with a glass of water. *One glass of cabernet won't hurt,* she convinced herself. Her levels had been stable for well over a week. Their initial meeting notwithstanding, she found herself becoming more attracted to him. Still, she wasn't ready for full disclosure.

Ondie began to feel transparent. It wasn't as if she was wearing a sign that screamed *I have a mental imbalance.* She glanced at the women at some of the tables around them. In her estimation, she was just as put together as any of them. Her hair was pinned up into a twist, her dress revealing, but not overtly so. *Maybe it's the wine.* She coyly pushed her glass to the side and decided to stick to water.

"Are you bored?"

She reined her thoughts in. "No, not at all."

"You look beautiful."

"Thank you, so do you. Uh . . . I mean . . ."

"I know what you meant." He chuckled. "So, tell me more about your daughter."

"Her name's Maya. She's my heart."

"What about her father? Is he still in the picture?"

"We share custody."

"And?"

"And that's it."

There was a certain amount of ambiguity that Ondie still felt as it related to her feelings about Dexter. She couldn't allow her unresolved emotions to overshadow the evening. "What about you, Paul? Any children?"

"Two boys, one seventeen and the other fourteen. They live with my ex-wife in Negril."

"How long were you married?"

"Five years. Most of which we were separated by distance. I wanted to study abroad, and she preferred I be content with life in Jamaica. Needless to say, things didn't work out. She's remarried. My sons and I are estranged. Even though I try to maintain a relationship with them, it's hard being so far away."

"Have you ever invited them to come visit you here?"

"Several times. But conflicts with their school and my work kept us apart. I wanted to be the best of the best, and I felt that I could not make that happen in Jamaica. My priorities were very different as a young man; the finest education was paramount. I couldn't give my wife what she wanted; I never anticipated driving my sons away. I regret being too busy for them. I am very proud of my eldest, Brendon; he is very intelligent, much like his father."

"Does he share your modesty, too?"

Paul smiled. "He's been accepted at NYU and will be attending in the fall. I think having a relationship with him will be much easier once he is here. In the meantime I plan to go to Negril in June for his high school graduation."

Ondie could hear the remorse behind Paul's pride as he spoke about his children. His vulnerability was surprising.

"So, other than the fact that you share Maya, what is your relationship like with your ex-husband?"

"Well, first of all, we were never married. And what there is between us is complicated."

"Meaning you still have feelings for him?"

Busted. Confess to her feelings and keep the rest under lock and key. "Yes, I do. But it doesn't matter, we're ancient history."

"Good. I was beginning to think that I didn't have a chance. Now I see that his loss may very well be my gain."

*Oh my God,* Ondie thought. *There has to be something wrong with him other than the fact that he's alienated from his children. He's good looking, educated, suave; there's no way he could be all he appears to be. There has to be a crack in the facade somewhere. If he's gay it's not blatant. Maybe he's on the down low. That has to be it; he wouldn't be the first man to shroud himself in a secret only Victoria could tell. But maybe I'm the only liar here.*

"You've drifted again. Where did you go?"

"I'm sorry. I was thinking about what you said."

"Should I take it back?"

"You may want to once you get to know me."

"I thought that's what we were doing now, getting to know each other."

"So why me?"

"I hope this doesn't come off as conceit, but if I wanted to be with just any woman I could do that. Since I'm here having dinner and conversation with you, I should think it would be clear that I want much more."

Their entrees arrived. Paul dined on steak-cut Alaskan halibut, while Ondie was seduced by the pecan-crusted salmon.

"More wine?" their server asked.

"None for me," Ondie injected.

"You've hardly touched your first glass at all. Don't you like it?"

"No, it's fine. I just don't want any more."

Paul gave her a look that she took to mean he understood. She was sure he wouldn't want a repeat of their first night together. Neither did she, but for very different reasons. This was one fairy tale she wasn't ready to let go of.

Hand in hand, they took a stroll through midtown after dinner. It was a balmy May night. Traffic, both pedestrian and otherwise, bustled with energy. They got a kick out of seeing young couples that appeared to be dressed up for a prom. They laughed and shared horror stories about their own experiences.

Paul admitted that he had not been quite the man that he'd grown to be. "I believe you call it being a nerd. You should have seen my glasses."

Ondie preferred to make up a story about having the flu, rather than to reveal the fact that she had had one of her episodes that caused her night to end earlier than anticipated.

Not wanting anything to ruin their evening, she pushed the recollection to the back of her mind where all such memories were forced.

Before they started into the crosswalk, she decided to have some fun with some of the passing teens. "Who are you wearing?" she asked, serving as fashion critic, while Paul playfully conducted faux interviews with those who dared to engage them. There was no stress, no pressure, and no self-doubt, just a man and a woman having a good time.

It was after eleven by the time Paul escorted Ondie home. He walked her to the front door and they kissed.

"That was nice," she said.

"Yes, it was."

"Do you want to come in?"

"Only if you're sure you want me to."

Ondie stepped inside, kicked off her shoes, and took Paul's hand. Their kisses were electrifying; their breathing intense.

"Ondrea."

"Yes."

"Maybe we should slow down."

"I don't want to." She fondled his crotch. "And apparently you really don't, either."

She turned around and pressed into him. He grabbed her and ravenously sucked on her neck like a vampire, being careful not to leave a mark. He then slowly unzipped her dress and it fell to the floor. She took him by the hand again and led him to her bedroom. She then stretched out on the bed as he hurriedly undressed and lay down beside her. His chest was smooth and hard. His touch masculine and sensitive simultaneously; no directive required. He kissed her all over, bringing special attention to the areas that needed it most. As amazing as his technique was, she nearly lost her mind when he massaged her feet and sucked her toes.

"I want you so much, right now," he whispered as he reached over to pull a condom from his pants.

He tore open the packet and prepared to enter. Ondie lay there, exposed, vulnerable. Tears pooled in her eyes. Had it really been so long since a man moved her this way?

"Do you really want this?" he asked.

"Yes."

Ondie threw her head back as the sensation of his abundantly endowed penis sent tremors through her body. Slowly and rhythmically, he slid into her. She held her breath and pulled at the comforter.

"I'll stop if you want me to."

"No," she said, almost laughing. She thought that he'd probably be the first man in history to really pull out after only getting the head in; that made her relax enough to accept the rest of him.

He braced himself on the bed, rolled his hips in a stirring motion, and moaned sensually. She pressed her pelvis upward to meet his impact with equal enthusiasm. Their bodies meshed for what seemed an eternity until the sweet release of anticipation and climax.

To feel human. To feel like a woman. At long last, this was what she needed, and it was good.

* * *

"You're smiling."

"I know."

"You want to tell me about it?"

"I've been seeing Paul."

"Really?"

"Are you shocked?"

"Surprised mostly."

"Why? Didn't you encourage me to get out and meet people?"

"Yes."

"Then you should be glad that your wise counsel is working."

"I'm curious. Have you put your feelings for Dexter aside?"

Ondie sighed, stood up, and moved to the window. "I'm still working that out."

"So he's still part of the equation?"

"He's Maya's father."

"That's a predictable place to hide."

"What do you want me to say?"

"If there were the slightest chance for you to get back with Dexter, where would that leave Paul?"

"Paul and I are just seeing each other, it's not like we registered at Macy's. Besides, I think Dexter may be seeing someone himself."

"Do you know who?"

"No." Ondie rubbed her hands over her eyes. The voices implicated someone. She didn't want to believe it could be true.

"Are you all right?"

"What's the matter with you?" Ondie yelled. "I came in here with good news and you're talking to me as if

I'm making a mistake. You told me to get over Dexter. You told me to move on with my life. Now you're questioning my decisions to do that. Which way is it, Doctor? Left or right? Up or down? What does everybody want from me?"

Dr. Mathis sat contemplating for a moment and then he stood and slowly moved toward her. "I apologize if it seems as if I'm raining on your parade. I did tell you not to be afraid to open yourself up. But my concern is the feelings you may be suppressing for Dexter."

"You said as long as I took my meds, there was no reason I couldn't live a normal life. Well, I've been taking them. And now when I look in the mirror it's not as dark. I don't see what I used to see. Isn't that what you want?"

"I'm glad that you're getting to know that woman. I just want you to be happy, Ondie. Whatever that looks like for you, that's what I hope you'll find."

Ondie walked toward the aquarium.

"Have you talked to this man about your disorder?"

"No."

The doctor scratched his head and sat back down.

"I don't know how to tell him. Being with him, every part of me feels so alive. I don't want to go back to the way that I was. But I know I'm going to have to say something eventually. I just wanted the ride to last a little while longer."

"I understand."

"Do you? Then please don't analyze this to death. Let me enjoy what I have while I have it."

# 10

Since early afternoon the air wafting from Reid's backyard was thick with the smell of hickory-smoked meat. Kenny was in his element, drinking beer and flipping ribs, hamburgers, and hot dogs. Music blasted from the stereo as he sang badly and bopped to the sound of the '70s. Ruth was in the kitchen gyrating to the groove and prepping the fixings for her renowned macaroni and cheese. Maya laughed while doing her bit to help Pop-pop with the sauce.

Earth, Wind, and Fire's "September" was abruptly interrupted by the harsh driving thump of the Ying Yang Twins.

"Who the hell touched my record?" Kenny yelled.

Serita breezed into the kitchen. "C'mon, Daddy, can we please listen to something in this century?"

Kenny slid open the patio screen and stepped inside. "Girl, if you don't keep your hands off my records. You call that music? What the hell is all that whisperin' about, anyway?"

"It's called 'Wait,' Daddy."

"Did he just say what I think he said? Wait till you see my what? Girl, you better turn that mess off. You see Maya sittin' in here."

"Serita," Ruth cautioned. "You know your daddy doesn't like anybody to touch those old albums."

"That's the problem, Mama, they're old, and you're not."

"Well, you can always take your young tail and get your own place. Then you can listen to whatever you want to, whenever you want."

"C'mon, Daddy. Loosen up." Serita shook and swiveled toward Kenny, pumping her fists in the air in rapid succession, trying to get him to join in.

"Are you dancin' or havin' a conniption?"

"Daddy!"

Kenny was unimpressed.

"Okay, fine." Serita went back into the living room and reluctantly replaced the CD.

"Daddy," Maya shrieked as Dexter entered the house. She dropped the wooden spoon she held, jumped down off her stool, and ran over to him.

Dexter cautiously held her at bay until he adequately cleaned her hands. He then bounced her in his arms and asked Kenny if he needed help.

No, was his standard response. He was the captain of this particular ship and everyone knew it.

Serita hung around the kitchen exchanging furtive glances with Dexter. No one noticed as they were preoccupied with their individual tasks. Dexter's eyes and subtle head movement indicated that he wanted her to make an excuse to leave the room and he would follow. Her exit would take care of itself as she was suddenly overpowered by the smell of boiled eggs and mayonnaise. That, too, went unnoticed.

Dexter moved to put Maya down with her toys in the living room just as Kenny called him out to the patio. "Damn," he whispered under his breath.

As the afternoon progressed, relatives, friends, and neighbors converged on the Reids' lawn. Concerned that Ondie had not yet arrived, Ruth tried her home and cell, just as she walked in with Paul.

Ruth's surprise was notable.

"Hi, Mama, this is my friend Paul."

"How are you?"

Paul extended his hand. "Mrs. Reid, very nice to meet you. I've heard a lot about you."

"Well, you have me at a disadvantage, because I haven't heard enough about you." She cut her eyes to Ondie.

"Mama."

Ruth took Paul's arm. "Do you mind if I have a minute with my daughter?"

"No, not at all."

Ruth caught Kenny's attention as he came in to refill a bottle of water. "This is Ondie's *friend*, Paul."

Kenny shook his hand. "How are you there, young man?"

"I'm fine, sir."

"Kenny, can you take Paul out back and make sure he's having a good time? I just need a couple of minutes with Ondie."

Kenny slapped Paul on the back and led him toward the patio. Ruth took Ondie's hand and dragged her to the den.

"Ondie, he's fine." Ruth beamed. "Is this the man you told me you met when you went out with Serita?"

"Yes, Mama."

"He seems very nice."

"I wasn't sure that I wanted to bring him here today, but he insisted."

"Does that mean you've told him?"

Ondie tugged nervously at the straps of her top.

Ruth frowned. "You didn't tell him?"

"No, I didn't."

"Oh, Ondie."

"Please, don't use that poor pathetic Ondie tone, Mama. What should I have said to him? Hi, my name is Ondie. I have a four-year-old daughter, and I have to take psychotropic drugs every day to keep from going crazy. That first date would have lasted all of two seconds. Hell, I wouldn't even have gotten to a first date with an introduction like that."

"Okay, I'm not going to lecture you, and I'm not going to butt in. You do what you feel is best. But, baby, if you want to get serious with this man you need to tell him."

A couple of Ondie's aunts and cousins swarmed around Paul like bees to honey. They got a kick out of his accent, and he got a kick out some of theirs.

Ondie found Maya playing; she excitedly jumped into her mother's arms. They then went to find Paul, who was hunkered over a plate of food. "You havin' fun?"

"I'm having a great time." He smiled and licked barbecue sauce from his fingers. "And who is this delightful creature?"

"This bundle of energy is Maya."

"Hello, Maya. Nice to meet you."

Maya bashfully buried her face in Ondie's shoulder and squirmed.

"She's shy," Paul noted.

"No, she's not. Maya, can you say hello to my friend Paul?"

"Hi."

Paul knew he won the little girl over when he made a cartoonish face and she laughed. "So, how did it go with your mother? I take it she gave you the third degree?"

"You know how mothers can be."

"Yes, I have one of my own."

Uproarious laughter drew their attention to the east end of the yard. After fueling up his courage, Ondie's uncle Frank started the traditional Soul Train line. It didn't matter what your music taste was, young and old alike came together. No Reid party was complete without the Electric Slide.

Ondie rolled her eyes. "Oh Lord, not that again."

"We should do it," Paul encouraged.

"No, I don't think so. But you go ahead."

He stood and reached for Maya. "How bout it, Maya? Care to get jiggy?"

Maya climbed into his arms.

"Wow, you do have a way with the ladies," Ondie noted.

Paul leaned down and whispered, "I like Maya, but I would much rather boogie with you."

Ondie blushed. Just as she decided to join them,

Dexter approached. Maya quickly abandoned Paul for her father's embrace.

"Hi, Ondie."

"Dexter."

The two men sized each other up as if it were some sort of pissing contest. *A manwich,* Ondie mused. Paul stood sure and confident in his cream linen, and Dexter cocky and arrogant, displaying his defined biceps and muscular calves. She got a charge thinking that he must have been watching Paul from the time they arrived.

"Dexter, this is my friend Paul. Paul, this is Maya's father."

Paul nodded. "What's up, man?"

"It's all good, doc."

Why did men only show an interest when it seemed someone else was sniffing around their supposed territory?

"Maya, Paul, and I were just about to go do the Electric Slide."

"Okay, I was just wondering where she was, that's all."

"You don't have to worry, man," Paul injected. "She's in good hands, they both are."

Dexter kissed Maya, passed her back to Ondie, and the trio walked off.

Ondie smirked. "That was wicked."

"Did I embarrass you?"

"Not at all. I liked it—a lot."

Dexter observed Serita going into the house. He eased past a riotous spades game and followed her up to her room.

He knocked. "Serita, it's me. Open up."

She didn't respond.

"Serita?"

The lock on the door clicked and it opened. She pulled him inside and checked to see if anyone might be prowling in the hallway. "Are you out of your mind coming up here?"

"I've been tryin' to get some time alone with you all day. Why have you been avoiding me?"

"I'm not, Dexter. I just don't think it's a great idea for us to be sneaking around in the house like this."

"But, baby, I haven't seen you in over a week. I called you and left messages and you didn't call back."

"I was busy working."

"That never stopped you before."

He leaned in for a kiss. She pressed her hand to his chest to stop him. "You're drunk."

"I had a couple of drinks. I'm not drunk."

"Not here, okay? You shouldn't even be up here. Ondie's downstairs."

"In case you haven't noticed, your sister is occupied."

"So is that supposed to let us off the hook or something?"

"Maybe."

Dexter wrapped his arms around her and pulled her toward him. She resisted.

"Baby, what's wrong?"

"This whole damned thing is wrong, Dexter. Look, we need to talk, but not now. You have to get out of here and go back downstairs before anybody sees you."

"Serita?"

"Go. Now."

Dexter went to the door, eased it open, and slipped out just as Ruth was coming up the hall.

"Dexter? What are you doing?"

He jumped and buried his face in his hands. Serita poked her head out the door.

"What is going on?" Ruth demanded. "Dexter, there's no reason for you to be up here. Somebody better say something, 'cause I sure the hell don't like what I'm thinking."

"Mama."

"Dexter, go downstairs."

Dexter knew not to argue with her. He did as he was told.

"Serita. Inside."

Ruth marched behind her as Serita stepped back into the room. The silence was caustic. The muted laughter and the music outside underscored the visible tension.

"Please tell me that there is nothing going on between you and that man."

Tears welled in Serita's eyes and informed her guilt. She'd honed her skills telling little white lies as a child. She got away with a lot more with Kenny, but Ruth was another matter. Once faced with her infraction, Serita couldn't hold it together.

"What in the world?"

Nauseated, Serita bolted for the bathroom. Ruth was troubled and followed behind her. Giving up what little she'd managed to eat that day seemed a clear indicator that something more was afoot.

"Lord," Ruth sighed. "Please tell me you're not pregnant?"

Serita turned on the faucet, splashed water on her

face, and cupped her hands to drink some down. She grabbed a towel from the rack, dried her face, and sat down on the rim of the bathtub.

Silence fell over them. Ruth leaned on the wall and covered her face with her hands. Physically drained from the day's activities, she lumbered back into Serita's bedroom and took a seat at the foot of her bed.

Serita eventually came out of the bathroom with her eyes downcast, too ashamed to look at her mother. "Would it make any difference if I said it wasn't planned?"

"When your father had an affair I remember him saying pretty much the same thing you just did. He didn't know I knew. He thought I was too busy with you and Ondie to pay much attention to what he was doing. I tried to ignore his trips to Macon. I let him think whatever he needed to in order to sleep at night, until I couldn't sleep anymore. I felt so betrayed when I found out he had a son by that woman. I wanted to crawl into a hole. I knew it wouldn't have hurt so bad if I didn't love him so much. It took a long time for me to be able to trust him again. When you're young you think you know what love is, and that you would die without it. Sometimes it takes maturity to understand that if you love someone you don't go out of your way to hurt them. I don't know how long this thing has been going on with you and Dexter, but you know what this is going to do to your sister when she finds out. Whatever you feel for him, is it worth what you're doing behind Ondie's back?"

Serita trembled and sank down on the bed. "We started seeing each other last year. We met at this party and one thing led to another. . . . Ondie and Dexter weren't together then and they aren't now, Mama. I really do love him, and I don't think we have anything to be ashamed about."

"If you feel that way, then you wouldn't have needed to sneak around."

Serita sobbed in her mother's arms.

"I wish I had the answers, but I just don't. I could tell you what I think you should do, but you're not a little girl anymore. This is something you need to work through on your own. But just know whatever you decide I'll be here for you."

Ruth held on to Serita and rocked her as if she were a baby. It was upsetting to have history repeat itself in such a way. Because of Kenny's indiscretion, she had learned what giving yourself over to temptation could do, despite the reasons.

Once you allow it, you set yourself on a course that is not easily altered. The result of one's misguided decisions can destroy the lives of everyone else involved in the blink of an eye.

# 11

"Maya's finally asleep," Ondie said.

"She's a sweetheart."

"Yes, she is."

Ondie sat next to Paul on the sofa and he poured her a glass of wine from the bottle he'd opened while she was putting Maya to bed. She anxiously bit her lip as he passed her the glass. She'd been doing so well; did she want to continue pushing the limits?

He toasted and she put the glass to her lips and pretended to sip. "I had a really good time today. Your family is terrific. They remind me a lot of my own, especially your father. It's hard to believe that he and your mother are separated. They seem to be so in love."

"Things are not always what they seem."

"What do you mean?"

"There are reasons people separate. My father had an affair that produced a son."

"Seriously?"

"I don't know that I could be as forgiving as my mother."

"I see. So you have a brother?"

"Who I haven't seen, and we really don't talk about. Does Kenny still remind you of your father?"

"Well, my father never stepped out on my mother that I know of. I just meant that Kenny was a lot like him in his manner."

"Are you close?"

"Were; he passed away seven years ago. He was a much better father than I've been for my own children. You can't imagine what it's like to hear your sons give homage to another man. It was my own fault. I should have tried harder to be a part of their lives, no matter the distance."

There it was again. The same remorse she saw in his eyes when he spoke about his children at the restaurant. He was so distracted he didn't notice that she wasn't drinking.

"Paul, I need to be honest with you about something." Ondie braced herself and readjusted. "I like you very much, maybe more than I should."

"I like you, too, Ondrea. I want what's developing between us to continue to grow." He took her hands. "You're freezing."

"I'm nervous." She inhaled deeply. "We've only known each other for a short while and what I need to say to you may scare you off, but I want to clear the air."

He looked at her intently and said nothing.

"When I was seventeen I was diagnosed with schizoaffective disorder. I get confused sometimes, and see or hear things that aren't there. I can get extremely angry and agitated. It's like the real you being trapped inside a person that you don't recognize. My symptoms are controlled with medication, and counseling, and as long as I'm on this regimen I'm stable."

"And if you're not?"

"You've seen a little of who that person is when we first met, remember?"

Paul sat up on the edge of the sofa and rubbed his hand across his chin as he tried to absorb what she said.

"That's pretty much it. I understand if you don't want to see me again. I just really needed to tell you the truth."

"Everybody has problems, Ondrea. Telling me took courage. I don't know what it's like to have shouldered the load that you have, especially while raising a child. But from what I can see you've done an extraordinary job."

"I had a lot of help."

"But no one can live your life. No one was inside your head." He brushed her tears away with his thumbs. "I'm happy with the woman that you are. If you want me to stay, just tell me whatever it is I need to know to support you."

"You could have any woman in Atlanta that you want. Hell, any woman in the world; why would you want to stick around me and my problems?"

"I'm thirty-six years old. I've had my share of female companionship, and been around the block a few times. I'm a little tired of the quick fix. I want something that will last—something real. You're a captivating woman, in and out of bed. I want us to get to know each other better. I'm willing to try, if you are."

His kiss assured her that he meant exactly what he said and he was man enough to back it up. Unencumbered, she wept as he touched more than her body; he reached out to touch her soul.

* * *

It was almost two in the morning by the time Ruth finished cleaning up the remains of a Memorial Day celebration that was more memorable than she would have liked. Despite Kenny's continued pleas, she refused to come to bed. He was feeling overly amorous, but Ruth was in no mood. He was snoring ten minutes after his head hit the pillow. She was still reeling from the discovery of Dexter and Serita's affair; cleaning was therapeutic.

Ruth fixed herself a cup of tea and sat down at the table. Kenny stumbled into the kitchen and found her crying.

"Ruthie, what's wrong?"

"Nothing, go back to bed."

"Why are you sittin' in here like this, baby? C'mon, tell me what's wrong."

"Kenny, there's nothing you can do about it, so you may as well go back to bed."

"How do you know what I can do if you don't tell me? Is it Ondie?"

"No."

"Is it Serita?"

"Kenny."

"Ruthie, tell me."

Ruth wrung her hands and stared into her cup. "Yes, it's about Serita."

Kenny eased into a chair next to her and took her hand. "Talk to me."

"She's pregnant."

"She's what? How do you know?"

"She told me. And I've been a nurse long enough to know the signs."

"Who's the father?"

"You don't want to know."

"Ruthie?"

"Kenny, I don't want you to do anything."

"What is it that you think I'm gonna do?"

Ruth pursed her lips and looked at him. He could see what her eyes were saying.

"Woman, you can't just drop a bomb like this and not tell me the rest."

"It's Dexter."

The transferred weight became Kenny's to bear and he was livid. He charged cursing up the stairs and Ruth chased after him.

"Kenny, where are you going?"

"I'm gonna do what I should have done when that son of a bitch walked out on Ondie."

He pulled on his pants and shirt, slipped into his shoes, and grabbed the keys to his truck.

Ruth threw herself in front of him. "Kenny, it's late. You don't need to be drivin' to Dexter's at this hour."

"Ruthie, he messed up Ondie's life. I'll be damned if I let him do the same to Serita."

"Kenny, we need to think about this."

"All I'm gonna be thinkin' about is how I'm gonna whup that boy's ass!"

With that he pushed her aside and bolted from the house. He then jumped in his truck and sped off.

"Mama, what's going on? Where's Daddy going?"

Ruth turned around to see Serita standing on the stairs.

"Oh no. You told him about Dexter, didn't you? He's on his way over there. I gotta call him."

Serita ran back up to her room; Ruth followed.

"It went to voice mail," Serita sighed. "He must have turned off his phone. I need to go over there."

Ruth stopped her. "You're not going anywhere."

"Mama, Daddy could hurt him."

"And what do you think you going over there will do?"

"I can try and stop him."

"You know Kenny's temper. It would take a lot more than you to stop him now."

Serita threw her head back. "Mama, why did you tell him?"

"I don't know. I didn't intend for him to react this way."

"What did you think he was gonna do, invite Dexter over for a beer? We should call the police."

"You are not going to call the police on your father."

"Then I need to try and call Dexter back. I gotta warn him."

Thirty minutes later Kenny's truck screamed into the parking lot of Dexter's complex. The night air cleared his head, but made his anger burn hotter. "Open up, boy!" He pounded on Dexter's door for nearly five minutes. Irritated neighbors threatened bodily harm, but he didn't back down. "Mothafucka, open this damn door before I kick it in!"

The door finally opened and Kenny pushed in, knocking Dexter to the floor.

He stood up and adjusted his boxers. "Man, what the hell is wrong with you? Do you know what time it is?"

Without warning Kenny hit him in the mouth. He flipped over the coffee table and landed awkwardly on the sofa.

"That's for messin' with Ondie's head and gettin' Serita pregnant."

Dexter shook himself. He tasted blood in his mouth and wiped it away. "What? Pregnant? What the hell are you talkin' about?"

"Don't act like you don't know. You been screwin' my little girl for months and it's gonna stop, you hear me?"

"Have you lost your damn mind?"

"I don't want you comin' to my house no more. I don't want you around Serita or Ondie, do you understand?"

"Your house? You don't live there no more. You just stop by every now and then for a quick nut."

Kenny charged Dexter, and Dexter punched him in the stomach, sending him to his knees. "You wanna come up in my shit and play hero when you ain't no better than me. You've screwed women all over Georgia, and now you want to act all holier than thou 'cause you supposed to be some kind of reformed player. How many other little bastards you got runnin' around without a daddy besides Ondie and Serita?"

Kenny clumsily rose to his feet coughing. "I meant what I said."

"Man, you better get on outta here with that before I hurt your old ass!"

Deflated, Kenny slunk away like a wounded dog.

Truth is not for the faint of heart. The sword cuts both ways.

After Kenny left, Dexter slipped into his blue jean shorts and tore up his apartment looking for his cell phone. "Shit, where is it?" He rubbed his hands over his face, mentally retracing his steps since getting home. The search led him to his Jeep, where he found it wedged between the front seats. There were two messages and three missed calls; all from Serita. He went back into his apartment and dialed her back.

"Dexter?"

"Serita, what the hell—"

"Did Daddy come over there?"

"He just left."

"Did he hurt you?"

"No, I'm cool." He heard a sigh of relief.

"Serita, are you pregnant?"

"I think so. I took one of those home pregnancy tests; it came out positive. I made an appointment with my doctor to be sure."

"I thought we were being careful." Dexter slumped on his sofa and buried his face in his hand. He winced when his hand brushed up against the cut on his lip.

"Dexter, are you there?"

"Yeah."

"What happened with Daddy? What did he say?"

"We came to an understanding."

"What does that mean?"

"Does Ondie know?"

"No, and I don't think Mama is gonna tell her, but maybe I should."

"What?"

"I'm sick of the lies, Dexter. Now everything's changed."

"Serita, we need to think about this."

"What do you want to do?"

"We can't . . . You can't have this baby."

"You want me to get rid of it?"

He said nothing.

"Dexter?"

"I don't see any other way."

"You just want to wash your hands of this whole thing, and get rid of this baby so there's nothing to remind you of what we did, is that it? So all that love talk didn't mean shit, huh?"

"Serita, you know I love you."

"Yeah, right. When it was convenient."

"Serita."

"Good-bye, Dexter."

# 12

Ondie sat patiently in Dr. Mathis's office and waited. He was running late, which was unusual for the habitually prompt doctor. As she waited she flipped through a number of pamphlets spread out on a table in front of her. One in particular caught her attention. It referenced an article written by her very own therapist.

> "For now we see through a mirror, dimly, but then face to face. Now I know in part; but then shall I know just as I also am known." *Into the Looking Glass and Beyond, by Dr. Lewis Mathis.*

Dr. Mathis entered as Ondie began reading.

"I'm sorry. I got hung up in traffic."

"That's all right." She held up his pamphlet. "I'm impressed. All this time I've known you and I didn't know you were a religious man."

He sat facing her and took a sip of the coffee he had brought in with him. "Is that important to you?"

"Well, I've said some really awful things in this room."

"Do you feel I was offended?"

"Clearly not."

"Do you think my believing in God should make a difference in how I treat you?"

She started to put the brochure back on the table.

"Feel free to keep it. That's what it's there for."

"Okay." She stuffed it in her purse. "Maybe it should change how I've treated you."

"Why?"

"I don't know."

"Then don't do it. This is a place for you to be honest. I don't hide behind my faith, and I don't want you to feel threatened by it. Deal?"

She nodded.

"So, what's been going on with you?"

"I told Paul."

"How did he take it?"

"He seems okay with it. He asked to come to a couple of these sessions with me so that he can better understand this disorder."

Dr. Mathis stroked his beard. "How do you feel about that?"

"I don't think I'm ready for you to meet, if that's what you're getting at. This is uncharted territory for me. I feel like I always have to be on around him. If I slip up and he sees the other side of me, he'll realize that he made a mistake."

"Well, you told him and he didn't run; that's encouraging."

"It is, isn't it?"

"So you know what my next question is, right?"

She looked at him as he sipped from his cup, smiled, and turned away. "I'm trying to put Dexter in perspective. I know he'll always be part of Maya's life, but that doesn't mean he has to be part of mine. Opening up to Paul helps a lot. They actually met at the barbecue."

"How did that turn out?"

"Dexter acted all weird with him, almost like he was jealous. But I think his attitude had more to do with the fact that Paul was getting along with Maya."

"Maya likes him. That's a good sign."

"I know it's too soon to be thinking about a future with Paul, but just maybe . . ."

"He could be the one?"

"I don't want who I am to be defined by my relationship with this man."

"Then don't let it. You are your person. You were before you met him, and you will be if he doesn't stick around."

"Dare to dream, right?"

After leaving Dr. Mathis's office, Ondie stopped by her mother's. Ruth was a great asset. Because of her appointments, Thursday was usually the only day Ondie couldn't pick Maya up herself. When Ruth wasn't available the task usually fell to Dexter. On those rare occasions when neither was able to collect Maya, Ondie made other arrangements with Dr. Mathis. It was a good system; everyone's schedules generally complied.

When she entered the house she found Maya

propped in front of the television eating a cookie, watching her favorite Aladdin video for the umpteenth time, and pretending to feed her toy parrot. "You want a bite, Iago?"

Ondie's jangling keys drew her attention to the door. She dropped the toy bird, ran to her, and leaped into her arms. With her mouth covered with chocolate and the crumbs of her feast, Maya planted a big sloppy kiss on her mother's cheek.

"Well, I see somebody's havin' a good time." Ondie brushed the crumbs from her face. "How many of those have you eaten?"

Maya sheepishly held up one finger, then two.

"Oh Lord. Where's Grandma?"

"In the kitchen with Auntie 'Rita."

Ondie continued on to the kitchen, where she found Ruth and Serita engaged in an intense exchange; they abruptly stopped when she entered.

"Hey, baby, I didn't hear you come in."

Ondie's brow furrowed. "Y'all look guilty as hell about something. What's going on?"

"Nothing." Ruth wiped her hands on a towel and returned to a boiling pot of turnip and mustard greens on the stove. "How was your day?"

Ondie put Maya down in a chair. "My day was fine. My session was good. The drive home wasn't even that bad. But that doesn't answer my question."

"Serita and I were just talkin' about the company she keeps sometimes, that's all."

"Oh, I should've known. This is about a man, right, Serita? Who is it this time? Somebody you met on a flight, or somebody you met when the plane landed?"

Serita didn't look directly at Ondie. "It was, uh, some guy I met last year."

Ruth cleared her throat and cut her eyes toward Serita. "You know I'm glad I bagged some of those greens we had at the barbecue. I know your daddy is gonna be hungry when he gets here."

"Yeah," Serita agreed. "He's probably gonna want some beer, too. I better go to the store. See you later, Ondie."

Serita sailed out of the kitchen.

"What is this about some guy she met?"

Ruth sighed and took a damp paper towel to clean Maya's hands. "You know your sister."

"She'll find the right man when she's ready. Arguing with her about it isn't going to help."

"You're right, Ondie. No sense gettin' my pressure up. Are you staying for dinner?"

"No, Paul's coming over. I told him about the disorder, and he still wants to be with me."

Ruth looked surprised. She and Ondie embraced. "I am so glad you told him. I hope it all works out."

"Me, too, Mama. Now I've got to get going." She took Maya in her arms. "Tell Serita I'll call her later. I want to hear all about this man of hers."

Ondie gathered up Maya's things, and Ruth saw them to the door, "Bye." Ondie and Maya waved and drove off.

The mouthwatering aroma of the roast she'd started in the Crock-Pot before leaving that morning saturated the air. Ondie changed clothes, put some jazz on the stereo, and finished dinner; as unusual Maya found a way to help. She pulled a chair up to the sink to stand on and sprayed water all over herself trying to wash lettuce for the salad. Ondie laughed, picked her up, and took her back to the room to change.

Paul showed up at seven o'clock, right on schedule. In her haste and preparation, Ondie remembered that she hadn't taken her medication since earlier that morning. While Paul played with Maya, she went to her bathroom to find that she'd forgotten to refill the prescription. A wave of anxiety seized her; she sat on the edge of her bed. She'd been doing so well. Surely missing one dose wouldn't affect her too drastically. In either case there was nothing she could do about it now. She pulled herself together and joined them in the living room.

Dinner went on without a hitch. After Maya was bathed and put to bed, Ondie and Paul curled up together on the sofa to watch an episode of *ER*. Paul yawned as the closing credits rolled. Ondie knew she should be getting to bed, too.

He slipped back into his shoes and she walked him to the door.

"Can I see you this weekend?"

"Of course." She smiled. "Are we going to sit around the house watching TV like an old married couple?"

Paul leaned in and kissed her. "What would be wrong with that?"

"Nothing, except we're not old, and we're not married."

"That could change, you know."

"So, what are we going to do, then?"

"I thought I would take you and Maya to dinner. How does the Cheesecake Factory sound to you?"

"It sounds great, except Maya will be with her father all day Saturday. He's taking her to the Aquarium."

"Well, I guess it will just be the two of us. How very fortunate for me. Maybe after dinner we can go dancing at this little reggae club I know about in Decatur. I do a mean *Jonkonnu*." He wrapped his arms around her waist. "Or perhaps we could manage more sensual moves."

"If you're anything like you are in bed I can hardly wait."

He chuckled and kissed her again. "I'll call you later."

Ondie watched him drive off until he disappeared up the street. She closed the door, leaned against it, and waited as if she expected some sort of metamorphosis. Everything was all right. There was nothing to worry about. Maybe she'd turned a corner. Maybe she wouldn't have to be so dependant on brain-altering pharmaceuticals to pull her through. There was light. At long last there was something to look forward to.

# 13

Serita sat in the sterile room after she'd finished dressing and waited for confirmation. Besieged by posters of expectant mothers, newborns, and tips on healthy eating, she felt that it was all a sign that she had indeed deceived her sister in a most profound way.

The door opened and her bubbly redheaded ob/gyn entered. "The sonogram was good. You look to be about ten, maybe eleven weeks along, which should put your due date around November. Barring any complications there's no reason you can't have a healthy pregnancy."

Serita closed her eyes and teared up. "Am I too far along to schedule an abortion?"

The doctor's smile dissipated. The room fell silent. "Is that what you want to do?"

"It's what I have to do."

"Do you mind if I ask why?"

"It's complicated, and I would really rather not go into it."

"You are a lot further along than I feel comfortable

with performing a procedure like this. Are you sure you'd rather not give this a little more thought?"

"I can't do anything but think about it."

"Serita, are you absolutely sure?"

"Yes," squeaked out in a whisper.

"There are other options."

"Not for me."

"So, when would you like me to set something up for you?"

"The sooner the better."

Ondie had been feeling good all day. There was a much more relaxed dress code at work on Fridays. It was payday, and her levels were stable. She'd been trading e-mails with Paul. His latest correspondence was an invitation to listen to some music and enjoy a picnic under the stars at the park later. He argued that it was casual day and he knew she'd have on blue jeans, so there was no need to fight traffic and go home. He also shot down her objection that she needed to pick Maya up from day care; it was Dexter's weekend with her. *There's nothing standing in your way,* he wrote. *Drive your car to my place and we'll go from there.* Ondie was sure that meant she'd be spending the night. With all her excuses taken away, there was no recourse except to oblige.

The twenty-one-acre Centennial Olympic Park was perfect for a lovers' stroll. The warm June sun showed no sign of relinquishing its pocket in the sky as the day lazily drifted toward evening. Ondie felt like a teenager as she and Paul gorged on Polish sausages, pretzels, and ice-cold lemonade near the Fountain Side Café. It was hysterical watching him frolic barefoot in the Fountain of Rings with other children, encouraging her to join in. She opted to stay dry if for no other reason than the sake of her hair. Still, she marveled at his ability to abandon his stiff corporate persona and become utterly carefree. That playful adolescence in him had to be what Maya was drawn to.

"I hope none of these parents thought you were some kind of child molester or something the way you were running around with those kids," Ondie joked.

"Who cares what they think? The only opinion that matters to me is yours."

"Is that right?"

"You light up when you smile. Perhaps I could do something to keep that look in your eyes."

"You keep talking like that and I'm never going to let you leave for Jamaica."

"Then you'll just have to come with me."

"I can't."

"I'm serious, Ondrea. After Brendon's graduation, we can spend time together and I can show you my Jamaica. We can romp naked on the beach eating mangos and making love to our hearts content."

"Paul, I appreciate the offer, but I really can't. Besides, you haven't seen either of your sons for almost a year. Since you're making the effort to go, you don't need to be distracted by me."

He kissed her. "You are the most enchanting distraction that any man can hope to have, Ondrea Reid."

They walked around Centennial Plaza until his T-shirt and jeans had dried enough for him to put his sandals and shirt back on. It was almost as if they were the only two people in the world; no one else existed, no one mattered.

Serita's cell phone rang. It was Dexter. In her state of mind she really didn't feel up to talking to him. She let it ring into voice mail. He immediately called back.

"Hello."

"Hey, how are you?"

"How should I be?"

"Did you . . ."

"No. Not yet."

There was a long, loud silence.

"Can I see you later?"

"Why do you want to see me, Dexter? Are you gonna try and pressure me into going through with it?"

"I just want to see you."

"Don't you have Maya this weekend?"

"Yes, but I'm stuck at work for two more hours. I was gonna call Ruth and ask her if she could pick Maya up and watch her tonight. Then maybe we could have some time together."

"Mama's at the hospital."

"Damn. Can you pick her up for me? I hate to ask, but I'm not callin' Kenny."

Serita sighed. "Yeah, I guess. Do you want me to keep her here?"

"What time does Ruth get home?"

"Seven o'clock, I think."

"So maybe I'll call Ruth and ask her to keep Maya and then you and I can talk."

"Talk? About what, Dexter? There's nothing left to say. Look, I'll pick Maya up, but that's about it."

Serita hung up the phone, grabbed her shoes and purse, and headed out the door.

As Ondie's sister, she was put on the list as one of those designated to take Maya from day care, though the opportunity hadn't come her way until now. When she entered the building she found her niece among a passel of other little girls waiting for their parents, too. For the first time it struck a chord that if she chose to be, she would be a mother soon. Maya would have a little cousin. The pitiable irony almost made Serita laugh; her baby would actually be Maya's half brother or sister. She shook it off.

"Auntie 'Rita!"

"Hey, munchkin. Are you ready to go?"

"Where's Daddy?"

"He's coming to get you later. I'm going to take you to Grandma Ruth's with me."

Maya grabbed her pint-sized book bag and threw it over her shoulder. Serita took her hand, shepherded her to the car, and strapped her in the backseat.

Serita glanced back at Maya. "Did you have fun today?"

"Yes. I drew a picture of Grandma and Pop-pop." Maya fished the work of art from her book bag. "See?"

"That looks just like them, except I think Pop-pop has a bigger stomach." Serita chuckled.

She handed Maya back the picture, buckled up, and pulled off.

"Auntie 'Rita, can I have some ice cream?"

"I think there's some at the house."

"Yay!"

The light at a crosswalk two blocks away had just turned green and Serita continued on without stopping. As she accelerated through the intersection a small pickup truck sped through the red light and collided into the back right side of her Civic, sending them into a tailspin. Maya screamed. Serita struggled to gain control of the wheel. Other vehicles spun out as the Civic screeched to a halt just before slamming into a utility pole.

The air bag deployed and Serita's head smacked against the driver's-side window. The wreckage of twisted metal and shattered glass lay in the wake of ruin.

Though she was dazed, Serita could hear a congregation of terrified voices; off in the distance the piercing sound of sirens.

"Maya? Maya, baby, are you all right?"

Serita looked up into the rearview mirror, barely able to move. There she saw Maya's motionless body slumped over in the seat, bloodied and covered with debris.

"Oh God. Maya, can you hear me?"

Serita struggled to pull up, but the seat belt held her in place. She soon lost consciousness.

# 14

A hectic morning at Kenenstone Hospital had finally given way to calm on the floor where Ruth worked. With thirty minutes left on her shift, all she could think about was a long hot soak in her garden tub.

"I swear," huffed a fellow nurse. "That Mr. Morton is gonna make me yank out his catheter if he rings that call button one more time."

Ruth laughed and returned to her charts. "I'm glad that I'm almost out of here."

"I know you are, girl. Got any plans for the weekend?"

"Kenny and I are going to Savannah in the morning."

"Must be nice."

"What about you?"

"I got a hot date with Mr. Morton."

"Is that the best you can do?"

"Hell, yeah, until I get twenty-plus years under my belt like you."

Ruth pulled away from her paperwork, took off her reading glasses, and massaged her eyes. She then stood and stretched. "I'm going down to get a Coke. This feels like it's going to be a long half hour. You want anything?"

"Girl, what I want they don't have in that machine."

They both laughed. The telephone rang.

"Fifth floor, this is Angelia . . . Yeah, she's right here."

The woman handed the phone to Ruth.

"Hello." Ruth's expression blanched. She grabbed on to the desk to keep from falling.

"Ruth, are you all right?"

"There's been an accident."

Ruth tore from the elevator in the emergency room practically before the doors had a chance to open. The nurse who had called to alert her was waiting.

"Where is she?"

"Curtain two."

Serita was being examined by an attendant when Ruth rushed in. "Serita, are you okay?"

The pimply faced doctor who looked like he'd just graduated from medical school assured Ruth that Serita was fine. "She bumped her head, and she's got a slight concussion. We'll do a head CT and an ultrasound to make sure there's no damage to the fetus. I put a call out to Dr. Brunner, just to make sure we cover all our bases. I'm sure she's going to want her to stay for observation."

Ruth moved to her side and took her hand. "What happened?"

Serita held her mother's hand tightly and burst into tears. "I had just picked Maya up, and I was on the way to the house when this truck came out of nowhere."

Ruth clutched her chest. "Maya was in the car with you?"

"Dexter called me because he had to work late."

"Wh-where is she? Is she all right?"

The young doctor shot the nurse a side glance and she squeezed Ruth's shoulder. There was no misinterpreting their body language. In her profession she'd had to deliver her share of bad news, too. That had been her least favorite thing about her job. Ruth moaned and tears sprang forth simultaneously. "No, Lord, not my grandbaby."

Ondie and Paul sat passionately kissing at the Water Gardens oblivious of time and space. Never one to be bothered by public displays of affection, he urged Ondie to let go of her inhibitions. She was like a flower budding in the spring, opening up to new experiences that she thought she'd never be able to take pleasure in.

"Maybe we should take this back to my place," Paul whispered, nuzzling her neck.

"Oh, really? And why exactly should we do that?"

"A lot more privacy and we can get naked. What I want to do with you I don't think you want all these people to see."

Suddenly overcome with dread, Ondie jerked away. "Something's wrong."

"What is it? Are you okay?"

"No. Something doesn't feel right."

Ondie's cell phone vibrated in her pocket; Ruth's name displayed on the caller ID.

"Mama, what is it?"

"Ondie, where are you?"

"I'm at Centennial Park with Paul."

There was silence on the other end of the line.

"Mama?"

"Can I speak to him, please?"

"Mama, what's going on? I don't like what I'm hearing in your voice."

"I just want to talk to Paul."

Ondie held the phone before she finally passed it to him. What could Ruth possibly want to speak to Paul for?

Paul listened without words. His expression conveyed nothing. He scratched his head and ran his hand over his face. When he got off the phone he stood up and put on his sandals.

"Paul, what is it? Why do you look like that? What did she say to you?"

"Ondrea, we have to go."

"Go where?"

"There's no easy way to put this." Paul inhaled deeply and held on to her. "There was an accident."

That's all he needed to say. She knew in an instant that it was Maya. Ondie's gut-wrenching scream echoed throughout the park and alarmed everyone within earshot. She clung to Paul and sank to the ground.

Despite the fact that Ruth asked Paul to bring Ondie to her house, she insisted on going to the hospital. Ruth, Kenny, and Dexter were waiting for them when they arrived. Dexter was in a state of shock. And when Ondie saw Maya in the morgue she was inconsolable.

"Do you think we should call Dr. Mathis?" Kenny asked Ruth.

"I already did. He's on his way."

Ruth was numb as she waited for the doctor to emerge from Ondie's room. It's no easier being on this side of a patient's door than it is being on the other, especially when the patient is your own flesh and blood. Maya's death could potentially drive Ondie over the edge. The image of her daughter being locked away just as her mother had been over thirty years earlier regurgitated in her mind, and tears ran down her stricken face.

Distorted flickers of her childhood raced though her mind as she heard Earth, Wind, and Fire's "Shining Star" faintly in the distance, growing progressively louder as the blurred pictures of history came into focus. She was thirteen years old standing in the kitchen of her family's shotgun South Carolina home preparing to make dinner, bopping to the tune on the radio. Her brother, Frank, and some of the boys in the neighborhood were shooting hoops in the backyard. Just after her father came in from work, her mother, who'd been lying down most of the day, emerged from their bedroom.

"Where the hell you been, John D.?"

"Naomi, don't start with me."

"You been with that bitch again, haven't you?"

Her father sighed. "No, in case you hadn't noticed I just got off work."

"John D., don't lie to me! You get off work at four; it's almost six thirty. It don't take you no two and a half hours to get from the paper mill to here."

"Naomi, you know what, I'm too tired to deal with you right now."

"What the hell do you mean deal with me?"

Her father blew her off and turned toward the kitchen.

Ruth could see the ire in her mother's eyes and knew to steer clear when she was like this. She backed away from the stove and cowered in a corner. Her mother became hysterical, balled up her fists, and started beating her father in the back and yelling. Ruth peered out the window toward her brother, who had dismissed his friends and stood outside too afraid to move. Naomi and John D.'s fight quickly escalated to an all-out brawl; she picked up the pot of scalding water from the stove and threw it at him. Ruth's eyes sprang open at hearing her father's agonizing screams as he fell to the linoleum floor.

John D.'s face was blistered and he almost lost his sight in one eye. It wasn't long after that that he took Naomi for a scheduled doctor's appointment; she didn't come back.

Despite the fact that Ruth was told the same could happen to Ondie, she never believed it would. She fought long and hard to keep her beautiful girl from suffering for as long as she could; it was part of the reason she wanted to become a nurse. Because of the turmoil she had lived with growing up.

Nothing Ruth ever trained for had prepared her for what was happening with her family now. The loss was devastating.

"Dr. Vasquez, how is she?"

"She's resting. I gave her a sedative. She should sleep through the night. Why don't you all go on home and get some rest as well?"

How were any of them expected to rest? Maya was dead. Serita was pregnant. The family was being torn apart; the worst had not yet come. There would be no rest any time in the foreseeable future.

# 15

Kenny slumped uncomfortably in a chair next to Serita's hospital bed and watched her sleep. His eyes were heavy and bloodshot. He thought about how horrible the accident was that snatched his grandchild's life, and almost took his daughter's.

The police told them that the driver of the truck that hit them had just come from a bar. Kenny's remorse over his own recklessness weighed on him. How many times had he escaped calamity, getting behind the wheel of a car after one too many beers? Was this how he would have bulldozed another family if he'd inflicted this suffering on them?

Serita's eyes fluttered awake. "Daddy."

He eased down on the side of the bed. "How are you feeling?"

She burst into tears and he gently cradled her in his arms. It was as if she'd never grown up. He still needed to protect her.

"It's all right, baby girl."

"No, it's not. It won't ever be again."

"Do you remember what happened?"

Serita pulled away and fell back onto the pillows. "I was distracted. I had gone to see my doctor; we discussed an abortion. Then when I picked Maya up and saw her and her little friends, I thought about how great it would be to have one of my own. When I saw my baby on the ultrasound, I knew that I wanted to keep it."

"Serita, have you really thought this through?"

"Yes."

"What about this disease your grandmother had? And what about what Ondie's had to live with? There's a chance your baby could inherit this thing."

"And there's a chance he or she won't. Maya didn't."

"You know that this disorder doesn't even show up until later in life. We'll never know whether Maya would have had it or not. Do you really want to gamble with your baby's future?"

"What have I done, Daddy?"

"You didn't do anything."

"Ondie won't see it that way, and neither will Mama."

"Do you think your mother is gonna blame you for this?"

Serita wiped her face with the backs of her hands. "Ondie has always been her favorite."

"That's not true."

"It is true, and you know it. She's always gotten the extra attention because of her mental problems, and I thought I was okay with that. I tried to make peace with the fact that Ondie needed Mama in a way that

I never did. Like right now. Maya is gone and I'm responsible."

As Kenny consoled Serita the door opened and Dexter entered. He swallowed his anger. Whatever their differences, this shared tragedy bound them together now.

Kenny dried his eyes. "I'm going to go check on Ondie." He kissed Serita's forehead. "I'll be back in a little while." He paused as he passed by Dexter; there was nothing he could say. The only kindness he offered was a compassionate pat on his shoulder.

After he was gone, Dexter stood at the door staring at Serita. His soft brown eyes glazed over with sorrow. Neither could speak. Their anguish was too profound. She could see it all over him, whether he said anything or not. This was their punishment. They were sentenced to live—and remember.

Dr. Mathis stepped off the elevator and whisked by Kenny and Paul, who stood just outside Ondie's room.

Paul knew that he wasn't helping just standing around. He started toward the waiting area and Kenny followed.

"You all right?" Kenny asked.

Paul sat, rested his elbows on his thighs, and buried his face in his hands. "Was that the therapist? You don't have to worry, Mr. Reid. Ondie told me about her condition."

Kenny sat facing him. "So that didn't spook you. You're still here. That says a lot about how you feel about her."

"If I walk away from her now, what kind of man would I be? I am very fond of your daughter. I think she's a brave woman to have endured all she has. To be honest with you, given what she's told me, and what I've read online, it scares me a little. Any mother would be distraught after losing her child, but Ondrea is not just any mother."

"She has to pull through this. I don't want to even think about what could happen if she doesn't."

"What the hell is he doing here?"

Kenny and Paul looked up to see Dexter.

Paul stood. "I'm here because of Ondrea."

"This is a family matter. You don't belong."

"I think that is for Ondrea to decide."

"We just lost our daughter. Ondie doesn't need some island fling hangin' on to her right now."

Paul's gaze narrowed. "Galang 'bout yuh business, bwoy. I think you know that I'm more than that."

"I got yo' *bwoy*. You ain't nothin'. How long have you known her, for like two minutes?"

"I may not have shared a child with Ondrea, but that doesn't mean I don't care about her."

"Yeah, whatever." Dexter turned to leave.

"Walking away seems to be a pattern with you."

Dexter spun back around. "You don't know a damn thing about me, man!"

"I know enough to have an opinion."

"What the hell is that supposed to mean?"

Kenny intervened. "All right, this ain't the time. Look, we're all on edge. We're all worried about Ondie." Kenny pulled Dexter back. "Why don't you go take a walk and cool off?"

"Why should I go anywhere? I belong here. Not like this jive-ass Jamaican."

"C'mon now, don't do this."

Dexter blew Kenny off, huffed, and stormed out.

Ondie was frantic. She threw back the covers and tried to get out of bed as Ruth and Dr. Mathis attempted to calm her. "I got to get to Maya. She needs me."

"Ondie, baby, don't."

"Let go of me! Why are you trying to keep me from my baby? She's crying. Can't you hear her?" Ondie kicked and struggled to pull away from them. A nurse rushed into the room and prepped a syringe.

Ruth was torn. She knew what had to be done, and she hated it. "Lewis, is this really necessary?"

"I'm sorry, but it is."

Ondie cringed when the needle plunged into her arm. She was subdued quickly. "Maya needs me. Maya needs me."

It wasn't long before the sedative began to take affect.

"I tried to tell her." Ruth's voice cracked. "I tried to make her understand."

"This was a lot for her to handle," Dr. Mathis said.

"She doesn't want to accept it. I don't, either."

"I know this is hard for you, Ruth. But you've got to be strong now."

"I buried my mother and my father. I don't want to have to plan my granddaughter's funeral."

Kenny quietly entered the room and Ruth fell into his arms and sobbed.

"I can't do this. I won't lose Ondie. Why did this have to happen? I don't understand."

"It's gonna be all right."

"You don't know that."

"I've got you, Ruthie. We'll get through this together this time, all right? Lean on me, baby. That's what I'm here for."

# 16

Later that day, Dr. Mathis stopped by to check on Ondie. He found her up and standing at the window staring off over the horizon. The sun was a blazing ball of warmth that illuminated her anguish and mocked her misery. Still, drifting in a haze of tranquilizers couldn't keep her from facing what was, and what was not.

"I see you're up."

Ondie didn't turn around or acknowledge him.

"Are you feeling any better? Have you eaten anything?"

"We don't go to church," Ondie whispered; her voice was hoarse. "We should have my baby's funeral in a church, but there isn't one. I never knew why—never asked. It was just something that wasn't a part of our lives. I know that there are a lot of people in the world with a lot bigger problems than mine. I just wish it didn't feel like God was ignoring me. I guess it's only fair since I've been ignoring him."

"Is that what you think?"

"I don't know what to think, or how to feel. I just

want my Maya back. She was the best thing in my life. She was all I had to live for."

"You're wrong about that."

"Yeah, well, that's your opinion."

Dr. Mathis walked cautiously to the window. Ondie slowly turned to face him.

"Why don't you let me help you get back in bed?"

"Don't handle me, Doctor! I'm so damn sick of everybody trying to handle me! You've always been the one person I've been able to talk to. Please, don't treat me like I'm gonna break, or I just might."

"If you want to talk I'll be more than happy to listen."

Ondie rubbed her tired eyes and moved slowly to the bed and sat down. "Maya was in the car with Serita; did you know that? Why was she in her car? She was supposed to be with Dexter for the weekend."

"Dexter couldn't make it on time to get Maya, so he called your sister."

"Yeah, I guess they were planning to meet later, and she was just using Maya as an excuse to go over to his apartment. There's only so many buddy passes she can lie about."

"Ondie."

"Do you believe in divine retribution, Doctor?"

"Serita didn't kill Maya. It was an accident. You understand that, don't you?"

Ondie looked at him as if he'd said something foreign that she couldn't quite comprehend. "Serita's alive and my Maya is dead. Do you understand that? She was supposed to be with Dexter. Why was she in that car?"

The hospital room door opened and Dexter poked his head in. When he saw that she was up he continued on inside.

Ondie flew into a rage and charged at him with a wild look in her eyes. She slapped him hard across the face. "Where the hell were you? Why was Maya in the car with Serita? She wasn't even in a car seat, damn it!"

Dexter recoiled as Dr. Mathis reached out and took hold of Ondie.

"Were you in on this, too?"

"Ondie, I had to work late. I called the house to see if Ruth could pick Maya up, but she wasn't there."

"Are you fucking my sister?"

Dexter was stunned. He looked at Dr. Mathis and then back to Ondie.

"You are, aren't you? You didn't think I knew. You didn't think I saw you together. Maya saw you. You had the nerve to throw that shit up in my daughter's face. That's why you did it, isn't it?"

"Ondie."

"Get the hell out of here! You make me sick!"

Dexter left the room without hesitation.

Ondie shook and ran her fingers through her tangled mop of curls. Dr. Mathis helped her back to bed.

"I don't want to stay here. I want to go home. I need to get everything ready."

"You need your rest, Ondie. You trust me, don't you? I'm not going to let anybody hurt you."

Dr. Mathis sat at her side until she was asleep again. He then quietly exited the room and rang for the elevator.

"Dr. Mathis?"

"Yes."

"Paul St. James. I'm a friend of Ondrea's."

The two shook hands.

"How is she?"

"I'm sorry, Mr. St. James. You'll understand that I can't really discuss this with you."

"I'm not looking for details. I just want to know if she's all right."

"I'm sure you can appreciate how difficult this has been for her. But she's surrounded by people that love her. She'll be fine, she just needs time."

"Is there anything I can do?"

"I've known Ondie for quite a few years, and I've grown to care about her, too. Be patient; that's the best advice I can give you. If you can't do that, don't lead her on."

*I'll settle down someday. But until then a girl's gotta do what a girl's gotta do. . . . Auntie 'Rita came over and made splaghettis. . . . Yeah, I was there. He wanted a buddy pass for one of his friends and I took it by on my way home. . . . Are you really seeing things that aren't there? Are you fucking my sister?*

Ondie gasped and her eyes flew open. The room was dark with the exception of pale moonlight streaming in through opened blinds and casting eerie shadows all around her.

"Ondie?"

She shrank back in fear, trying to focus on the silhouette sitting in the corner.

"Are you all right?"

The figure moved into the light.

"Serita, what are you doing here?"

"I had to see you. I had to make you understand that it was an accident. I never meant for it to happen."

"What are you talking about?"

"Me and Dexter. You know firsthand how irresistible he is."

"You stabbed me in the back. How could you do that?"

"You weren't together. The only reason you ever saw him at all was because of Maya. Now Maya's gone."

"You killed her to get to him?"

"It was an accident."

"Liar!"

"Dexter's heart is broken, too. But you're so damned selfish you can't see that the world doesn't revolve around Ondie's problems. He needs what you can't give him."

"Shut up!" Ondie picked up the telephone and threw it at her apparition. "Get out of here and leave me alone!"

Ondie switched on the light and curled up in bed; her erratic breathing bordered on histrionics. The darkness was closing in, trying to swallow her up.

"They won't win. I won't let them."

# 17

Kenny took Serita home the next morning after she was discharged. She hadn't seen or spoken to Ondie since the accident. She couldn't face her. She wouldn't know what to say, or how to say it. *I'm sorry* was such an overused and disingenuous platitude, and nothing she could do or say would bring Maya back. But she knew the time was coming, and soon, that she wouldn't be able to evade her any longer.

Ruth and Paul saw to it that Ondie got home safely. There was a strange emptiness to the house now. Everywhere she looked she was reminded of the little girl with the bright smile and dimpled cheeks that made a huge impact in all their lives and left a hole too big to ever be filled again. Maya had enough toys and clothes for three children. And there were literally hundreds of Polaroid memories of her short life crammed into stacks of photo albums.

"You don't have to stay here, Ondie. I wish you'd come home with me."

"No, I want to be in my own house."

"Then I'll go get some things and come stay with you."

"No, Mama, you don't have to do that. Paul has to leave in the morning. He's spending the night."

"Then at least let me fix you something to eat."

"I'm not hungry."

"You should try to put something in your stomach so the medicine doesn't make you sick."

"Okay, Mama."

Paul sat quietly watching Ondie flip through a book of photographs.

Ruth went into the kitchen and found a couple of cans of soup (mothers' fail-safe remedy for just about everything.) While the soup simmered she looked into the refrigerator to see if there was anything to make sandwiches with. The sight of all of Maya's drawings plastered on the refrigerator disturbed her, and she decided that it wouldn't do Ondie any good to be reminded in such a way. Ruth choked up as she reverently removed each one and neatly stacked them in a drawer.

"Soup's on." Despite how she felt inside, Ruth tried to sound cheery. "C'mon, you two, before it gets cold. It's not homemade, but it'll do."

She set out three piping-hot bowls of chicken and noodle soup, accompanied with grilled cheese sandwiches.

"It smells good," Ondie said, taking a seat at the dining room table.

"Yes, it does, Mrs. Reid," Paul agreed. "I must admit I'm a bit hungry myself."

With the exception of spoons clanking on glass bowls, they ate in relative silence.

Some time passed before Ruth finally spoke again. "I hope you don't mind that I called Williams Funeral Home and talked about possible arrangements, and a time that might be good to have the service. Kenny asked Clyde Brown to officiate. You remember him, don't you? He's the minister that works with your father."

"Yeah, I remember. I guess Williams will have to do," Ondie sighed.

"Of course everything is left up to you and Dexter to finalize."

"Dexter," Ondie scoffed.

She spilled soup on the leg of her jeans and got up to go to the kitchen for paper towels.

"I can get that for you, baby."

"I'm not disabled, Mama. I can still do stuff for myself."

Ruth pressed her lips together and absently tore at bits of her sandwich. Paul remained quiet.

Ondie went into the kitchen and returned in a fury. "Where are they?"

"Where's what?" Ruth asked.

"Maya's drawings. What did you do with them?"

"Sweetie, I'm sorry. I didn't think—"

"Did you throw them away?"

"No." Ruth hurried uneasily into the kitchen with Ondie dead on her heels.

Paul moved uncomfortably in his seat witnessing what was happening.

Ruth took the pictures from the drawer. Ondie snatched them from her, and frantically reattached them to the refrigerator door with magnets. "You don't touch my things, ever!"

"I didn't mean to upset you."

Ondie regained her composure and walked over and leaned on the counter. "Mama, I know you meant well. Everybody means well; tiptoeing around me like I'm on some kind of suicide watch. I don't expect Maya to come running in here any minute asking for cookies and milk. She's gone. I know that in my head, and as soon as I feel it in my heart I'll be okay. I'm not ready to let go yet."

"Ondie, there's no time limit for grieving. You have to feel how you feel for as long as you need to. I know what it's like to lose someone you love. I've been afraid of losing you practically every day since you were born."

Ondie looked into Ruth's eyes and knew she wasn't talking about death. Tearfully, she walked over to her and they embraced.

"Mama, I'm not going anywhere."

Paul finally got up and stepped toward the kitchen. "I should probably get going. It looks like you two could use some time together."

Ruth and Ondie pulled apart and wiped their eyes. Ondie went to him. "Please don't. We're okay, aren't we, Mama?"

"Yes, we are." Ruth smiled and took Paul's hand. "I want to thank you for everything that you've done for my baby."

Paul embraced Ruth. "It was my pleasure to do it."

# 18

The time had come for the Reids, Wheelers, and Campbells to say good-bye to the tiniest jewel in the family crown.

Dexter's mother and father had arrived from Jacksonville the night before. Since hearing about their granddaughter, the buxom, fair-skinned, sandy-haired Vivian Campbell had been as distraught as anyone. She wanted to be there for her son from the moment they got the news. She barely spoke to her husband the entire ride for dragging his feet and insisting they give Dexter his space. Her maternal instincts were in overdrive long before they crossed the state line. Not even Dexter's repentant revelation that Serita was pregnant jarred her. "You're still my son. I love you, and that's never gonna change."

"Two women from the same crazy-ass family. Boy, you can't be that hard up." Dexter's father cracked. Orvillo Campbell (nicknamed Bumper) was a strident ex-marine with a deep southern drawl and a low tolerance for BS.

"Leave him alone, Bumper. It ain't like you been no saint all your life. Dexter's already down. He needs our support. You don't need to make him feel any worse. Poor Ondie must be beside herself."

"When ain't that woman beside herself?"

"Stop it, Bumper. I don't want you carryin' on like that when we get to the service."

"That's another thing, I don't know why the hell we're havin' this thing in a funeral home instead of a church, just a bunch of damned heathens. We should have buried Maya in Florida, at least that way we could've had a descent service at Second Baptist."

Dexter's sullen temperament wasn't made any better by his father's acerbic jabs. After blowing his basketball scholarship, Dexter knew that he was little more than a disappointment to his dogmatic father. He just needed to keep himself in check long enough to get through the day. Given the fact that he'd have to be in the same space as both Ondie and Serita, his parents, and theirs, the potential for a major dustup loomed large.

Serita was in her bedroom packing when Ruth knocked at the door. She froze and contemplated ignoring it. She knew full well how her mother would respond to what she was doing, especially today.

"Serita, your father just went down to the car. Are you ready to go to the mortuary?"

"Uh, no, Mama. I'm not going."

"Serita, let me in. I want to talk to you."

She hesitantly unlocked and opened the door. Ruth

tugged at her jacket and smoothed down her skirt as she entered and looked around at the disarray. "Are you still feeling queasy?"

"Not as much."

"Can I get you a 7up, or some saltines?"

She shook her head.

"You're not working today, are you?"

Serita moved to her bed and continued to pack. "No, I took an extended leave."

"So, what are you doing?"

"I'm moving out."

"Serita, your sister is burying her baby today. The whole family needs to be there."

Serita stepped around Ruth to get to a box of shoes. "Ondie won't want me there."

"Will you stop long enough for me to talk to you?"

"I've made up my mind, Mama. I'm going to stay with a girlfriend for a few days until I find a place. I don't want to stay around here with you looking at me the way you have been since this whole thing started."

"What way?"

"That look that says this is all my fault."

Serita maintained her frenetic pace. She pulled a stack of sweaters from the closet and Ruth grabbed on to them.

"Please, stop."

"Why?"

"I talked to your father. I'm so sorry that you think I blame you for this. I never meant to make you feel like I loved you any less than I love your sister. I was so caught up with Ondie all these years that I wasn't paying as much attention to you as I could have. I didn't realize what I was doing to you." Ruth stroked Serita's cheek. "You're my baby girl. I don't want you to hurt, either, and if I could take the pain away from either of you, I would. This is a bad situation, but you can't run from it."

Serita melted in Ruth's arms.

"Will you get dressed and come with us?"

"I can't look at her."

"It'll be all right, baby. We can't let this tear us apart. We'll find a way to heal."

Ondie was up early; she hadn't slept much, anyway. She lay there trying to find the will to get out of bed. She knew what she had to do; she just didn't know if she could. She watched the clock display as the numbers flipped by, thinking that she would move at the next turn of the dial. *Mommy*. She popped straight up, hearing Maya's cry, threw the covers back, and ran to her room. She went to Maya's bed and pulled the blanket off, held it to her nose, and inhaled. Emptiness hit her in the stomach like the destruction of a wrecking ball; she sank to her knees and wailed.

The telephone rang and scared her. She ignored it, labored to her feet, and robotically made her way to the bathroom. After showering, she found a simple scoop-neck, short-sleeved, black pencil dress in her closet and slipped into it. She had issues with her hair, opting to pull it back and tie it up. Her makeup was simple, applying just enough concealer under her puffy eyes to camouflage the dark circles; glamour was not the objective.

She listened to Ruth's voice mail stating that they

would come by to pick her up on the way to the funeral home, but opted to drive herself. Strength and weakness collided. She needed some time alone before being hassled by family.

The oppressive morning heat rose defiantly against the air-conditioned anteroom of the mortuary. When Ondie entered the Slumber Room, she wavered. There, nestled among the sprays and floral arrangements was a small white box that held the remains of her heart. She removed a handkerchief from her handbag and sat quietly in a seat at the back of the room. As she remembered Maya's contagious laughter, she summoned the courage to continue to the altar for one last look.

Ondie took note of the condolences. There was an array of cards and flowers sent from her job, UPS, where Dexter worked, and the hospital. She peered into the casket and straightened the ruffles on Maya's white satin dress. She then leaned in and kissed her. "I love you."

Ondie's attention was drawn to the door as Dexter and his family entered. He slowly approached and she glared at him coldly. Vivian rushed over to her blubbering and pulled her into an embrace. Bumper squeezed her hand and joined his son at Maya's casket.

The car carrying the rest of the family motored up to the door as others assembled. All the well-meaning hugs and pitying looks were draining.

Ruth entered on Kenny's arm; Serita trailed behind.

"What are you doing here?" Ondie barked at her sister.

Kenny interceded. "Serita's here for the same reason we all are."

"None of us would be here if it wasn't for her!"

Some of the mourners gathered around them pretended not to hear, but couldn't look away.

"Ondie, you need to stop it now," Ruth cautioned.

"Why? It's the truth."

"She's right, Mama," Serita admitted. "I shouldn't have come."

She turned to leave and Kenny blocked her. "Ondie, this is a sad and terrible day. We got to get through it the best way we can, the whole family. This is for Maya; don't make a scene."

"You're right, Daddy. I'll deal with you later, lil' sista."

Dr. Mathis, who'd come for Ondie's support, stepped out to see if there was anything he could do. Ondie assured him that she was fine; she then went back inside with Kenny and Ruth. Serita sat a safe distance behind them.

The service was somber. No one was unaffected. How do you say good-bye to innocence? The unspoken grief that flooded the room was palpable. The sickeningly morose funeral dirge didn't help. Ondie wept aloud in Ruth's arms, triggering a wave of empathy and tears. Unable to remain still any longer, Serita bolted. Kenny ran after her.

"Serita, wait. Please come back inside."

"I gotta get outta here, Daddy."

"Don't go."

"How can you expect me to sit there with everybody staring at me? Blaming me? I can't be here. I can't take this." Serita pulled away from him, darted up the street, and hailed a cab.

Kenny was torn; go after her, or go back inside to be with Ondie and the rest of the family. He glanced at his watch. The service would be over soon, and then he could see what, if anything, he could do for Serita.

One of the things that can be counted on at most any funeral is the feast that is certain to follow. After leaving the internment, Dexter opted to go back to his place. His parents didn't argue. Other relatives and friends descended on the Reid house intent upon feeding their troubled souls. There was enough food prepared for a legion of mourners; death had a way of making people hungry. Ondie, however, was not one of them.

As Ruth tended to the guests, and ensured that anything her sister-in-law had prepared stayed clear of those who wanted to avoid diarrhea, Ondie made her way upstairs to Serita's room.

Serita was alarmed when the door opened; she thought she'd locked it behind her.

"I saw your car outside when we pulled up. Looks like you're moving out."

Serita couldn't look at her. All her fears from childhood flooded her senses. She held a box of her things in front of her as if to hide her secret. "I thought I'd be gone before anybody got back. I was just about to leave."

"That's pretty cowardly of you, isn't it?"

"I guess it is."

"You guess?"

Serita closed her eyes and swallowed. Ondie blocked

the exit. The only way out was through her, or out the window.

"How long have you and Dexter been . . . together?"

"What?"

"Let me make it plain enough for someone of your considerable talents to understand; how long have you been fucking?"

Serita's lids brimmed with tears. Her nonverbal communication bore the truth.

"How long?"

"Ondie."

"Answer me."

Serita's mouth opened, but there was no sound.

"Were you with him when we were together?"

"No, Ondie. It wasn't like that."

"Then what was it like? We shared clothes. We may as well share a dick, too; is that what you thought?"

"Please don't do this."

"What in the hell do you mean don't do this? Don't do what? Do you have any idea what I'm feeling right now? This is not a dress, Serita! This was my child. My baby. I can't go out and buy another one!"

"Ondie, please," Serita cried.

Ondie closed the door and locked it behind her.

There was enough noise coming from downstairs to mask what was going on in Serita's room. Ruth came out of the kitchen looking around frantically. Kenny looked up to notice panic on her face.

"Ruthie, what is it?"

"Have you seen Ondie?"

"Not since we got back from the cemetery."

"Is Serita's car still outside?"

Kenny moved to the window and peered out into the driveway. "Yeah, it's still there."

"Oh, Lord Jesus."

Ruth dashed up the stairs with Kenny in tow. They could hear screaming coming from Serita's room as they approached the landing.

Ruth unsuccessfully tried the knob. "It's locked."

Kenny pounded. "Open this damn door!"

Ruth trembled listening to Ondie's abusive tirade, praying that she would do Serita no bodily harm.

"Open this door right now before I break it in!"

Morbid curiosity drew others up to the landing as they waited anxiously, like crows on a farmer's fence, for what was to come next.

Ruth turned sharply and angrily shooed them away. "This don't concern y'all. Go on back downstairs!"

Kenny took several steps back and charged the door; it didn't give. Ruth shrieked.

"Ondie! Ondie, open this damn door! Do you hear me?"

Punctuated by an ominous silence, the lock on the door finally clicked. It was mere seconds, but it felt as if time stood still. The door flung open. Ruth grabbed Ondie as she tried to run off.

"Let go of me," Ondie screamed. She shook Ruth loose, plowed down the stairs, and out of the house. Someone's car had her almost penned in, but she managed to navigate out of the space and speed off.

Kenny rushed inside the room to find Serita whimpering and balled up in the corner like a rag doll. "Serita, are you all right?"

She nodded.

"Are you hurt?"

She shook her head and grabbed on to him, shaking.

Ruth stood in the doorway grateful that nothing was done that couldn't be undone. The belief that she could keep Ondie from self-destructing was quickly slipping away.

# 19

"It's been a couple of days since we've seen each other; how are you feeling?"

Ondie didn't answer. She stood quietly at the window idly watching yet another construction delay on the interstate below. She hadn't gone back to work. Her usual tidy appearance was unkempt. "If you livc in Atlanta long enough you almost become immune to all the barricades. Driving is like being on an assembly line, or in a rat's maze going nowhere fast."

Dr. Mathis seemed to sense Ondie's reluctance. He knew the process all too well and decided to hold back and give her the space she needed to open up.

Time seemed to stagnate, empty minutes holding them both hostage.

"I can't resolve myself to cleaning out Maya's room. Everything is just the way it was that Friday morning when we left the house."

"Do you feel there's any particular urgency to get rid of her belongings?"

"No. I guess there isn't."

"Have you spoken to Paul?"

"He's called a couple of times from Jamaica. He said he'd be in late tonight, but I don't think I can see him."

"Why not?"

Ondie turned to face him. "Look at me. I'm a mess. I can barely get out of bed, let alone do something with my hair."

"It takes time."

"I haven't spoken to my mother in two days. She calls and I won't answer. She comes by and I won't open the door."

"You're still processing. I'm sure they all understand that."

Ondie rubbed her weary eyes and leaned against the window. "I almost hurt my sister after the memorial. I wonder if she understands that. I felt angry enough to kill her."

"But you didn't."

"No."

"Were you angrier because you still hold her responsible for Maya's death, or because of Dexter?"

"Both, I suppose. Their mendacity is stifling. Mendacity; don't you love that word? It seems so appropriate, almost biblical. I'm sure you can appreciate that, can't you, Doctor? For now I see through the mirror dimly, and I hate what I see."

Ondie left Dr. Mathis's office and for the first time in a long while she didn't feel any better. The bitterness inside her waxed cold. When she got home the alarm reminding her to take her meds set her off. "To hell with it," she spat, and flushed them down the toilet. "I don't want to numb the pain. I want to feel it."

She went into Maya's room and stood in the middle of the floor. All her dolls were neatly lined up on top of her massive toy chest as if waiting for her to come and play with them. Ondie wanted to tell them that Maya wasn't coming back, but she wasn't crazy enough to believe that they would understand. She barely did herself.

She sat down on Maya's bed and looked at the picture of her in a Princess Jasmine costume that was taken while she was in Florida. She picked up the picture expecting to cry, but there were no tears. *Iago,* she thought, referring to Maya's talking toy parrot. "Where's Iago?"

Whatever the reason, Ondie fixated on that particular toy. She searched all over, but it was nowhere to be found. The harder she looked, the more determined she was to locate it. "Where is it?" She was becoming unhinged. She knew that it wasn't with her the day she died. Perhaps her mother had it. *No,* she thought. *It had to be at Dexter's.* Ondie remembered Maya taking the damnable toy with her to his apartment the weekend he took her to the Aquarium.

"Hi, it's me. I was wondering if I could come by."

Dexter held the phone for a long moment without answering.

"Dexter?"

"Yeah, I guess."

Serita hung up and within minutes she was at his door. He was naturally taken aback.

"I've been sitting outside for almost an hour," Serita began. "I wasn't sure whether I wanted to come up or not."

Dexter stepped back from the door and let her in. He dashed into his bedroom to grab the T-shirt he'd just taken off. He looked into her eyes and still felt her undeniable attraction. There was power in the forbidden fruit. But the invisible line that he'd crossed had become a rope, and that rope had become a noose, and that noose was the guilt that strangled him.

"You were at the gym?"

"Yeah, earlier; I needed to clear my head. I was just about to jump in the shower."

"I won't stay long. I just wanted to tell you that I moved out. I'm staying at Tonja's for a while. I'm looking for a place of my own, and I've decided I should go back to work. With things the way they are at Delta, it's not a good time for me to be off. I need the insurance."

Dexter's jaws tightened. "So you're keeping the baby?"

"You don't have to worry. I don't expect anything from you."

"I can't think about what bringing another child into the world would mean right now."

He sat pensively on the edge of his sofa and picked up the toy parrot. His eyes misted. "This was Maya's favorite. She loved this damn thing." He broke. "I miss her so much."

Serita's heart reached out to him, and he reached out for her. They found comfort in each other's embrace.

He pulled away from her, wiped his face with his forearm, and stilled his inner man. In spite of the fact that he had a right to his pain, he despised his weakness. "It's too soon. I can't think about you right now. You should probably go."

Blaring car alarms penetrated the awkward space between them. Dexter threw open the door and ran out onto the landing. He spotted Ondie with a large stick in her hands pummeling his Jeep. "What the fuck!"

He dashed back inside and grabbed the keys off the counter and sprinted down two flights of concrete steps with no shoes on. He pressed the button on the keyless remote and the noise halted. But his was not the only alarm that sounded. Serita spied her smashed windshield and the brick that laid it to waste. Ondie zeroed in on her standing there when the clamor from her car ceased. Serita backed into the apartment like a frightened rabbit.

"Ondie, what the hell are you doing?" Dexter raged.

"Three days," Ondie shot back. "It hasn't been a good three days and the two of you are going at it already!"

Titillated neighbors hung out doors, and some of the more emboldened moved closer, unapologetically intrigued by the unfolding drama.

"We just put our little girl in the ground, and you couldn't keep your dick in your pants long enough to respect that?"

Dexter tried to reason with her. "Ondie, nothing was going on."

"You're a damned liar. The hypocrisy and the

sneaking around has been going on, and apparently hasn't stopped."

Jeers and snaps encouraging a fight rose from the mostly female mob. A couple of the men that knew Dexter well wanted to come to his aid, but they didn't dare get any closer than the fringe of the crowd that formed on the lawn of the complex.

As Dexter stepped cautiously around the broken glass of his headlights to survey the scope of the damage, Ondie started up to his apartment. A collective "uh-oh" resonated in the late June air.

Consumed with anger, Ondie took to the stairs with the stick in her hand, fully prepared to use it.

Someone yelled Dexter's name and diverted his attention from his Jeep and he locked in on Ondie. A piece of glass sliced into his foot as he gave chase. "Shit!" He hopped around balancing himself on one leg until he extracted it, then hobbled after her. "Ondie, wait! Don't do nothin' you're gonna regret."

Dexter caught up to her by the time she reached the top of the landing. He reached out and grabbed her arm and she swung around violently, smacking him in the head with the stick. He lost his footing and flailed backward, tumbling down the jagged concrete.

The sirens of approaching police cars drew Serita out from hiding and she screamed. Ondie stood frozen and detached as the horde congregated around Dexter's twisted body lying at the base of the stairs like vultures preparing to pick at his remains.

* * *

Kenny belched his approval after polishing off a meal of fried chicken, mashed potatoes, and corn on the cob. He leaned back in his chair and washed it down with a beer. "Baby, that was good," he proclaimed as he patted his stomach.

Still dressed from work, and preoccupied with her girls, Ruth had barely touched her plate.

"Ruthie, are you all right?"

"I was just thinking about Maya. I've been so used to picking her up and bringing her here after work that I almost forgot. When I left the hospital I started to go by the day care."

"Have you talked to Ondie?"

"She won't return my calls. Lewis says to give her time, but I'm scared to let her stay in that house all by herself."

"What else can you do, Ruthie? She'll come around when she comes around. You can't force her."

Ruth shook her head and stood up to clear the table. "You want some more to eat?"

Kenny took her hand and gently pulled her over to sit on his lap.

"What are you doing, man?"

He kissed her. "You're always so busy takin' care of everybody else that you never take time to take care of yourself."

Ruth hugged his neck and kissed his forehead. "I'm all right."

"You know, Ruthie, I've made a lot of mistakes in my life, but the one thing that I got right was falling in love with you. Do you remember when I wanted to take you away to Savannah?"

"Yes."

"I was tryin' to get you away from everything and everybody so I could ask you to marry me again."

"Kenny."

"I want to stand up in front of God and everybody and tell them how much I love you, and how much I appreciate your taking me back in your life. I never should have taken you for granted."

Ruth's eyes clouded and she smiled sadly.

"C'mon, woman. Don't act like you're surprised. I'm over here all the time. I got more clothes in your closet than I got in mine. We're too old to play games, and I want to be more to you. There ain't been no other woman that can hold a candle to you. I want my address and my heart to be in the same place."

"Kenny, there's just too much going on right now to be thinking about something like this."

"A little bit of happiness may be just what this family needs to pull us back together. C'mon, Ruthie. What do you want me to do, beg? All right, then."

He nudged her from his lap, got down on his knees, and took her hands.

Ruth chuckled. "I think you're supposed to be on one knee."

"Naw, I wanna show you how serious I am."

She caressed his face.

"Ruth Anne Wheeler Reid, will you marry me—again?"

Her eyes brimmed with emotion. "How can I say no? Now get up before you get stuck down there."

Kenny jumped up, embraced her, and playfully whirled her around. Laughter reverberated through the echoes of sadness. They were like two young lovers making a commitment to be together for the first time.

The telephone rang.

"Kenny, put me down, I need to get that."

"Let 'em leave a message."

"It could be important. It might be one of the girls."

Kenny released Ruth and she pulled herself together and answered the call; and just like that, reality stole its way into her core and ripped it to shreds.

In a very short span of time the Reids found themselves revisiting the same nightmare that they thought they'd just awakened from; only this time there was going to be a very different outcome.

Ruth and Kenny exited the elevator at Dekalb Medical Center and ran up the corridor to find Serita pacing nervously in the surgical waiting area.

"Serita, what happened?" Kenny asked. "Are you all right?"

"It's Dexter," she cried. "He's being operated on."

"Calm down and tell me what happened."

"Ondie came over to his place. She was completely out of control. She hit him in the face with a stick or something, and he fell down the stairs outside his apartment."

"Ondie?" Ruth queried. "What was she doing there? For that matter, what were you doing there?"

"Ruthie."

Ruth pushed Kenny aside and approached Serita. "Where is Ondie now?"

Serita inhaled. "She's been arrested."

"Arrested?"

"Mama, I haven't seen her like this in a long time. I know she wanted to kill me."

"What? Oh, Serita, don't be ridiculous. Ondie wouldn't hurt you."

Serita scoffed. "I figured you'd take her side."

"I'm not taking anybody's side. I just want to know what happened. Something had to set her off."

"You know as well as I do that it doesn't take much. Whatever she thinks is real is real in her mind. There's nothing you can say to stop her once she gets a thought in her head."

Ruth knew better than anyone how acutely a skewed perception could be twisted into reality. She needed to get to Ondie and know that she was all right.

They tracked down one of the arresting officers, who was still at the hospital. He informed them of the specifics concerning the account of several witnesses and the destruction of property.

Ruth didn't have time to process what he told her. The only fact she focused on was that Ondie was in jail. "I've got to get down there."

The officer tried to placate her. "Ma'am, there really isn't a whole lot you can do at this point."

"Don't you tell me that there isn't anything I can do. We can get a lawyer. We can fight this."

"Ruthie."

"No, I'm not leaving her in that place!"

Ruth left Kenny with Serita and took off. It was nearly eight o'clock when she finally was able to get in touch with Dr. Mathis. He promised to meet her there and that he would call the detention center to ensure that they knew that Ondie was under his care.

Once she made it to the Dekalb County facility, Ruth discovered that Ondie was being held in the mental health unit pending an evaluation to determine her competence. Dr. Mathis advised them of the medications that Ondie was prescribed so they would know how best to treat her. He wasn't optimistic. The options were minimal. Other than prison, being kept in an institution equipped to deal with her needs would be the worst-case scenario.

Ruth's greatest fears were being realized. "Lewis, why can't you continue to treat her?"

"Unfortunately, Ruth, it's out of my hands now. We're just going to have to wait and see."

Ruth was near hysterics. "They're going to lock her away, just like my mother." Again the visage of the shell of a woman she had visited in the asylum at eighteen haunted her.

"Ondie isn't going to end up like your mother," Dr. Mathis assured her.

It didn't allay any of Ruth's doubts.

Kenny joined Ruth at the police station, but their efforts to do anything were futile. Just as Dr. Mathis stated, they would just have to wait.

Visiting hours were well over by the time Bumper and Vivian arrived at the hospital. They were told that Dexter had suffered a concussion, a broken arm, and a fractured rib that punctured a lung, but he made it through surgery and was expected to make a full recovery. Bumper demanded that they be allowed to see him. Vivian sat at his bedside and prayed. Bumper was too furious to talk to anybody but the police. He was adamant that Ondie pay for what she'd done to their son. His rancor was intimidating. If he had his way, Ondie would never taste freedom again.

# 20

Kenny and Ruth stepped off the elevator and stopped at the nurse's station to find out what room Dexter was in. Bumper, who was with Vivian in the waiting room, spotted them. "What the hell is this?"

Vivian stepped between him and Kenny. "Bumper, not now."

"Naw, Vivian. Dexter damned near died and these two waltz up in here like everything is all right. You ain't gon' soothe your conscience with no damn flowers. Y'all can just get on outta here with that!"

"Ruthie, I told you this was a dumb idea. Let's go," Kenny said.

"You think that was a dumb idea?" Bumper sneered. "Your crazy-ass daughter was the dumb idea!"

"Bumper!"

Kenny stepped to Bumper. "Man, I ain't gonna stand here and let you disrespect me or my wife."

"Kenny, let's go," Ruth pleaded.

"Oh, you bad now? You gon' hit me. Try it, big man, and you can end up in one of these hospital beds, too."

Kenny flashed with rage and snatched Bumper by the collar and threw him into the wall. Ruth and Vivian tried unsuccessfully to come between them. A male nurse and two security guards bounded into the room.

"Hey—hey—hey, break it up!"

The guards pinned both Dexter and Bumper and they struggled to free themselves.

"You all need to take this outta here," the nurse demanded.

Kenny broke free of the guard that held him, grabbed Ruth's arm, and headed back toward the elevator.

Bumper calmed down and was released.

Dexter awoke bruised and sore, but glad to be alive. The first thing he focused on was his mother's smiling face and it brought tears to his eyes. It seems that no matter how old a man gets, his mother, if she's a good one, will always be the first love of his heart.

She gently kissed his cheek. "How's my boy?"

"Okay," he whispered. The snug bandages around his torso caused him discomfort.

"Can I get you anything?"

He shook his head, entwined the fingers of his left hand in hers, and gave her a gentle squeeze. "I'm glad you're here."

"Your father's here, too. He's out there somewhere raisin' hell with the nurses, I'm sure."

Dexter tried to laugh and choked. Vivian jumped and poured some water in a cup, stuck a straw in it, and put it to his lips. He lifted his head slightly.

"Not so fast, baby. Do you want me to raise your bed a little?"

He nodded.

Vivian was extra careful. She didn't want to hurt his bandaged head. She examined the monitors and IV drips as if she knew what she was looking at. "You know, with that busted wing of yours it looks like I'm gonna have to feed you, just like I did when you were a little boy."

"I still got one good arm and hand, Mama."

"I know. Thank God for that."

She sat quietly, anticipating a need that never came.

A nurse walked in, checked his vitals, and gave him an oral painkiller. Vivian watched her like a hawk as if waiting for her to make some kind of mistake so she could call her on it.

When she left, Serita entered carrying a planter decorated with get-well balloons.

Vivian's forbearance of the Reid sisters started to mirror that of her husband. She arched her brow and pursed her lips as an outward symbol of disdain. She and Bumper were in full agreement that their only son's involvement with this family was his undoing.

"Hello, Mrs. Campbell."

"Serita."

"How are you feeling, Dexter?"

"I'm good."

Serita set the planter down on the bureau across the room and stepped to Dexter's side.

"I don't mean to be rude, but my son needs his rest."

"I'm not staying. I'm scheduled for a flight this afternoon and I just wanted to stop by and see if there's anything you needed."

Vivian butted in before Dexter could respond. "Haven't you and your sister done enough already?"

Dexter cut his eyes toward his mother and then looked back to Serita. "I'm fine. I got everything I need right here. Are you sure you're in condition to be flying?"

Serita nodded. "I'm gonna get going. I'll check on you when I get back."

Serita quickly exited without looking back.

"Did you have to do that?" Dexter asked.

"It ain't no worse than your father would have done if he had caught her in here."

"She didn't put me in here."

"She had a hand in it."

"Ondie didn't put me in here, either. I tripped and fell."

"Well, that's not how the police saw it."

"What do you mean?"

"Ondie was arrested last night."

"What?" Dexter's sudden jolt caused a sharp pain to shoot through his chest, and he recoiled.

"Now, you know you can't get out of bed, I don't know why you'd even try."

Dexter coughed. "Ondie's in jail?"

Vivian poured more water and assisted him in drinking it. "Several people told the police what they saw. Even her own sister told them that she was afraid of what Ondie would have done to her."

"Ondie didn't do this. I have to tell the police."

Dexter tried to reach for the phone. Vivian stopped him.

"Dexter, you need to calm down."

"Ondie didn't push me. I tripped and fell. End of story."

"Did you bash yourself in the head, too?"

"I hit my head on the stairwell."

"Why do you want to protect that girl?"

"Because I owe her that much."

"You don't owe her anything. She could have killed you."

"But she didn't. So can we just drop this, Mama? I'm not lookin' for revenge, and I don't want Ondie in jail."

"Well, that's exactly where she's gonna be until God or the court says different."

Dr. Mathis recommended an attorney to assist the Reids with Ondie's case. Temporary insanity was the lawyer's defense. Citing her family history, he argued that the witnesses did not have all the facts, and that the death of her only daughter was so heinous and incendiary that it quite literally drove her to madness. Dr. Mathis also defended her by testifying that Ondie had been under tremendous duress. He demonstrated that up until her daughter's tragic accident, Ondie's malady was handled successfully through medication and therapy. Dexter and Serita's affair was also disgracefully brought to the court's attention in order to further establish Ondie's frame of mind at the time of the alleged attempt on their lives. All of that coupled with the fact that Serita told the police that she hid in the apartment because she was afraid for her safety was evidence enough for the judge to declare there was probable cause to detain Ondie, despite Dexter's claims that he slipped and lost his footing.

After considering Ondie's psychological assessment, she stood before the bench. She was ordered to undergo a ninety-day inpatient treatment program at the Peach State Psychiatric Hospital. At the end of her confinement she was to be reevaluated, and if so deemed the attempted murder charge would be reviewed.

Bumper was unnerved. "I don't give a damn what that court says; that lunatic deserves to go straight to jail!"

"All Dexter wants is for Ondie to get the help she needs."

"I'll tell you another thing, Vivian. I don't care if that Serita has a litter of puppies, Dexter needs to leave those people alone."

"He's a grown man, Bumper, and he's as stubborn as you are. So as much as you don't like it, he's not gonna listen to you."

"He needs to listen to somebody or else the next time he could wind up with more than a broken arm and a cracked skull."

"Well, then it's a good thing he inherited your hard head, too."

It had been a week and Ondie still hadn't allowed herself to become acclimated to the Stepford existence of the hospital. Being deprived of certain personal liberties she'd taken for granted was quite an awakening. Her regimented routine consisted of breakfast, lunch, dinner, and group therapy. She longed for the attention and intimacy of Dr. Mathis's office. He knew her, maybe even better than she knew herself most days. Kate Bennett, the staff clinician, seemed nice enough, but Ondie felt no urgent need to talk to her—or to anyone else there. She'd transferred from one jail cell to another; this one just had better food.

She had eighty-three days left to prove to a judge that she was sane enough to live among the regular, law-abiding, taxpaying, moral, backstabbing, and legalistic degenerates of society. She decided that the only *normal* thing to do was play along.

"Ondie, you have visitors."

Ondie caught a glimpse of her haggard reflection, massaged her face, and combed her fingers through her hair to appear more presentable.

Ruth ran to her and hugged her so tightly she nearly took her breath away. Kenny was a bit gentler in his approach. She hadn't been allowed to see them until now. They found an available table and sat down.

"How are you feeling?" Kenny asked.

"I'm okay, just tired. I'd rather be home in my own bed."

Ruth looked at her surroundings. Attendants seemed to lurk around every corner. Surveillance cameras were not too subtly posted at the entrance and other strategic areas of the building. It was a lot like the sanitarium that her mother had been relegated to. There was no mistaking that Ondie was not free to leave.

Ruth squeezed Ondie's hand. "Are you being treated all right?"

"So far."

"We were told we could bring you some things. I wasn't sure what you needed, but if you give me a list I'll be sure and pick them up for next time."

"I can't think of anything right now."

"Paul's been calling for you," Kenny injected. "He wants to come."

"No. I can't let him see me in here like this."

"Ondie, he really seems to care about you," Ruth added. "Don't push him away."

"I thought Dexter cared about me, too. You see where that got me."

"You can't judge Paul by what you and Dexter had or didn't have. You said he was interested enough to research your disorder. If he wants to come here and see you, that has to mean something."

"It means he wants to see the animals in their natural habitat," Ondie cracked.

"Don't joke like that," Kenny frowned.

"I'm sorry, Daddy. But I got to find the humor in all this somehow."

Deep down, Ondie was thrilled that Paul wanted to see her, even if it was here. She was equally aghast that he knew why she was there. She surmised that everybody must have been talking about it by now, including all those that observed her meltdown at Dexter's. At the end of her detention, how was she to return to the life she'd known? Where would she begin to pick up the pieces that remained?

"Mama, can you do something for me?"

"Of course."

"I'm going to give you my bank account information. I need you to take care of my bills and stuff while I'm in here."

"Don't worry about that, Ondie. We've got that covered," Kenny assured her.

"Would you do something else for me? Would you go and pack up Maya's things?"

Ruth's eyes clouded. "Yes. I'll take care of it."

Kenny wrapped his arm around Ondie. She rested her head on his shoulder and wiped the moisture from her face. It was time to let go.

# 21

Nine diverse individuals made up what one of them cynically referred to as the psychologically challenged circle. This was the third session that Ondie sat in on and scrutinized as the group laid their issues bare. Kate Bennett had been patient, but Ondie knew that she was regularly reporting back to the court about her involvement, or the lack thereof.

"Okay," the mannish brunette began, taking her seat. "Let's get started."

Everyone noisily made their way to their seats. An overweight soccer-mom type sat on one side of Ondie, and a balding manic-depressive sat on the other. Ondie scanned the circle and recalled everyone's names. She counted eight. Melissa, a mousy middle-aged diagnosed schizophrenic, was missing.

"So, we're going to go around the room, and I'd like you to introduce yourselves and tell me why you're here."

The woman waited, but no one wanted to be the first to speak. She locked eyes on a young man directly in front of her. He was a swarthy grunge-rock type, with an array of piercings and tattoos, who couldn't have been more than twenty years old.

"What?" he barked.

"Do you want to start us off?"

"I don't know why the fuck you asked me. You asked the same question yesterday, and the day before that."

"So, tell me again."

The man slouched farther in his seat and threw his arm over the back of his chair. "Billy . . . Billy Badass."

"And why are you here, Mr. *Badass*?"

Some in the group were amused and chuckled. Kate Bennett wasn't too concerned that anything volatile would jump off. She appeared to be a woman that could easily handle herself. However, if things got too out of hand, there were a couple of massive attendants at her beck and call. She repeated her question. "Billy, tell us why you're here."

"You know why I'm here. You know why we're all here."

The woman was not moved. They stared at each other as seconds ticked away. When he realized she was not moving on he sat up and answered, "My drunken stepfather tried to put his cock where it didn't belong, and I did my best to cut the damn thing off!"

The boy's irritation was excruciatingly clear.

One by one the group opened up. Mary, the soccer mom, confessed to being bipolar, and she was there because she refused to take her medication. Another relayed that her family didn't want her around, so they had her committed.

Kate scribbled some notes on a pad of paper. "How about you, Ondie?"

Ondie's eyes shifted nervously from side to side. She shook her head and said nothing.

"Why do we all have to talk and she just sits there day after day like some deaf-mute or somethin'?"

Charley Butts was an angry and overly aggressive man that, among other things, took out his frustrations behind the wheel of a car. In a fit of road rage he had driven an elderly woman into an interstate guardrail. No one cared for him, and given his gruff and abusive conduct it was easy to see why.

"Ondie will talk when she's ready," Kate defended.

"Maybe she should be ready now."

Ondie rolled her eyes and looked away.

"Hey, where's that Melissa chick?" another of the men asked.

"Didn't you hear?" Mary whispered anxiously. "She cut her wrists last night. They rushed her to emergency. I think she died."

Everyone turned to Kate for confirmation. Her evasion was the answer.

Despite Melissa's rumored suicide, Ondie was more ambivalent about the people she was forced to share space with. Even though they were no less human or fallible than she was, their psychoses and the methods by which they chose to deal with them were all very different; or were they? She certainly thought so, and felt no allegiance to their so-called psychologically challenged circle.

* * *

Ondie finally agreed to a visit from Paul. Against her better judgment was a phrase that would have applied under ordinary circumstances, but her judgment was suspect. She was as uneasy as she was the first time they'd gone out together. Fussing with her hair and what little makeup she was allowed to have was not enough to cover up the fact that she was in a mental hospital, but she needed to make the best of her appearance.

She watched him from across the room as he entered the common area: tall, dark, and as confident as ever. Her pulse raced and her heart felt as if it would beat right out of her chest. He looked almost edible in a starched white button-down and jeans. His embrace was sorely missed. She wanted to linger in that moment forever. Her libido cried out for attention, but this was neither the time nor the place.

"I've missed you, Ondrea," he whispered. His deep resonant accent caressed her ears like music.

"I've missed you, too."

Under supervision, she was allowed to walk out into the gardens with him. It was a sweltering July afternoon, but Ondie didn't care. The heat made her feel alive.

"I could hardly believe it when I heard what happened," he said.

"I can hardly believe it myself."

"It is good to see you."

"Letting you come here was a bad idea."

"Why?"

"Don't get me wrong, I wanted to see you, but now

that you're here I'm too ashamed to even look at you. I know you drove a long way, but maybe you should go."

"I didn't come all this way just to turn around and go back home. I spoke with your mother and I was prepared for what I would find. I'm just sorry that I wasn't here for you to lean on when you needed me."

"Paul, you were where you had to be."

"But perhaps it would have been better for me to have never left."

"There wasn't anything you could have done."

They stopped walking and he turned to her.

"Look at me. Ondrea, look at me."

Ondie reluctantly did as she was asked.

"I could have held you. I could have told you that you are not alone. I would have made you believe that."

"Why would you want to be bothered with me at all?"

"You've become very important to me, and if nothing else, this trip has taught me to cherish the people that are significant in my life. Don't turn me away. Let me in."

He leaned in and kissed her. "I have something for you."

Paul removed a small cloth sack from his pocket, took her hand, and poured its contents into it.

"Sand?"

"Not just any sand. This is from the beach in Negril. Since you couldn't come to Jamaica, I wanted to bring a little of it to you."

Ondie's eyes misted. "Are you for real, or are you just something I made up in my head?"

"Last time I checked I was very real." He took her free hand and put it inside his shirt to feel his heartbeat. "What do you think, Doctor?"

"You feel like a survivor."

"Believe it or not, Ondrea, so do you. We all cope in our own way. I have no doubt that you miss Maya, and nothing will ever take her place in your heart, but trust that you will endure this. It's just a season, and seasons change."

A lifeline is all most of us need to get from one day to the next. In the face of incredible loss, Ondie was given another lifeline to help her weather the storm.

"Um . . . my name is Ondie. I'm here because when I don't take my meds I have crazy thoughts."

"Don't we all?" Mary cracked.

"I recently found out that my sister was sleeping with a man that I was involved with, a man that I had a child with."

"What did you do?" Kate asked.

"I wanted to kill them."

"Did you?"

"I tried."

"So, do you feel bad about what you did?"

"She probably feels worse that she didn't get away with it," Charley Butts interjected.

Everyone laughed.

"My four-year-old daughter was riding in a car with my sister without a child safety seat and she was killed in a horrible accident. So in essence my sister is just as responsible for her death as the drunk bastard that plowed into them."

"Do you think your sister did it on purpose?"

"There's no doubt in my mind."

"When you get out of here—"

"Don't you mean *if* she gets out of here?" Billy interrupted.

Kate shot the man a cutting glance. "I was speaking to Ondie."

"Sir! Yes, sir!" he snapped.

Kate ignored him and turned back to Ondie. "When you are released do you think you'd try to hurt your sister again?"

Ondie sat thoughtfully, considering her answer. All eyes were on her.

"I honestly don't know. I guess that's part of the reason I'm here. When I'm done with all these one-on-one, feel-good group sessions, do you think I'll try to hurt her again?"

"Well, I'm hoping that you won't. But, honestly, when the time comes, unless you can convince me that your answer is no, you and I will be getting to know each other a lot better."

# 22

Serita immersed herself in work by taking as many flights as she could handle in her condition, but she was wearing herself down. When the first off day she'd had in two weeks rolled around, she decided to take the opportunity to sleep in as a present to herself. Her cell phone rang and she felt around on the nightstand without opening her eyes.

"Hello."

"Happy birthday!"

"Hi, Mama."

"Uh-oh, I woke you up, didn't I?"

"It's okay." Serita rolled over and propped herself up on pillows.

"Are you working today?"

"No, I'm off."

"Do you have any plans?"

"Not really."

"Can I take you to lunch?"

"You want to take me to lunch? After what I did to Ondie?"

"You're not to blame for that."

"I'm the reason she's locked up in that place. I shouldn't have said anything to the police."

"You were just scared, that's all. I understand that."

*Somehow I doubt that,* Serita thought.

"Can we have lunch together?"

Serita glanced at the clock, thinking about Ruth's aversion to the restaurant experience. "It's almost noon now. What time were you thinking about?"

"How does two o'clock sound? Any place you want to go."

"I've had a taste for seafood. What do you think about Spondivits?"

"I'll see you then."

Serita ended the call and lay back for a few minutes more wondering what Ruth's real motives were for asking her to lunch. *Don't be so suspicious,* she thought. She then forced herself to get up. When she got out of the shower she found that she had voice mail from a few other well-wishers, Kenny among them. But it was the message from Dexter that surprised her most.

"Hey, it's me. I'd like to see you. Call me."

Serita wasted no time returning the call. The timbre of his voice was a gift. When he asked her to meet so they could talk, she couldn't say yes fast enough.

She was preoccupied with Dexter all through lunch with Ruth. Idle chitchat seemed all they could muster.

"Did you get a new car?" Ruth asked.

"Yeah, I could've gotten my Civic fixed, but I really didn't want to after everything that happened."

"An SUV like that isn't too much for you, is it?"

"No, I'm managing."

"Your hair's grown out, it looks nice. Are you feeling okay?"

"Keeping busy for as long as I can. Unless anything goes wrong, I'll be able to fly until I'm at least six months. Then I'll work in reservations or something."

"Have you heard from Kenny?"

"He called right after you did. He's in South Carolina. He said he wanted us to do something special when he got back."

"He and Frank went up there to look at that property."

"Is Uncle Frank still trying to build a house on that land your father left you?"

"Frank has been talking about building that house for years, and that's all it's been is talk.

"We miss you around the house. It's really empty with everybody gone. Have you found a place yet?"

"Honestly, I haven't had time to look. But I will soon. I need my own space, and I know Tonja's about tired of me."

"You two up under each other's feet?"

"No, actually we hardly see each other. Her flight schedule is a little different than mine. Every once in a while we'll be on the same leg of a trip."

"You can always move back to the house."

"With the baby?"

Without hesitation Ruth answered yes.

"You don't really want us there."

"Yes, I do. Kenny and I both want you to move back."

"Tell me something, what would you have said if Daddy wanted to bring his son home?"

"I would have told him no."

"Why?"

"Because it would remind me of what he did. . . ."

"I guess I made my point."

"Your situation is different."

"How is what I did any different than what Daddy did?"

"I love you, Serita."

"You love Daddy, too. But in almost ten years you've never once wanted to see his son, you don't even want to know that he exists, because it would remind you that Daddy was unfaithful. You don't think you'd look at me and Dexter's baby any differently?"

Ruth was speechless. She wasn't sure that Serita wasn't right in her assessment. They finished practically an entire meal in silence before Serita spoke again.

"So, what did you all do for the Fourth?"

"I didn't feel like cooking, so we ended up at Frank's house."

"How did that go?"

"I knew it was a mistake from the minute I said yes. You know Maxine can't cook, and your daddy was mad."

"I guess that's why Uncle Frank is so skinny. Good thing he knows how to cook, or they all would starve to death."

They laughed and the tension eased a bit, until their conversation turned serious again.

"How's Ondie?"

"She's good."

It was an awkward topic given the circumstances.

"Dr. Mathis thinks it's a good idea to tell her about

your pregnancy while she's in the hospital to give her enough time to absorb it."

"Why, so she can try and hurt me again, or worse? And what about what she could do to my baby?"

"Ondie would never deliberately hurt you."

"Really? Do you remember what happened after Maya's funeral? If you and Daddy hadn't come in when you did . . ." Serita's voice trailed off and she shook. "Maybe I should just leave town."

Ruth reached across the table and took her hand. "Please don't do that. I don't want to lose you, too."

"Mama, you're not gonna lose me just because I move away. Staying in Atlanta isn't gonna work."

"We'll find a way, baby. Ondie will come to terms with this situation eventually. She's not obsessing over Dexter anymore. She's met this really nice man. Do you remember, Paul?"

"The guy that she brought to the barbecue?"

"Right now I think he's just what your sister needs."

Serita doubted that a man like Paul, or any man for that matter, would help to relieve the strain that would forever live between her and Ondie.

"Oh, I almost forgot. I got some good news." Ruth beamed.

"Really, what is it?"

"Kenny asked me to marry him."

Serita almost choked on her water. "What? Are you serious?"

"We're thinking about October. Ondie will be home by then, and we want the whole family to be together."

"Mama."

"I know it's going to be hard. But we've got to get past this, Serita. All of us have got to try."

They purposely steered clear of talking about the baby, Ondie, or Dexter for the rest of the afternoon, even though Dexter was all Serita could think about.

Ruth went on about her wedding plans and how intimate she wanted it to be. She even pulled out magazines showing the dresses she was considering. She asked Serita her opinion regarding each choice, and then spent ten minutes raising objections about why a particular style wasn't right for her. It was a viable distraction, but not a lasting one.

Serita agreed to meet Dexter for ice cream at a shop in Decatur. She didn't dare return to the scene of the crime, certain that his neighbors had not forgotten her last visit. They sat under an umbrella to shade themselves from the heat. The ice cream was refreshing.

"How are you feeling?" she asked.

He moved uncomfortably. "I'm still a little sore, but I'll be all right."

"I was surprised to hear from you today. It's been three weeks."

"Three long weeks. I've had nothing on my hands but time. Time to think about my mistakes, and time to regret. Then I remembered that it was your birthday."

Serita smirked thinking that she had to have fallen into his regret category. "So, are you healing up pretty good?"

"With the exception of this scar on my head, and

an immobile left arm, I'm on top of the world. The Vicodin helps, trust me."

"Are your mother and father still here?"

"No, I kicked them out two weeks ago. My father was driving my mother crazy, and she was driving me crazy."

They laughed.

"I miss you, Serita."

Heat rushed into her face. "I miss you, too."

"You know, losing Maya was hard as hell, but when you're faced with your own mortality you get a whole different perspective on things. I know how we started out, and it was a pretty dog-ass thing to do, but I love you, girl. I want us to be together. We've got some tough shit to deal with, your parents, my parents, Ondie, but I think we can do it. I really didn't know what I wanted when I hooked up with Ondie, but I do now. I messed up with Maya, but I don't wanna mess up like that again. I want this baby to be born with my name."

"Maya had your name."

"No, I mean in every way. I want you to have my name, too."

"Dexter."

"I know I'm gonna have to deal with Kenny and Bumper, but I'll do what I have to do. I care about Ondie, but I never felt about her the way I feel about you. If we gotta move out of Atlanta for this to work, then I'm willing to do that."

"Funny, I was just telling Mama earlier that I wanted to move away. She asked me not to."

"Let's get married. We don't have to do anything

extravagant, but I do want to make it right with you. We can fly off to Vegas or something; just name it."

"Is this the painkillers talking?"

"No, it's just a man who's trying to step up and do the right thing for once."

"If we do this our families are going to be angrier than they are right now. Do you really want that?"

"I'm not trying to tear you away from your family, but we gotta live our lives, Serita. We don't have to tell them right away. We can ease them into it."

"Like we did when they found out we were seeing each other to begin with, or when they found out I was pregnant? Why don't we just bash them in the head with a sledgehammer? We snuck around for over a year and look where that got us. As much as I want to be with you, I don't want to do things the same way we have been."

Dexter took Serita's hand. "You're right. We'll be up front with them. We can stand a hell of a lot stronger together than we ever could apart."

# 23

The distant cries of a baby caused Ondie to have another restless night. Sleep had become an enemy. The shadows dancing on the ceiling taunted her. Rolling out of bed, she picked up Maya's framed picture from the nightstand, clutched it to her chest, and rocked back and forth. "Shhhh—everything's gonna be okay."

When she realized what she was doing, she put the picture back in its place and called herself to task. She then got up and moved to the bureau and stared into the mirror.

*Girl, if you don't get it together you'll never leave here.*

Swallowed up in uncertainty, she was convinced that there were forces conspiring against what was left of her sanity. With heavy lids, she climbed back into bed and sat with her knees pulled up to her chest. She had to fight harder.

Fifty-two days, four hours, and twenty-eight minutes: that was how much of her sentence that had been served. Thirty-seven was the magic number. If she could endure the calculated persecution of her current condition for that much longer, she could breathe freely again.

Paul allowed her escape, if only for a brief time, between the mind-probing group sessions and the monotony of puzzle books. Frequent visits from Ruth and Kenny kept her grounded and connected to the outside. The end was close—just not close enough.

Ondie was excited to hear that Dr. Mathis, who'd been strangely absent, called for a visit. "Well, look who finally decided to show up."

"How are you, Ondie?"

Despite the fact that she wanted to be angry with him, she couldn't bring herself to lash out. She detected a camera in the corner of the room and knew that her every move was being watched. "Are you here to break me out?"

"Now, you know I can't do that. I just wanted to see how you were. And I wanted to apologize for staying away for so long."

"I thought you'd forgotten about me now that I've become this hardened criminal."

"This place isn't that bad, is it?"

"I suppose it could be worse. Dexter could have pressed charges."

"How are your sessions going with Dr. Bennett?"

Ondie shrugged. "All right, I guess. I'm sorry I disappointed you, though."

"What would make you say that?"

"Because I'm in here. That must make you feel like you failed. You didn't. I did."

Ondie looked over Dr. Mathis's shoulder to see Ruth. "Mama?"

She noted the looks exchanged between her mother and Dr. Mathis, which gave her pause. His expression conveyed little, but Ruth's was telling.

"Okay, something's up. What's going on?"

As Ondie scanned their faces for answers, Kate Bennett approached. Dr. Mathis stood and greeted her.

"Why don't we use my office?" she said.

"Use your office for what?" Ondie snapped. "Mama, what's going on?"

"Ondie."

A chill ran down her spine. "Oh my God! Is it Daddy?"

The three of them looked at her as if she were going to implode. Ondie closed her eyes and inhaled and exhaled slowly. Whatever was about to be said was bad and she needed to be prepared. Ruth reached out and took her hand. Ondie stood and absently walked with them to Kate's office.

Ruth sat on a sofa and Ondie reluctantly joined her. Dr. Mathis knelt in front of them. Kate hovered.

"Ruth had something to tell you and she asked that I be here," Dr. Mathis began.

Ondie needed to keep herself in check. *Fight harder*, she thought. "Okay, what is it?"

Ruth cleared her throat. "It's about Serita."

"What about her?"

Their lack of immediate response spoke volumes.

"She's pregnant."

Their cloak-and-dagger routine made it all more sinister than it needed to be.

"They've been screwing each other for God knows how long," Ondie said calmly. "She was either going to get pregnant or contract a venereal disease. Too bad it's not VD."

With that Ondie got up and left the room, leaving them perplexed by her reaction. She hustled to her bedroom, locked the door, and sank to the floor in a puddle of tears. Naturally news of this magnitude was going to affect her, but she would not give them the satisfaction of watching her fall apart. She would jump through whatever emotional hoops she had to in order to keep that from happening. The anticipation of thirty-seven days would not permit anyone to see otherwise.

Kate perched on the side of her desk and folded her arms. "She took that surprisingly well."

Ruth cut her eyes and scoffed at the flippant remark. "Lewis, what do you think?"

Dr. Mathis stood thoughtfully and shook his head. "She's wounded, and she's doing her best to suppress it."

"Will you talk to her?"

Dr. Mathis shot Kate a side glance and sighed. Ruth interpreted the look.

"Please," Ruth pleaded.

"This goes against policy," Kate responded.

"My daughter's mental health is more important than some damn policy—please."

Kate made a call, and a few minutes later she accompanied Dr. Mathis to Ondie's room.

He knocked. "Ondie, it's Dr. Mathis. May I talk to you?"

Ondie opened the door.

"I'll be right out here," Kate said as Dr. Mathis stepped inside.

"Did you come to see if I hung myself?" Ondie snapped. "Well, I didn't. I'm being a good little girl. I'm taking my meds and I'm going to group."

"This news about your sister has to have thrown you for a loop, especially in lieu of what you've had to deal with losing Maya."

"What do you expect me to say?"

"Say what you feel."

Ondie laughed disdainfully. "How would you feel, Doctor?"

"This isn't about me."

"Apparently it's not about me, either. Look, I thought you could only treat me as an outpatient; what is this about?"

"I'm not trying to treat you. I just want to talk."

Ondie sat brooding on the edge of the bed. "I'm pissed. I want to hurt them as much as they've hurt me."

"That's understandable."

"Is it?"

"Hurting people, hurt people."

"That's cute. Did you get that off a match book cover or something?"

Dr. Mathis smirked. "It wasn't my best work, but I gave it a shot."

"You know that Kenny isn't my birth father, right?"

"Yes, your mother told me when I first started treating you. Lee Earl Samuels?"

"Since I've been in here I've been thinking a lot

about him and wondering how much of him is in me. He's in prison for murder."

"Yes, I know. However, I don't believe that one act of violence brands him some sort of sociopath. And I don't believe that you inherited anything of that nature from him. He didn't raise you. You don't know him."

"So you don't think that some part of his darkness is in me just like the parts of me that come from my mother's family?"

"Why are you bringing this up now?"

"If I tell you something, would it still be confidential?"

"Of course."

"As much as I want to get out of this hellhole, I'm afraid what I'd do if I saw either one of them right now."

"Ondie, there's a certain amount of comfort that comes from holding on to this hatred that you're feeling. But it's not hurting them, it's hurting you. I don't believe you want to kill them."

"I can't forgive them."

"If you're ever going to move on with your life, you have to. It's not a question of *can* you, but *will* you."

# 24

"Okay, I'm here," Kenny announced as he entered the kitchen to find Ruth at the stove. He wrapped his arms around her from behind and nuzzled her neck.

"Kenny, stop now. You're gonna make me burn myself."

"The stove ain't the only thing that's hot. Why don't you turn that off and come upstairs with me?"

"Kenny." Ruth laughed and turned into him for a kiss. "You need to slow down, Mr. Man. Serita is gonna be here any minute."

Kenny swatted Ruth on the rear and stepped over to the refrigerator. "Do you have any idea why she wanted to see both of us?"

"She didn't say. I just hope she's not going to tell us she's moving out of Atlanta."

"Well, at least she'll be away from Dexter."

Ruth shot him a look that suggested her leaving and separating from Dexter were not synonymous.

"I can dream, can't I?"

"Mama! Daddy! Are you here?"

Ruth turned the fire off from the pot of pasta that she'd started, and wiped her hands on a towel. Kenny followed her into the living room with a beer in his hand. They were both stunned to see Serita standing there with Dexter.

"Boy, you must have some kind of death wish," Kenny spat.

"Daddy, don't."

Ruth held Kenny back.

"Daddy, we came here to talk. Can we please just have a civilized conversation?"

Ruth sat on the sofa and pulled on Kenny; he followed suit. Serita eased down in a wingback chair facing them. Dexter took the matching one beside her, but remained guarded in case the situation escalated to violence.

Kenny grimaced and sucked his teeth. His eyes narrowed. "What's this about?"

"Daddy, me and . . ."

Dexter looked at her and she stopped. "Kenny, I came to talk to you man to man."

Kenny sneered. "Man."

"Kenny," Ruth cautioned.

Dexter wiped his hand over his face and cleared his throat. "Serita and I have been talkin'. I want you both to know that I really love your daughter. Everything is really fucked up right now—no disrespect." He glanced at Ruth. "I can't undo what's been done, but I've matured from it. I can only try to do the right thing now. That's why I wanna marry Serita."

Ruth looked to Kenny, whose jaws were tight. "You know I got issues with you, boy. You runnin' up in both my girls, and you ain't done right by Ondie, as far as I'm concerned. I appreciate the fact that you didn't hold her to the fire for what she did. I want Serita to be happy, but this shit don't sit well with me."

"Look, Kenny, man. We're grown. I'm not askin' permission. I'm tryin' to respect you and Ruth enough to be straight up and let you know the deal."

Kenny jumped up from the sofa, causing Dexter to react in kind. Ruth and Serita sprang to attention as well.

"Have you thought about what this is going to do to Ondie?"

"Ondie! Everything is always about Ondie with you, Mama," Serita injected. "You have another daughter, in case you've forgotten. What we do, or don't do, is not going to make Ondie better. I accept the fact that I messed up. But how long am I going to have to pay for it? If you can forgive Daddy, why can't you forgive me? We could have run off and gotten married and moved away and never seen any of you again, but Dexter didn't want this to become another wall between us. I'm having this baby. We want you both to be a part of its life. I'm not walking away from him. If you can't accept that, then maybe I need to walk away from you." She then grabbed her purse, grabbed Dexter's hand and the two left the house.

A conundrum: sacrifice one daughter's happiness over another's, or let Serita move away with the man she claimed to love. Embrace Dexter, or shun him, and bear Serita's contempt. Any choice made was not going to be an easy one for anybody. One thing was certain: another child was coming into their lives, and if by chance the same destiny that had traversed the generations should befall him or her, Serita would need her mother.

"Can you believe that boy, Ruthie? Comin' in here like he was callin' the shots."

"Kenny, you may not like what he did, but it took a lot of guts for him to do it. Deep down Dexter's a good man. He was a good father to Maya. He'll be a good father to Serita's child."

"Are you sayin' we should just stand by and let them run off together?"

"We don't really have a say in this, Kenny. They're going to do whatever it is they want to do, and we can't stop them."

Kenny threw up his hands and sat down on the sofa.

Ruth perched on his lap and put her arms around him. "Have you ever thought about what my daddy would say to you if he knew you wanted to marry me again? For that matter, what he would have said the first go-round? That man probably would have hog-tied you and hung you from the I-75 overpass. Every father wants the best for his little girl. For me, it's you. Is Dexter the one for Serita? Who's to say? Ondie was one thing. Serita is another. All we can do is pray that he doesn't hurt her."

"I can do a hell of a lot more than pray."

"You know you may not want to hear this, Kenneth Reid, but I think the reason you don't get along with Dexter is that he reminds you a lot of yourself."

"Now, why the hell would you go and say somethin' like that?"

"Because he's more like you than you're willing to admit."

"Now look what you did. You done gone and ruined the mood."

"I'm sorry." She kissed him. "Is this better?" She then unbuttoned his shirt and kissed down his neck to his chest. "How about this?"

Kenny was aroused. "Hmmmm, now, that's what I'm talkin' bout."

Ruth laughed and got up.

"Where you goin'?"

"To finish dinner."

"Dinner ain't goin' nowhere. C'mere, woman."

Kenny grabbed Ruth's hand and pulled her back to him. He then tickled her and playfully wrestled her onto the sofa. They kissed; he fumbled with the buttons of her blouse and stretched out on top of her.

"Kenny, not in the living room."

"Why not? Ain't nobody here."

"Kenny, no."

"Then let's go upstairs."

Ruth pushed him up, pulled her top back together, and darted up to her bedroom. Kenny trailed her, snapping at her heels. They fell onto the bed and Ruth giggled like a schoolgirl. Her cares momentarily took a backseat to pleasing her man, and as Kenny pointed out—taking care of herself.

The next morning Kenny awoke to the smell of bacon and eggs. He made his way to the bathroom to relieve himself and then went down to the kitchen to find Ruth hovered over a cup of coffee.

He yawned. "Mornin', baby."

Ruth glanced up at him with a halfhearted smile.

"What's wrong with you?"

"Nothing. Breakfast is on the stove. Help yourself."

Kenny poured himself a cup of coffee and then fixed his plate. He started shoveling food in his mouth practically before he could sit down. "I'm so hungry. You know you wore me out last night. We never even got to eat dinner."

"It's in the refrigerator. You can eat it tonight."

He detected a tone in her voice, put down his fork, and took a swig from his coffee mug. "Okay, what's wrong? And don't say nothin', 'cause I can see it all over you."

"I've been doing a lot of thinking. I don't know that it's the right time for us to be planning a wedding."

"What?"

"Hear me out. I thought it would be good to bring the family together, but now I'm not so sure. Ondie will just be getting out of the hospital and now this mess with Serita and Dexter. We could just be asking for trouble."

"Do you wanna postpone it until all the stars are aligned and the troops are back from Iraq and there's no more black-on-black crime?"

"I'm serious."

"Me, too, baby. Everything is never gonna be just right. There's always gonna be somethin' goin' on with Ondie, or Serita. But this is about me and you, Ruthie. It's right for us to do this, and it's the right time. Or we can just keep livin' in sin if that's what you want."

Ruth smiled. "All right, I guess I need to make an honest man out of you."

"You ain't gettin' no younger," he laughed.

"I ain't gettin' no younger? Man, you're five years older than me."

"Yeah, but I still look good. I'm still a catch."

"Kenneth Reid, are you trying to talk me in or out of marrying you?"

He lunged forward and kissed her. "I was a fool the first time I let you go. I'm not gonna be that same dumb-ass fool again."

"There's something else. I think it's time I met your son."

Kenny was aghast. "Woman, you never cease to amaze me."

"He knows about us, doesn't he?"

"Yeah, he does."

"Then maybe we should know more about him. You go off to Macon and you spend time with one family, and then you come back here to another. Why don't you bring him to the wedding?"

Kenny took Ruth's hand. "I know it was hard for you, but despite how you felt about it, you never stood in the way of me getting to know my son. I don't know what I did to deserve a woman like you. But whatever it was, it damn sure wasn't good enough. I love you, Ruth, with all my heart and soul."

# 25

Ondie's inexorable captivity was nearing an end. She was eager to rejoin civilization and regain ownership of her life. She had been the model prisoner for almost three months. In four days, six hours, and thirty-two minutes there would be a payoff.

"So, how are we feeling today?"

Ondie felt Kate's pronouncement of "we" was condescending, and wondered if *she* saw people that weren't there. "I don't know about *we*, but I'm good."

"No more nightmares? No headaches?"

"Not one."

"And how are you feeling about your sister?"

*Trick question? Tell her what she needs to hear. Dance with her.* "Serita and I have a problematic relationship. There will undoubtedly be a lot of friction between us. But what siblings' relationship isn't strained after going through what we've been through?"

"She hasn't come to see you the entire time you've been here; does that bother you?"

"Should it?"

"Do you think she's afraid to see you?"

"Probably. I'd be afraid of me, too, right about now."

"What do you mean by that?"

"Just that when I get out of here she and I should maybe stay as far away from each other as possible for a very long time."

"Does this mean that you still have a great deal of animosity toward her? Do you still want to harm her?"

"I've had a horrible few months, and that's putting it mildly. I was bitter and angry and all I wanted to do was lash out at someone."

"Specifically your sister."

"Yes. But I've had time to sort through all that. I'm not as angry as I was when I went to Dexter's apartment that night. I was off my meds and I know that was a mistake and it triggered my psychotic break, but I know it won't happen again."

"How can you be so sure?"

"Because I'm sticking to my routine and I'm taking my meds, and in time I just may come to forgive my sister."

"And if you don't?"

"Then I guess I'll go my way, and she can go hers. There's no law that says I have to have a good relationship with her, is there?"

"No, there are plenty of brothers and sisters that don't get along."

"There, you see? In that regard I'm not so different than most anybody else."

And just like that the dance was over.

* * *

Ondie made sure to quiet the voices in her head for her final evaluation. After all was said and done, she couldn't chance the court's denying her discharge. Paul's visit the night before was reason enough to stifle the noise. He'd been unbelievably supportive through the entire ordeal and she looked forward to seeing what lay ahead for them. She needed to block out anything that would undermine her concentration. She recalled Dr. Mathis's words: "You have to find a way to coexist with the woman in the mirror." *Coexist.* She couldn't be allowed to take over ever again.

For a second time she found herself before the bench as the judge rendered a ruling.

"Ms. Reid, I've reviewed your case file and Dr. Bennett's evaluation. I have also interviewed your family, and Dr. Mathis. Provided you adhere to your outpatient therapy schedule and continue with your medication, I see no reason to keep you in custody any further. Dr. Mathis will see to it that this court is kept up to speed on your progress over the next six months. If for any reason we find that you are not abiding by the court's mandate, you will be remanded back to the Peach State facility for a period of no less that twenty-four months. I trust that the court's indulgence is not going to be abused or else you will find yourself in a great deal of trouble. For now, you're free to go."

Ondie squealed with glee as the judge's gavel rang out. Paul made his way to her and she leaped into his arms. Ruth, Kenny, and Dr. Mathis all gathered around her and offered a congratulatory hug.

"I can't believe it," Ondie sighed. "I am so glad to get out of here."

"I made a special welcome-home dinner at the house for you. Lewis, I'd like you to come, too," Ruth enthused.

"Ruth, I appreciate it, but I really can't," Dr. Mathis replied. "I've got a patient coming by the office in an hour, and I really need to be going."

"Thank you, Dr. Mathis, for everything."

"Ondie, you just make sure you take care of yourself from here on out. I'll see you next week."

After Dr. Mathis darted out of the courtroom, Ruth turned back to Ondie and Paul. "Who's hungry?"

"Mama, I can't thank you enough for all you've done, but all I really want to do right now is go home and take a long hot bath, and sleep in my own bed."

"Ondie, your mother went to a lot of trouble," Kenny injected. "Please, just come by for a little while."

"It was nothing," Ruth countered. "I should have known that you might just want to go home after all this was over."

Ondie looked into her mother's eyes. There was just no way to disappoint her. "I can take a bath later." She smiled and took Ruth's hand. "I haven't had a good home-cooked meal in three months."

With renewed energy and a new sense of self, Ondie embraced her freedom, but the mirror was waiting, just as it always had been.

# 26

Dexter held Serita's hand and watched the ultrasound monitor with every expectation of positive results. They both breathed a sigh of relief as they were told that nothing appeared to be wrong with the baby. Concern over spotting struck fear in their hearts. At twenty-eight weeks, Dexter was already so in love with his little girl that losing another one at this juncture could potentially destroy him.

"Everything looks good," the doctor declared. "You seem to be right on schedule."

"What about the spotting?"

The doctor turned off the machine and handed Serita a towel to wipe away the excess gel. "It goes without saying that you need to try and avoid stress. Continue to watch your diet, make sure you rest, don't overexert yourself, and enjoy it. This is one of the most miraculous times in a woman's life."

Serita jumped as the baby kicked. "Oh my God!"

She took Dexter's hand and placed it on her stomach. He smiled when he felt it, too.

"It's just her way of telling you both not to worry," the doctor assured her.

"I'm so glad that's over," Serita signed as they motored away from the parking lot of the clinic and merged into traffic.

Dexter didn't respond.

"Baby, are you all right?"

"Yeah, I'm fine."

"Where'd you go just now?"

"I was just thinkin' about Maya, and how excited I was when she was born."

Serita turned away and stared out the window. Dexter glanced over at her and surmised what must be going through her mind. He reached over and took her hand.

"Mama says that Ondie's getting out of the hospital today. I was thinking that maybe we should take out a retraining order."

"Why would you want to do that after what you told the judge? I thought that 'she could never harm another living soul'?"

"I didn't want anyone to blame me if I was the cause of Ondie staying in that place. I couldn't tell the judge that I was afraid of her."

Dexter let go of her hand. "Serita, we talked about this. I thought we didn't want any more bad blood between you and Ondie."

"I don't want her coming after us again, especially now."

"Maybe I should go talk to her."

"Talk to her about what?"

"Just kind of get a feel for where she is right now. Some time has passed; she's obviously more stable or they wouldn't have considered letting her out of the hospital."

"And what if she isn't?"

"Maybe we should reconsider leaving Georgia. Now that we're married it doesn't matter what Kenny or anybody else says."

Serita gazed at the ring on her finger and smiled. "I still can't believe I let you talk me into it."

"I didn't talk you into anything. You wanted to do it just as much as I did."

"I wanted to wait until after the first of the year. We could have had a real ceremony with bridesmaids and groomsmen and tuxedos."

"We can still have all that. But right now it's important to me that you're my wife."

"Another secret we have to keep."

"Um . . . I kind of already let it slip," Dexter admitted.

"What? Dexter, I thought we agreed to wait. I don't want our news to overshadow Mama and Daddy's wedding."

"I know, baby, but I was talkin' to my mother, and Bumper got to runnin' you down again and I couldn't take it, so I told 'em."

"When?"

"Last week."

"What did they say?"

"Mama started cryin'. All I could hear was Bumper cussin' in the background. I told them why we did it the way we did." Dexter laughed. "Mama said it wasn't the real thing because we did it at the courthouse instead of in front of God at a church. I promised that when we had the *official* ceremony I would let them know."

"They're never going to accept me now."

"You're givin' them another grandchild. They'll come around. And you don't have to worry about them talkin' to Ruth and Kenny. After what happened when I was in the hospital, it's not like they're gonna be calling each other for a chat."

"This little girl is not going to be a replacement for Maya."

Dexter took Serita's hand again and kissed it. "I know that. Nothing will be."

They drove along for a few more miles until coming to their Smyrna exit and pulling off.

"Does it upset you that it's a girl and not a boy this time?" Serita asked.

"No, but are you thinking that she might develop this disorder?"

"I'd be lying if I said I hadn't thought about it. Hopefully there's a good chance Reese won't have it, either."

"Reese," Dexter repeated, and smiled, stopping at a light. "So that's the name you decided on."

"No, I want us to make the decision together. I was just saying it out loud to see how it sounded."

"Reese Campbell . . . R.C. I like it," Dexter affirmed. He leaned over and rubbed Serita's stomach. "Hey, Campbell soup, hurry up and get done. We're waitin'."

"Campbell soup?" Serita laughed.

"Yeah, that's what some of the kids used to call me when I was little."

"No." Serita grimaced. "You are not calling our daughter any kind of soup."

"Well, how about R.C.?"

"How about you just drive? The light's green."

Serita didn't want to share her anxiety with Dexter, but as her due date drew closer she obsessed more about the possibility of her daughter being diagnosed as schizophrenic or schizoaffective. Ruth rarely talked about how it was growing up with a mother with this condition, but she had to live through it to some degree with Ondie once she started showing symptoms. If by chance her daughter would be cursed to live a life of confusion, could she be the selfless caregiver that her mother had been?

# 27

"Your uncle is a very funny man," Paul mused as he wrapped his arm around Ondie's waist. "Dinner was fantastic, but I'm glad to finally have you all to myself."

He and Ondie shared a passionate kiss.

"Welcome home," he said.

Ondie smiled. "It is good to finally be back here. But don't you think we'd be more comfortable inside than standing here in the doorway for all the neighbors to see?"

"Let them look."

They kissed again.

Ondie finally broke away and stepped inside. It was clear that Ruth had been there earlier. The whole place smelled of pine cleanser and vanilla-scented candles. Ondie walked slowly through every room as if inspecting them for the very first time. Paul held back and let her take it all in. There were a few pictures of Maya displayed on the credenza that gave her pause, but she pressed on. She ran her hand gently over the neatly arrayed drawings mounted on the refrigerator.

She then proceeded to the most important room in the house. When she opened the door to what used to be Maya's bedroom she found no trace of her there: no toys, no clothes, no furniture. Instead she found that her desk had been moved into this room from her bedroom. The house was very still—lifeless—empty. Ruth told her that everything had been neatly packed away and stored in her garage for whenever she decided to do something with them, but the shock of not seeing Maya's familiar possessions brought tears to her eyes.

Paul startled her from behind. "Are you all right?"

Without saying anything, she went to him for comfort.

Ondie awoke the next morning wrapped in Paul's arms. They were lying atop her bed still fully clothed. Paul stirred when she moved to get up.

"Good morning."

Ondie covered her mouth and yawned. "Good morning."

"How did you sleep?"

"Okay."

"Just okay?"

"Well, I couldn't really get as comfortable as I would have liked with all these clothes on."

"We could take them off and try again."

"Sorry, but it's time to get up."

Under protest, Ondie got out of bed and started for the kitchen. "I'm going to start a pot of coffee." She stopped short after catching a glimpse of herself in the mirror. "I look terrible. I need to get something done to my hair and get a manicure and a pedicure. If I call the salon, maybe I can get my stylist to squeeze me in."

"You look fine."

"Don't try and make me feel good. I know how I look, and *fine* is not exactly the adjective you should be using."

Paul jumped up and pulled her into him. "So why don't you have your day of beauty treatments? I've got some work to catch up on at home. I'll call you later and then perhaps I could convince you to go out to dinner with me tonight, and maybe dancing to show you off."

"That sounds perfect, Mr. St. James. I would be glad to go out with you tonight."

Ondie pleaded until she got her stylist to squeeze her into her afternoon calendar. Unlike most of the professionals in this business who usually stacked their appointments, Delores Anderson tried her best to stick to a schedule. Add to that the fact that she'd heard the scuttlebutt surrounding Ondie's three-month hiatus and she was dying to hear the scoop firsthand.

Walking into the Kitchen Confidential Salon, Ondie felt as if she'd been in a coma instead of locked away in a psychiatric hospital. She'd missed July Fourth; Labor Day, and the renovations. The waiting area had been upgraded. The worn pleather chairs that were there before had been replaced by new royal-blue cloth furnishings that gave the place a warmer feel. Laminate wood floors were now visible where torn carpeting used to lie. Even the stylists' stations had been transformed. It almost felt as if she were in the wrong place, but when she heard Delores's unmistakable cackle she knew this was it. The business was picking up, or

Delores had a sugar daddy, Ondie mused. The thought of either was not beyond the realm of possibility.

Most of the chairs were filled with expectant customers who looked at Ondie as if she planned to usurp their positions in line. She knew that Saturday afternoons were the absolute worst time to try and get anything done in a place like this. Still, it would be worth it if she could make herself feel a little more feminine.

She spotted the stout and feisty Delores, whose station sat farthest from the door, and waved.

"Hey, girl. Long time no see. I got two in front of you," the woman yelled over the whirring of hair dryers.

Ondie nodded and found a seat as she thought about trying out another of the stylists. Delores was still as loud as ever, but nobody could do hair like she could, so Ondie resolved to wait it out.

Ondie glanced around the room and noticed that the manicurist's chair sat empty. She decided to have her nails done. When she got up, two women seated next to her laughed. She turned back. They shifted uncomfortably and looked away. Even though the manicurist's station was off center of the rest of the shop, Ondie began to feel as if she was the focus of attention. She got anxious when it seemed as though she was being whispered about. Even Delores appeared to have joined the folly. Ondie's throat tightened and her lips went dry. Her breathing intensified. Objects around her shifted in and out of focus. *This was a mistake. I have to get out of here.* She jumped up from the table and a bowl of cuticle solution spilled over. She bolted.

"Ondie, wait. I'm gonna get to you," Delores yelled. "Where're you goin'?"

Ondie didn't look back. She nearly ran into another car as she sped off. When she'd gotten a block away she pulled over to the curb, pounded the steering wheel, and cried. Deflated, she rested her head on the seat; a vagrant tapping at the window gave her a scare. She threw the car in Drive and took off.

Determined not to allow this minor setback to throw a monkey wrench into what promised to be a wonderful evening with Paul, Ondie stopped at a Wal-Mart and a beauty supply shop to buy what she needed to do her own thing. She was certainly resourceful enough to do her hair and nails. She even purchased facial scrubs and exfoliates. Her confidence was shaken, but what else should she have expected? Hair salons are notorious for backbiting and backstabbing; she was just among the casualities. Kitchen Confidential would not have to worry about ever seeing her business again.

A few hours later as she soaked in a tub of luxuriant bath salts with her hair pinned up and her nails polished, she had a real sense of accomplishment. Paul called and left a message that he was taking her back to the midtown seafood restaurant where they'd had so much fun the last time. That night was so long ago that she'd almost forgotten how incredible it made her feel. When she got out of the tub and toweled off she remembered a certain little something she had tucked away in her jewelry box that might help her rising anxiety. She wrapped the towel around her and found the marijuana she'd left there. "Just a couple of puffs. It's not like I'm drinking alcohol." Ondie sat on the edge of her bed and fired it up. Soon her entire being relaxed. "That's just what I needed."

It took almost an hour for her to finish dressing after her little leisure activity. Paul called to let her know he was just getting off the exit ramp and would be at her house shortly.

When she opened the door to let him in, the chill of late September enveloped her. She shivered in her short-sleeved frock and after greeting him, announced that she needed to change.

"Ondrea, you look fine. More than fine, you look fantastic."

"No," Ondie countered, still loopy from the marijuana. "I really need to put on something warmer. I'll be right back."

Paul noted her off behavior. "What's wrong with you?"

"Nothing more than usual."

He took her by the arm and looked into her eyes. Through the creams and perfume he could still detect the unmistakable aroma of cannabis in the air. "Are you high?"

"No, of course not. Now, just give me a few minutes and I'll be ready to go."

"Ondrea."

"All right, fine. I smoked a joint before you got here. Sue me!"

He looked at her disbelievingly. "Wow, I hadn't realized."

"Realized what, Paul? I'm not a dope addict, if that's what you're thinking. I had a shitty day, okay? I went to the salon and couldn't get my hair done and I ended up having to do it myself and it looks like crap."

"It looks fine, Ondrea."

"No, it doesn't, it looks like a pile of shit."

Paul took a step back to assess the situation. "All right, why don't you go and change? We don't have to go all the way back into Midtown. We can find a nice place to eat out here."

"Why? Are you ashamed to be seen with me in public?"

"No, Ondrea. That's not what I meant."

"Ondie! My name is Ondie, okay? Stop calling me Ondrea like I'm some fucking . . ."

The look in Paul's eyes halted her invective.

"Paul, I—I'm sorry. I don't know what came over me. I didn't mean to yell at you like that. You are the best thing that has happened to me out of this whole mess. I don't want to ruin what we have."

Paul reached out and caressed Ondie's cheek. "Maybe tonight is not the best night for us to go out. We should probably wait until you've had a chance to settle back in. You already said you didn't sleep that well last night."

Ondie teared up. "Paul, don't leave."

"I'm not leaving for good."

"Then what are you doing? Are you afraid of me? You think I'm crazy just like everybody else, don't you?"

"If I thought that, I wouldn't be here at all."

"Then what is it?"

"Ondre . . ." he kissed her cheek. "I'll call you tomorrow, all right?"

Ondie turned away from him and shook her head. "Go. Just go."

After Paul left, Ondie sat in the darkness of her living room willing herself not to cry. The telephone rang and she picked it up and looked at the caller ID. It was Ruth. Ondie started to answer, but changed her mind. She got up and went to her bedroom, changed into a pair of jeans and a cream-colored V-neck cable-knit sweater, and touched up her hair and makeup. She then grabbed a jacket and her car keys and left the house.

In her haste to make herself presentable for Paul, Ondie hadn't eaten all day. She drove to a nearby restaurant and went in to place a to-go order. When she sat down to peruse the menu the bartender asked her if she wanted something to drink. She looked at all the multicolored and various-sized bottles on display and contemplated having one while she waited. She'd been a good girl, and it had been a very long time. One couldn't hurt. Then she thought about her imposed check-ins with Dr. Mathis and decided that was the rationale that always got her into trouble. "I'll just have a Coke."

After serving her soda and taking her food order, the woman disappeared into the kitchen. A man across the bar, with one eye on the televised football game and another on her, winked and smiled when she looked in his direction. The fair-skinned brother was neatly groomed and had an athletic build. She thought he was cute, and after the day she'd had and the humiliation she'd just suffered, she wanted to feel needed. It had been a very long time for *that* as well.

"What's your name?"

"Ondie."

"I'm Ron."

"Nice to meet you, Ron."

"You stay around here?"

"Close by."

"That's what's up."

The stench of beer and cigarettes on the man's breath was a turnoff. Her food arrived just in time. She signed her credit card receipt and got up to leave.

"So, uh, Ondie, you wanna hang out? Maybe we can grab a drink, get into a lil' somethin'."

"You know, Ron, as tempting as your invitation might be, the only meat I'm leaving here with tonight is in this bag."

With that Ondie left the restaurant. The man's inept advances boosted her self-esteem. The fact that she was able to walk away without regret was an added bonus.

The hamburger and fries were suddenly not enough to subdue her hunger. She still had an itch that needed to be scratched, but she didn't want just anyone to do the honors. She took a chance and headed down to Atlantic Station. If nothing else she wanted to apologize again.

She saw the lights on in Paul's loft as she rounded the corner off the Seventeenth Street Bridge. Would he even entertain an apology from her now? Or would her attempt to make amends go unrewarded? There was no street parking; in this area there rarely was. She drove to the underground garage close to his building. Her cell phone rang. It was Paul.

"Hi," she said.

"Are you asleep?"

She smiled. "No."

"You've been on my mind. I don't like the way we left things."

"I know. I don't, either."

Ondie pressed the button on the outside intercom of the building.

"Hold on. There's someone at my door. . . . Who is it?"

"It's Ondie."

The buzzer rang, releasing the lock on the exterior door, and she went inside. He was waiting for her when she got off the elevator. He looked just as good in a faded Old Navy T-shirt as he did in one of his business suits, if not better.

She held up the bag. "I brought a peace offering, bacon cheeseburger and fries, but they're cold by now."

He smiled, took her hand, and led her into the apartment.

"Paul, I want you to understand that what happened earlier was not because I wasn't taking my meds. I was more overwhelmed by everything than I thought I would be. Getting out of the hospital and seeing that Maya's things were gone as though she never existed; I guess I just wasn't ready for that. And to top it off I was trying to get my hair done today so that I could look good for you tonight and the whole thing just came crashing in on me. I wasn't having some kind of psychotic episode. It was just a really bad day. I took it out on you and I'm sorry. Getting high didn't help as much as I thought it would, either."

"To be honest with you, Ondrea . . . Can I still call you that?"

"Yes," she responded shamefully.

"You did scare me tonight. I had hoped that you'd been able to work through the bad stuff that caused you to have to go to that hospital in the first place."

"I have. Everybody has a bad day once in awhile, even sane people."

"Why yu fe galang so? I wish you would stop that. You're not insane. You have issues and challenges, but you're dealing with them. This self-deprecation is not attractive on you."

"It's a defense mechanism. If I tear myself down before anyone else has a chance to, then it won't hurt so much."

"But you don't have to beat yourself up. You're a beautiful woman with a problem. You have to realize your own worth before you can expect anyone else to."

The building intercom buzzed again.

"It must be the pizza I ordered before you got here." Paul went to the door and let the deliveryman up. He paid and stepped back into the apartment. "Mmmmm, it's not the Oceanaire but it will do. Would you like a slice? It's got to be better than a cold hamburger."

"You want me to stay?"

"Would you rather leave?"

"No, I'm right where I want to be."

Not counting dinner with the family the night before, pepperoni, mushrooms, and sausage pizza was one of the best meals she'd eaten in weeks. They stuffed themselves on half a pie while watching some inane comedian on HBO. Paul appreciated the man's humor much more than Ondie did, but she laughed along anyway. Once the show was over, Paul went to his stereo and put on a CD.

"This song is called *Waiting in Vain*. You've heard of Bob Marley, haven't you?"

"Of course I have. What kind of question is that?"

Paul pulled Ondie from the sofa and twirled her around the floor as he bounced and sang along to the reggae flavor.

"I don't wanna wait in vain for your love . . . From the very first time I rest my eyes on you, girl, my heart says follow through."

Paul quickly discarded his T-shirt and undid his pants as the song continued. He then pulled Ondie's sweater up over her head and was delighted to discover that she wasn't wearing a bra. His large warm hands cupped her breasts as she turned her back and seductively ground her hips into him. She gasped when he unexpectedly swept her up in his arms and laid her atop a plush area rug, He then slowly pulled her jeans off. She countered by pushing his pants over his hips and released his rigid penis. Reveling in their sensuality, he gave her what she'd been waiting for—it was something he'd craved himself. It was the perfect end to an imperfect day.

# 28

Thanks to the intervention of her attorney, Ondie's job remained intact. He'd sent the appropriate documentation to the HR department of her employer, giving just enough information for her to be listed on short-term disability. When Monday rolled around she found herself once again mired in traffic and construction that could bring even the savviest of drivers to tears.

Unsure of how her coworkers would receive her, Ondie still felt she was ready to take on whatever the day threw at her. It was month-end close; time to make sure that accounts and payables of the company checked and balanced. Jack, the department manager, was already hard at work when she arrived. He was a gaunt unpretentious man who wore thick horn-rimmed glasses and had a crooked smile. He could be pleasant most of the time, but at month-end, he was higher strung. It was nothing for him to come in an hour or two earlier than everyone else, work through lunch, and stay until the custodial staff came to clean at night.

Ondie wanted to appear as if not so much time had

passed, and that nothing had changed in her absence. "Good morning, Jack."

He looked up from one of several manila folders that held his attention. "Ondie, you're back. Is everything all right?"

She wasn't sure how much of her personnel file he was privy to. She hadn't been to work since Maya died. There was a genuine tone of concern in his voice.

"Things are better, Jack. One day at a time, you know."

"Well, I'm glad you're back. We could use you around here. Make sure you check in with HR later this morning, okay?"

"Will do."

Ondie proceeded to her desk and saw that Linda, another of her coworkers, was already there as well.

"Welcome back." She smiled. The woman then reached into her desk drawer, pulled out an envelope, and handed it to Ondie. "I know we don't know each other very well, but we really felt bad about your little girl. We all chipped in. It's not much."

Ondie set her purse down and eased down in her chair to open the envelope. Inside she found a card that they all had signed and two hundred dollars that had been collected from the department. She choked up. They'd already sent an arrangement of flowers, which was enough of an expressed sentiment, but this was an unexpected benevolence.

She wiped her eyes. "Thank you, Linda."

The woman nodded and returned to her work. Ondie picked up the framed picture of Dexter and

Maya on her desk, sighed heavily, and slipped it into a drawer.

The morning was in full swing by nine. All of Ondie's passwords had been reset and her accounts reactivated. It was just like riding a bike, a little wobbly at first, but the more she pedaled, the more sure of herself she became.

Ruth called to see how her first day back at work was going. She was glad to report that there had been no major snafus.

"What time do you get off tonight?"

"Usually four, but everyone's been so nice and there is so much work to do that I think I'm gonna work some overtime. Why, what's up?"

"I need to go shopping. I've got some things I need to pick up for the wedding—my dress for one."

"Mama, I thought you already had your dress?"

"I ordered one, but I didn't like the way it fit so I'm taking it back. I sure could use your eye."

"Why don't you ask Aunt Maxine to go with you?"

"Maxine is sweet, but she has no taste in clothes. If I ask her opinion that woman will have me looking like Minnie Pearl."

"Who?"

"You remember *Hee Haw*, don't you?"

Ondie muffled a laugh. "No, Mama. I don't. Sorry I can't go shopping with you. I may stop by tonight on my way home."

"Okay, well, let me get off this phone so you can get back to work. I'll call you later."

When Ondie hung up, her e-mail notified her of a message. It was Paul checking in and asking her if she wanted to have lunch. She glanced at the clock and replied that she had plans and she would get back to him later.

She got up and stepped around her cubical wall. "Linda, are you busy for lunch?"

"I was just going to go to the cafeteria," the woman responded.

"Mind if I join you?"

"That would be nice."

The two went on to the cafeteria together and found a table. Ondie discovered Linda to be a bit more of a scandalmonger than she would have imagined. The woman was a walking tabloid. She filled Ondie in on who'd been fired, who she accidentally happened upon in a compromising position at the office picnic back in July, and that Jack's wife asked him for a divorce. Ondie listened with feigned interest and wondered what was being said about her behind her back. Did anyone really know the nature of her term of disability? She'd only asked Linda to lunch to repay a kindness, but it wasn't all that enjoyable. It would be the last time they ate together.

"Mama, you home?"

"Up here."

Ondie climbed the stairs and found Ruth in her room surrounded by piles of shopping bags. "Wow, did you leave anything in the store?"

"I couldn't make up my mind on half this stuff. Most of it's probably going back tomorrow after I leave the hospital."

Ondie picked through some of the lingerie and held them up for examination. "This is pretty."

"Yeah, that one I'm keeping for the wedding night."

"Ooooh, I hope you can stay in it."

"I'm gonna make your daddy beg for it."

They laughed.

"I'm sorry I wasn't able to go with you."

"It's okay. Serita came by and we—"

"Serita?"

Ondie cleared a space on the bed to sit. Ruth stopped what she was doing and joined her.

"Ondie, are you, okay?"

"Peachy."

"Are you sure?"

Ondie grabbed Ruth's hand. "Yes, Mama. I'm fine. I'm also starved."

"Well, I've got some baked chicken in the oven. I was fixing dinner for your father, but he drove up to Macon to see his son's basketball game."

"I suppose I should be asking you if you're okay."

"Don't worry. I'm a lot better with all this than I used to be. In fact, I asked Kenny to bring the boy to the wedding."

"You're kidding."

"No, I think it's time we all met him."

"It doesn't sound like you're sure."

Ruth thought about the implications of what Serita had said to her about not being able to look at her baby and accepting it as part of the family, because she would feel about it the way she felt about Kenny's son. She went to her bedside table, took out a photo, and handed it to Ondie.

"Is this him?" Ondie asked.

"His name's Anthony. He looks just like your father did at that age."

"I can't believe we're finally going to meet him, and that you're okay with it."

"As long as he doesn't bring that woman with him I'll be fine."

"I just don't know how you do it, Mama. I love Daddy, but if it were me I'm not sure that I could have a constant reminder of what he did hanging around."

"I do it because I love your father. The breakdown in our relationship wasn't just on him. When you started having these episodes I was putting all my energy into protecting you. I pushed Kenny away because I felt he didn't understand your special needs. I'm not saying that it was an excuse for him to cheat, but I certainly gave him reason."

"So this is my fault."

"No, baby, I don't blame you. That's not what I'm saying, either. I have been dealing with the fallout from this disease all my life in one way or another. My goal was to keep you out of institutions, and to help you be as normal a girl as you could be."

"Look how I turned out."

"You didn't ask for this. Sometimes your burdens pick you, and there's nothing you can do except to rise above them. I hate that you and Serita have problems, but we're family. We have to love each other, and if you can find it in your heart, I know there is a place there where you still love your sister."

"Like you found it for Daddy?"

"Just like I found it for Daddy."

# 29

Ruth and Kenny's wedding day had finally arrived, but there was a question as to whether or not the occasion would be the happy one she'd hoped for. She stood at the window staring up into the overcast October sky. The forecast reported a twenty percent chance of rain by noon. As if she didn't have enough to fret about, now the weather threatened to ruin her day.

The house had been cleaned and furniture was rearranged to accommodate the thirty or so invited guests. A tent was pitched on the back lawn where the ceremony was being held. It was decorated in shades of mauve and rich purple, and accented with cascading arrangements of assorted lilies. Ruth slid the patio door open and stepped out. It was fifty-eight degrees, and she could smell the moisture in the air. She walked into the tent and gave everything one last check. "Lord, should I really be doing this today?"

"Yes, you should."

She jumped and turned around to see Kenny standing behind her grinning like the Cheshire Cat.

"Kenny, you scared me."

"Sorry, baby." He pulled her into him and kissed her. "The place looks really good. Is everything ready?"

Ruth broke free. "No, the cake isn't here yet."

"Where is it?"

"Maxine was supposed to pick it up. She called and said she was stuck behind an accident on 285. I swear if one more thing goes wrong!"

"It's only nine thirty. Maxine will be here." Kenny tried to comfort Ruth, but she was having none of it.

"It's supposed to rain and the temperature is going to be dropping. Who in their right mind has a wedding in October—outside no less?"

"Baby, it's gonna be all right. Hey, there's somebody I want you to meet."

Kenny turned around and called for his boy, who stepped timidly from around the corner of the house. The scrawny ten-year-old did indeed resemble his father, with the exception of ears that protruded slightly, a contribution from his mother's side of the family.

Kenny nervously introduced them. "Ruthie, this is Anthony."

Ruth's throat went dry staring into the face of infidelity. She had said she wanted to meet him, and with him standing there in the flesh there was no turning back. She swallowed and managed a smile. "Hi, Anthony, how are you?"

"I'm okay."

Kenny patted the boy on the head. "Why don't you go get your stuff from the truck and go in the house? I'll be right in."

The boy darted out of sight.

"Are you sure you're okay with this, Ruthie?"

She clenched her teeth and nodded.

"Where's Ondie? I thought she stayed over here last night."

"She did. She went to the mall to buy me another pair of panty hose. I bought the wrong size and the wrong color. My stomach is all tied up in knots. You would think this was the first time I was getting married."

"Ruthie, you gotta calm down, baby. C'mere." Kenny pulled her to him. "Listen, if it rains we'll move the whole damn thing inside. I don't care if Maxine gets here with the cake or not. I don't even care that you got the wrong color panty hose. I would marry you in your bathrobe if I had to. I love you, Ruth Anne. And if I wasn't such an asshole all those years ago we wouldn't be goin' through this right now."

"You know you really shouldn't be here right now. It's bad luck."

"Let me tell you somethin', woman. You didn't want me here last night, but I ain't goin' nowhere now. You're stuck with me." He nibbled on her ears and neck.

"Kenny, stop now. You're going to mess up my hair."

"Just give me five minutes."

"In case you forgot, your son is in the house."

"Oh yeah, well, I guess we'll have to pick this up later. Let me go get him situated."

Ruth blew out a cleansing breath and wondered if she should have her head examined for allowing Kenny's two worlds to collide on this very important day.

* * *

Dexter walked into the bedroom to find Serita lying in bed. "You're not dressed."

"I'm not going."

"Why not?"

"For the same reason you're not going."

"You have to go. I'm not going to keep Kenny off my back."

"That's exactly why I'm not going. Plus, Ondie's going to be there and I can't face her. I don't want her to see me like this."

"She wouldn't do or say anything to ruin this for your mother."

"Ondie may or may not be in control."

"Serita, you can't disappoint Ruth. Just go and if Ondie starts up you can always leave."

"But what if something happens?"

"You're gonna be upset with yourself if you don't at least make the effort."

"Come with me."

"You really wanna kick up some shit, don't you?"

"All right, I'll get dressed." Serita moved to get out of bed and a sharp pain shot through her. She fell back onto the pillows and held on to her stomach. "Oooh! Reese is really active today."

Dexter laughed. "Maybe she heard me say you wanted to kick up some you-know-what."

Serita moved to stand again and broke into a cold sweat as another pain seized her. "This doesn't feel right. I think you better call Dr. Brunner."

Elegantly attired in a beaded ivory satin jacket and matching tea-length skirt, and accessorized with teardrop pearl earrings and a cultured pearl necklace, Ruth admired herself in front of the full-length mirror in her bedroom. The laughter of the guests assembling downstairs and out on the lawn sent chills through her. In little more than an hour she would be Mrs. Kenneth Reid again. Not that she'd been very far from that status as they both enjoyed the benefit of a mutually beneficial divorce.

"Knock, knock," Ondie said as she opened the bedroom door and entered. Decked out in a formfitting dusty gold Diane von Furstenberg knockoff, she was every bit as alluring as her mother. "Oh, wow! Mama, you look beautiful."

"I feel beautiful." Ruth beamed and smoothed back the loose hairs of her updo.

"You are going to knock Daddy's socks off."

Ruth sat down on the edge of the bed to adjust the ankle strap of her shoes. "Well, that is the idea."

"It's shaping up to be a real nice day. Aunt Maxine finally got here with the cake. Everybody's having a good time. The sun even came out for a while. See, you were worried for nothing."

"The day isn't over yet. Have you met Anthony?"

"Yes. He seems kind of quiet. Are you sure he's Daddy's son?"

Ruth chuckled.

Ondie sat next to her and took her hand. "Nothing is going to go wrong."

"You look good, baby. Are you happy?"

"I'm working on it. But you shouldn't be thinking about me. Today is all about you. So, tell me, what can I do to make things easier for you?"

Ruth lovingly picked at the loose curls that framed Ondie's face and caressed her cheek. "There is one thing that would make today complete."

"What's that?"

"When your sister gets here will you please put your differences aside, for me?"

"Are you sure she's even coming?"

"I've been calling her, but I haven't got an answer. I'm hoping she's on her way."

"Mama, I'm not going to do anything to ruin this for you, I swear."

"Thank you, baby."

Ondie stood and headed to the door. "I'm going to go down and check on Daddy. I'll be back in a few."

After she left, Ruth picked up the phone to try Serita again. No answer. She called Dexter's cell phone and there was no response from him, either.

Despite her resolve to stay calm, worry reared its ugly head.

"Braxton Hicks contractions," Dr. Brunner assured her. "It's false labor. You remember we talked about this. Your body's just preparing for what's coming."

"So there's nothin' to worry about," Dexter quipped.

"Well, it was still a good thing you called. The spotting you experienced a few weeks ago was something we definitely want to keep an eye on."

"Is this gestational diabetes still something to worry about?"

"I checked your glucose levels, and as long as you're

controlling your blood sugar, and watching what you eat, everything should be fine."

Serita inhaled and breathed out a sigh of relief.

Dr. Brunner removed her latex gloves and tossed them in the trash. "Just continue to take it easy. Stay away from stress if at all possible."

"That's about as easy as avoiding swollen feet and constipation," Serita cracked.

Dexter finally checked his cell phone and discovered the missed calls from Ruth. In all the excitement he'd forgotten to take it off vibrate. He glanced at his watch. "Ruth's called three times. We should at least call her and tell her what's happened."

"No, I'll call her later."

"You still have time to make it to the wedding."

"I'm supposed to be avoiding stress, remember?"

"You know how much it would mean for her to have you there."

"Dexter, I'm not even dressed."

"You look fine. The important thing is that you go."

Serita shook her head.

"I'll drop you over there, and I'll come back to pick you up after."

"All right, let's go."

On the ride to Ruth's, Serita combed her hair out from the ponytail she sported and applied mascara and a coat of fresh lip gloss to spruce up her appearance. "Why do you want me to go to this thing so bad?"

Dexter pretended not to notice when she removed her wedding ring and slipped it into her purse. "Because you love your family, and deep down I know you would kick yourself if you missed this. We dipped out and got married, and with the baby comin', you're gonna need all the support you can get. I don't want you on the outs with Ruth and Kenny, too."

The Sandy Springs cul-de-sac was peppered with parked cars. Dexter could barely pull close enough to let Serita out without having to walk a good distance to the house.

"I love you, you know that?" she said.

"I love you too, lil' Mama. Hey, bring me a plate back."

"I'll see what I can do."

He gave her a peck on the lips. "Call me when you're ready to go."

"I will."

As Serita got out of the Jeep, she could hear Kenny Lattimore's "For You" wafting from the back of the house. She stilled herself and followed the music.

There were people spilling out of the tent and watching in awe as Ruth proceeded up the makeshift aisle and stood by Kenny's side. Serita excused herself past several of the onlookers to get closer. Both Kenny and Ruth spotted her and smiled. Ondie, who was seated on the front row, followed their gaze. Serita swallowed hard and pulled her jacket closed as a man got up and offered her his seat.

The storm was rolling in. As the ceremony progressed, what little sun there was took cover behind a bank of clouds.

No sooner had the presiding minister uttered the words "you may kiss the bride" than the rains that were held back, seemingly by sheer will, refused to be put off any longer. The guests scurried from the tent, and into the house. Kenny removed his jacket and covered his wife as they made a mad dash as well. Just as Serita started from the tent, Ondie caught up to her.

"Glad you could make it."

That was it; that was all Ondie said to her before she ran into the house with Paul. Serita had expected a storm to rival the one that was happening around them. There had to be more, of that she was certain. But, unlike the ominous clouds that announced the pending downpour, Ondie would most likely strike without warning.

Food and liquor flowed endlessly from the kitchen. Maxine Wheeler acted as hostess, making sure that everything went as smoothly as possible, and instructing the women who had volunteered to help serve. A few of the men made it their business to collect chairs from the tent so that people had a place to sit. Nothing was going to dampen the spirit of this joyous occasion. They were prepared to transition.

Ruth heartily embraced Serita. "I'm so glad you made it."

"Sorry I was late. The baby gave us a little scare."

"Are you okay?"

"Just some unwelcome contractions. I wish I had had time to put myself together. A maternity top and stretch pants don't exactly make me a fashion plate."

"None of that is important," Ruth said as she hugged Serita again. "You're here. That's all that counts."

A familiar tune tickled Ruth's ears and made her smile. "Oh no, he didn't."

"Isn't that . . ."

"That man ought to know better."

"Careful," Serita teased. "We don't want to see nothin' we shouldn't see."

"Ah yeah, that's it right there." Kenny swayed toward Ruth, doing an admirable Billy Preston imitation. "C'mon, woman, you know what time it is!" He took her hand and pulled her to the center of the floor.

Cameras flashed and a circle formed around them as Kenny cuddled up close to Ruth and sang softly in her ear. *"Come bring me your softness. Comfort me through all this madness. Woman, don't you know with you I'm born again?"*

"You are a mess, Kenneth Reid."

"Did you ever tell Serita she was conceived to this song?"

"No. But she knows that this song was the reason we named her Serita. She doesn't need to know any more than that."

"So the day didn't turn out so bad after all."

"My girls are here. I got my man, and I couldn't be happier."

"Why don't we send these moochers home so we can do that married *thang*?"

"I've waited ten years to get you to come to your senses, man. I'm not going to rush through this moment."

The groove of the music changed, sending more people to the floor to dance. Ondie sat across the room glaring at Serita, jabbing her fork into a piece of wedding cake. It was hard not to notice her pregnancy and the fullness of her face because of the extra baby weight. It didn't take a mind reader to know what was going through Ondie's head.

"Are you all right?" Paul asked.

"Yeah, I'm fine."

"Your sister being here bothers you, doesn't it?"

"I haven't seen her in four months. When Mama told me she was pregnant it somehow didn't seem as real as it does right now."

"Do you want to go?"

"No." She put her plate down and stood up. "I'll be right back."

"Where are you going?"

"I want to talk to her. Don't worry, I promised Mama that I'd be a good girl."

Maxine and Serita were getting acquainted with Anthony when Ondie made her way over. Most everyone there was aware of the strife between the sisters. The matronly woman felt obligated to keep the peace. "Ondie, is everything all right?"

"It's fine, Aunt Maxine. I'm not here to cause trouble. I just want to talk to my sister."

Maxine shot Serita a look as if asking for permission to leave her alone. Serita nodded.

"Come on, Anthony," Maxine said. "Let's go get you another piece of cake."

Ondie waited until Maxine and the boy were clear. "Can we go upstairs and talk?"

"No, I'm good right here."

Ondie smirked. "You afraid I'm going to do something?"

"I don't know, Ondie, but I'd rather be safe than sorry."

"So my little sister is going to have a baby. Dexter must be thrilled. Of all the things you could say about him, he was a good father. Be careful, though, if he cheated on me with you . . . Well, it's just like that old saying, a tiger can't change his stripes."

"Dexter didn't cheat on you, Ondie."

"Is that the way you see it?"

"That's the way it is. Look, I'm sorry about all this. I don't know how to make any of it better. It happened. Dexter happened. We have to find a way to get on with our lives."

"Well, it's clear that you have."

"You can, too. This guy Paul, he seems nice."

"Don't try it, Serita. Paul is not your get-out-of-hell free card."

"Ondrea," Paul called out over the music. "Dance with me."

Paul led a reluctant Ondie through the crowd and onto the floor.

As the rain subsided, Serita stole away to the patio. She searched her purse for her cell phone, but couldn't find it. "Damn, I must have left it at home."

She stepped back into the house and used the kitchen phone to call Dexter.

"There's my girl." Kenny lit up as he wrapped his arms around her.

"Hey, Daddy."

"What's wrong?"

"Nothing, just a little tired. I think I'm going to head home and lie down. Dexter's on his way to pick me up."

"Dexter?" Kenny rolled his eyes. "Your mother told me that you two were livin' together now."

"Daddy, don't start."

"Do you really think it's wise?"

"Daddy, we're . . ."

"You're what?"

"I'm happy for you, why can't you be happy for me?"

"I would be if I thought you were makin' the right decision."

"It is right—for me."

"Did you meet Anthony?"

"Yeah, I did."

"What do you think?"

"I think if you and Mama can work it out, we can, too."

"So you're still gonna go through with this marriage foolishness?"

"Dexter should be here in a few minutes. I'm going to go say good-bye to Mama." She kissed his cheek. "Congratulations, old man."

# 30

"How was the wedding?" asked Dr. Mathis.

"It was fine. Daddy had his son there from Macon."

"So you all finally met. How did that go?"

"All right, I guess. We don't really know each other, so there wasn't any special connection or anything."

"Do you think he'll be coming around more?"

"Hard to say. That'll be up to Mama."

"What about you? Would you like to get to know your brother any better?"

"It's not on the top of my list right now."

"Any other issues?"

Ondie sat thoughtfully on the sofa in Dr. Mathis's office and didn't respond.

"Is something bothering you, Ondie?"

"Serita was there."

"How did that go?"

"I didn't realize how awkward it would be seeing her after so long a time. It was almost like being in the room with a stranger."

"Did something happen?"

"I told Mama that I wouldn't start anything. But just looking at her going on with her life as if nothing had changed, I just wanted to snatch her and shake her."

"Was Dexter there?"

"No. I'm glad. I really don't think I could have handled seeing him; it was hard enough seeing her. But you know what I finally realized . . . I'm the one with the problem. I'm the one that can't move past this place."

"Do you feel like you're stuck?"

"Yes."

"Is there anything that you think will help you get unstuck?"

"I don't know . . . maybe."

"Paul?"

"Why do people ask about Paul as if he's supposed to be some kind of savior or something? He's not Superman. He's not a magic wand that you can wave in front of my face and make me forget."

"I don't think he's in your life to make you forget. But he's obviously in it for a reason. Perhaps he's the bridge that will take you in a whole different direction."

"And what direction would that be?"

"That's up to the two of you to decide. Maybe it's marriage."

"Marriage?"

"Okay, what about the possibility of having another child? You're still young and strong enough."

"I can't begin to envision being a mother to a child who has this disease. What do you think would have happened if Maya had lived?"

"The probability that Maya would have been affected wasn't as high as it was when you were born."

"But you can't be sure of that."

"No."

"This is hopeless."

"It's manageable."

"Do you want to trade places with me?" Ondie walked over to the wall-encased aquarium and stared at the fish. "I don't have the kind of life that would be conducive to having another baby. Maybe I never did. I'm not the wide-eyed twenty-two-year-old anymore that got pregnant and was stupid enough to believe in a man that didn't believe in me. The only reason I wanted Maya was to hold on to Dexter. Then when I saw that beautiful little girl, she gave me purpose. I don't have that purpose anymore."

"Then find a new one."

Ondie glared at him as if she needed to choose her words more carefully. She chose not to respond. "Do you know I've barely spoken to Paul all week? When I call him his assistant tells me he's in a meeting, or whatever excuse she's been instructed to relay. When he calls me back it's a quick "I just wanted to say hi. I'll call you later." Or he'll call when I'm in the shower or it's too late to talk. I just think he's lost interest in playing nursemaid to an emotional cripple."

"So you don't believe that he's just busy?"

"He told me that I was important to him. You make time for the things you really want to make time for, don't you?"

"Try not to jump to conclusions. He took you to the wedding. It's only been a few days."

"Do you think I'm being paranoid?"

"Are you?"

"I don't want to go through the same thing with him that I did when I was with Dexter. If he's over it I just want him to be man enough to tell me."

"Could you handle it if he was?"

She didn't answer.

"Ondie, where is this coming from? There has to be more to what you're saying than a couple of missed phone calls."

"Sometimes when we're together I catch a look in his eyes. Dexter used to look at me like that after he found out about my disorder."

"Have you asked him about it?"

"I'm afraid of what he might say."

"Are you in love with him?"

"I don't know if you can call what I feel love. I thought I was in love with Dexter."

"It's obvious your feelings have definitely moved past the 'like' stage."

"I'm really trying not to be all weird with him, but I'm a girl, I can't help it. I like the way he makes me feel. I love his laugh, the way he touches me, his intelligence and sensitivity and passion, and he's sexy as hell."

"You don't think he could be feeling the same way?"

"What if he's not?"

"Why don't you just go to him and be honest? Tell him exactly how you feel, and if he's on a different page, deal with it. I'll help you. But don't cut him out of your life based on what you think without giving him a chance to answer."

* * *

"Go to him and be honest," Ondie repeated. That's exactly what she needed to do. She had to see for herself whether or not it was work that occupied Paul's time, or something else. It was nearly six o'clock when she left Dr. Mathis's office. It would take thirty minutes to get from Midtown to Buckhead in traffic. She called Paul's office to see if he still might be there. "Hi, it's me."

"How are you?"

"Fine. Although I half expected to get your voice mail; seems like I've had more time with it than you lately."

"Yes, I know. I'm sorry about that. We're just in the middle of handling all this paperwork for a merger and we've all had to log some really long hours this week."

"So you're still at your office?"

"Yes, I'll probably be here until about nine o'clock."

"Do you want to get together after?"

"Ondrea, I'm going to be really tired."

"What about this weekend?"

No response.

"Paul?"

"Sorry, I was looking over some notes. Saturday sounds cool. Do you want to get together for lunch? I could call you after I leave the barbershop."

"What time will that be?"

"Ondrea, I've got to go. Someone just came into my office."

Before she could respond he hung up. Several minutes later she found herself in the parking lot of the ultramodern Lenox Road building. She told herself this could be a mistake, but her heart overruled reason.

*Just a few minutes,* she thought as she stepped into

the elevator. All she needed to do was look into his eyes and she would know.

No one was sitting at the receptionist's desk when she entered. She heard voices just down the corridor; Paul's distinctive accent was notable. Ondie crept quietly toward the door to his office. She looked inside and spied Paul enjoying Chinese food with two of his colleagues, one an attractive blond female. The woman brazenly reached out and wiped away a spatter of soy sauce from Paul's tie. She then looked up and saw Ondie. She cleared her throat in order to draw Paul's attention to the door.

"Ondrea, what are you doing here?"

"I—I'm sorry. I was . . . I just wanted to see you, but I can see that you're busy with your merger."

Ondie turned and darted back toward the lobby. Paul excused himself and ran after her.

"Ondrea, wait. What is going on?"

"I don't know, Paul. You tell me."

"I'm working. I told you that. We're just taking a dinner break."

"I haven't seen you since Saturday. I just wanted to spend a little time with you, and I come in here to find . . . I don't know what."

"Three people eating Chinese food?" Paul put his hands on his hips, lowered his gaze, and sighed. "Ondrea, you can't possibly think that there's anything going on here."

"Is there?"

"What do you want me to tell you?"

"How about the truth? The people in my life seem to have a hard time with that."

"We're having dinner and we're working; that's all."

"Are you sure?"

"Look, I'm not going to stand here and try to defend what you *think* you saw. There is no reason for you to overreact."

"I'm not overreacting."

"Then what is this?"

She looked into his eyes. "That's what I'd like to know, Paul. What is this? What are we doing?"

"Ondrea, this is seriously not the time for this conversation."

"So when exactly is the time, Paul? Late at night when you're tired and I'm at home asleep, or in the middle of the day in an e-mail?"

"I can't do this here. I've got to get back to work."

"Just answer one question and I'll go."

Paul rubbed his face in frustration.

"Are you sleeping with that woman?"

"Please don't act like this."

"Like what, a crazy person?"

"No, damn it, like a typical black female."

"Is that what you think I am?"

"Are you going to blame this attitude on your disorder?"

"Are you going to stand there and tell me that that plastic Barbie doll in there doesn't want to get inside your *legal briefs*?"

"It wouldn't matter if she did, Ondrea. I'm not interested in being with that woman. What is it going to take for you to realize that I want to be with you? How many ways do I have to prove it?"

"Paul? Mr. Shenault is holding for the conference call."

They both turned to see the blonde standing in the doorway.

"I'll be right there."

Paul shook his head and sighed. "Ondrea, I've got to go."

Ondie's eyes clouded. "I'm sorry."

"Yes . . . me, too."

# 31

It was a busy Sunday afternoon. Serita's friend, Tonja, threw her a shower and she had quite a lot of baby-booty to haul back to her place. Ruth was there to lend a hand.

They could hear Dexter and some of his buddies jeering and yelling over a battle between the Atlanta Falcons and the Carolina Panthers as soon as they pulled up to the town house and got out of the car. Serita knew that it was going to be hard to tear him away from the television screen to help them unpack. Ruth decided to step in, knowing how useless Kenny could be during football season.

She grabbed the remote and flipped off the set; fortunately for everyone it was halftime.

"I'm going to need all of you to go out to the car and bring that stuff in." She stood her ground, daring any of his four beer-swilling comrades to balk. "Go on now, and don't break anything."

Dexter knew Ruth meant business. He kissed Serita, and then encouraged his associates to do as Ruth instructed. Serita was tickled as they submitted. Ruth pressed her lips together to contain her amusement. Within minutes the car was emptied and the men returned to their sport.

Serita and Ruth retreated to the bedroom. They sat on the edge of Serita's bed cooing over tiny dresses, sweaters, shoes, and lace-trimmed socks that were awaiting the baby's arrival.

"Thank you for coming with me today, Mama."

"Of course I was going to be there. Where else would I be?"

Serita's disposition took a downturn.

"What is it, baby?"

"I've been thinking about Ondie. I wish . . . I miss her."

Ruth patted her hand. "I'll be willing to bet that Ondie misses you, too. She's still in a dark place. Seeing you like this is hard for her."

"I know it is."

"She'll come out of this, just be patient."

A thunderous shout erupting from downstairs shook the walls as the football game heated up. The women laughed.

"Serita, I want you to know that in spite of the circumstances I've always liked Dexter. And if he makes you happy, then I'm happy."

"He does, Mama. He really does."

"Well, can I get a look at that ring?"

"Huh?"

"Don't huh me. I saw you struggling to get it off when I got here earlier today."

"Mama, I . . ."

"You don't have to say anything. I pretty much knew that you might try something like this when you and

Dexter showed up at the house that day. But you know your father is going to hit the roof."

"You're not going to tell him, are you?"

"No. You are."

"We just didn't want to steal your thunder. We were planning to have a real ceremony next year, maybe in the spring."

Serita pulled the ring from her purse and put it on.

Ruth smiled sadly. "Lord, have mercy. What am I going to do with you? Just wait until Reese grows up, you'll see."

"That's what I'm looking forward to."

Ruth stood up. "It's getting late. I better get on home. I probably won't have to cook since Kenny and Frank have probably gorged themselves on sub sandwiches and hot wings."

"They probably left a mess for you to clean up, too."

"Who? Oh no, Hazel is off duty. If your father knows what's good for him, there won't be a crumb or an empty beer can to be found when I get home."

After Ruth left and the game ended, Serita took a bath and got ready for bed. Dexter applied cocoa butter to her stomach and rubbed it in.

"Mama knows we're married," she said.

"Are you serious?"

"She saw me trying to take my ring off before we went to Tonja's."

"What did she say?"

"She was cool. It's Daddy and Ondie that we have to worry about."

Dexter began to massage Serita's feet without comment.

"Mmmmmm, that feels so good."

"Well, maybe when I'm done rubbin' you down you'll return the favor." Dexter smiled salaciously and pointed to his penis.

"You are so nasty."

"And you are so sexy. C'mon, baby. I thought you said it was okay."

"Dexter, my back hurts and I'm bloated and gassy. There's nothing sexy about that."

"So, what do you want me to do now that you got me all worked up?"

"I didn't do that," Serita laughed. "You did that to yourself."

Dexter wiped the residue of cocoa butter from his hands and snuggled up next to her and fondled her breasts. "C'mon, baby. It was good the last time we did it, right?"

"It's always good. But not tonight, okay?"

"Well, how 'bout I take a little trip downtown?"

"Ugh, Dexter."

"Are you all right?"

"Yeah, just a little heartburn. I think I ate something earlier that I shouldn't have."

"You want me to get you some Maalox?"

"Would you mind?"

"I'll be right back." Dexter hopped out of bed, darted to the kitchen, and returned with a bottle and a spoon. "Any better?"

Serita nodded. "I think I just need to get some sleep."

She curled up in Dexter's arms and he flipped the television on to ESPN and watched sports recaps until he fell asleep. Shortly after midnight Serita awoke in distress—the sheets were soaked with blood. "Oh God! Dexter, wake up!"

Serita was rushed to the hospital by ambulance. Panic seized Dexter. He called Ruth, and then he called his parents. Within the half hour Ruth and Kenny joined Dexter and fretfully waited. A nurse came out to speak with them.

"What's going on?" Kenny demanded.

"Dr. Brunner is going to have to perform an emergency C-section," she replied.

"Oh Lord," Ruth gasped.

"Is the baby gonna be all right?" Dexter injected.

"Mr. Campbell, your wife's in good health. Dr. Brunner is going to do everything she can for both her and the baby."

Kenny glared at Dexter. "What did she just say? Your wife?"

Ruth pulled on his arm. "Not now, Kenny."

The nurse looked at them as if she'd stepped into the line of fire. "Mr. Campbell, I just need you to sign these consent forms."

Dexter took the clipboard and signed off; Kenny fumed.

The nurse quickly disappeared through a set of doors leading back to the OR. Dexter rubbed his hands together and blew into them. Anticipating an attack, Ruth headed her husband off. "This is not the time, Kenny."

Kenny shook his head and turned away. "I'll be damned."

"Right now Serita and the baby are the only ones we need to be concerned with."

Two pints of blood and forty-five minutes later, Dr. Brunner found them in the waiting area.

Ruth and Kenny stirred. Dexter jumped to attention and wiped his eyes. "Dr. Brunner? What's going on?"

The petite redhead pulled off her surgical cap and smiled. "Both Serita and the baby are fine."

"Thank God," Ruth whispered.

"What happened?" Kenny asked.

"Serita's placenta separated from her uterine wall, causing an abruption. There was some hemorrhaging, but we got it under control and delivered a healthy seven-pound baby girl."

Ruth and Kenny embraced.

Relief washed over Dexter. "When can I see them?"

"Serita's in recovery. You can see her as soon as she wakes up and we move her to a room. The baby will be down in the nursery until then."

After Dr. Brunner left, Dexter called his mother and brought her up to speed.

"Get off the phone," Kenny demanded.

Dexter glared at him and rolled his eyes. "Mama, I gotta go. I'll see you when you get here."

"Kenny, calm down," Ruth cautioned.

"I am calm, Ruthie. I just wanna know if this jackass is really married to my baby."

"Yes, Kenny. This jackass is married to your daughter. I told you I wasn't askin' permission."

"You also said you wanted to respect me and Ruthie. And that you wanted to be straight with us. Is this what the hell you call bein' straight?"

"Look, I'm sorry for sneakin' off and marrying Serita behind your backs, but we both wanted to do it. We didn't want to take anything away from your and Ruth's celebration."

"That's bullshit!"

"Kenny!"

"It is, Ruthie."

"Kenny, Dexter was just trying to do the right thing. He may have gone about it the wrong way, but he loves Serita and she loves him."

"Wait a minute . . . you knew about this, didn't you?"

"I suspected it. Serita confirmed it after we left the baby shower."

"And you're all right with it?"

"They're married, Kenny. There's nothing we can do."

Dexter started out of the room. "I'm goin' to see my baby girl."

Kenny grabbed his arm as he walked by, and spun him around. "Let me tell you somethin', *son-in-law.* I swear to God if you hurt Serita the way you hurt Ondie I am gonna break my foot off in yo' ass! Do we understand each other?"

"You know what, man? I'm gettin' sick and damn tired of your threats!"

Kenny's brow arched. "If you think this is a threat—try me!"

Dexter snatched his arm out of Kenny's grasp and scoffed as he walked away.

Kenny and Ruth left the hospital after catching a peek at the newest addition to their family through the nursery window. Dexter tried to make himself as comfortable as possible propped up between two chairs in Serita's room.

The pain of Serita's incision stirred her around six in the morning. She rang the nurse for medication and woke Dexter.

Her voice was dry and raspy. "Hey."

Dexter took her hand and kissed her. "How are you feelin'?"

"I'm sore as hell, but other than that I'm okay. Have you seen the baby?"

"She beautiful. She's got a headful of curls." Dexter teared up.

"Dexter, what's wrong?"

He rubbed his neck and slowly rotated his head. "Just a little stiff. That chair's not as comfortable as our bed."

"Is that all that's bothering you?"

"No. I was thinkin' about . . ."

"Maya?"

"I'm not gonna blow it this time."

"Dexter, you didn't do anything wrong before."

"If I had just picked her up like I was supposed to."

Serita's eyes misted. "I have played the *what-if* game for months. I'm always going to bear the burden for what happened that day. But the one thing I know for sure is that you loved Maya, and she loved you more than anything."

The nurse entered with a tray of medication. "I'll bet you want to get a look at that little angel, don't you?"

"Yes."

"Well, I'll see to it that she gets brought in to you in a bit. Here, I brought you some ice chips."

"Thank you."

The nurse left the room and Dexter eased into bed next to Serita and wrapped his arm around her.

"Has Mama and Daddy seen her?"

"Yeah, they were here until two. Mama and Bumper should be rollin' in sometime this morning."

"Are you and Daddy getting along?"

"It was rough, but as soon as he found out I was your husband we came to an understanding."

"What? Did you tell him?"

Dexter chuckled. "I didn't have to; the nurse did it for me. She came out before your surgery to get these forms signed. You should have seen Kenny's face when she handed them to me."

Serita laid her head on Dexter's shoulder and closed her eyes. "I hope you two find a way to make peace now that he knows."

"I think it'll snow in hell before your daddy thinks of me as anything other than a bottom-feeding, blood-sucking pariah. But you know what, that's okay because I got you and Reese. And I got a second chance."

"Look who's up and I think she's hungry." A pediatric nurse wheeled the baby into the room and found both Dexter and Serita asleep. Dexter stretched and got up as the nurse scooped the baby up and gently laid her in Serita's arms.

Serita burst with elation. "Hi, Reese."

The baby squirmed and started to fuss. Serita looked up at the nurse as if for guidance.

"It's okay," the woman assured her. "She'll know what to do."

"I guess this is where those videos and classes come in handy."

Serita opened her gown and after some coaxing the little one found a home.

"Wow, I think I should be jealous," Dexter cracked.

The nurse laughed. "I'm going to give you guys some privacy. I'll be back in a little while."

Kenny and Ruth walked into the room just as the baby finished. Shortly after that Vivian came in.

"Mama, where's Dad?" Dexter asked.

Vivian seemed embarrassed. "He didn't come."

A knowing look passed between Kenny and Ruth.

"Mama, you drove up here by yourself?"

"I'm not handicapped. I do have a driver's license, you know." Vivian drew closer. "Will you look at that? She is an absolute doll. Can I hold her?"

"I think Reese's daddy should bond with her first," Serita replied.

Dexter cautiously picked her up and cradled her. Everybody gathered around acting like most people act when they see a newborn; as if it were the first one they'd ever seen. There was so much love waiting for this child.

Ruth turned her attention to Serita. "Are you all right? You look like you could use some rest."

Serita didn't respond.

Ruth noted the glazed expression in her eyes. Serita broke out into a sweat and began to shake.

"Serita? Serita, baby, it's Mama. Can you hear me?"

Dr. Brunner entered the room with a nurse and saw Ruth's panic.

"She's nonreactive," Ruth said.

"I'm going to need everybody to clear out," Dr. Brunner barked. "Barbara, can you get the baby back to the nursery?"

Dexter passed the baby to the nurse and rushed to Serita's side.

"Dexter, I'm going to need you to step out with the others," Dr. Brunner insisted.

"I'm not going anywhere!"

She didn't waste time arguing with him. Quickly assessing the situation, she administered glycogen in order to restore Serita's glucose levels.

Ruth and Dexter stayed with Serita until she responded to the medication. They left her resting and Dexter took his mother back to the town house. Ruth and Kenny went to the cafeteria for breakfast. Just as the elevator reached the basement level of the hospital, Ruth's cell phone rang.

"Hello."

"Hi, Mama. Where are you?"

"I'm at the hospital."

"I just called; they said you weren't working today."

"I'm not working. I'm at Piedmont with your sister."

"Serita had the baby?"

Ruth paused, realizing that Ondie would not be as thrilled as the rest of them, but it was senseless to backpedal.

"Mama?"

"Yes, she had to have a caesarian early this morning."

"Boy or girl?"

"She had a girl."

There was no response from the other end of the line as if it had gone dead.

"Ondie, are you there?"

"Yeah, I'm here."

"Are you okay?"

"I'm fabulous. Why shouldn't I be?"

After hanging up the phone Ondie went into her manager's office and asked for the rest of the day off. He gave his permission without a second thought. She quickly gathered her things and turned off her computer. Within minutes she was headed to the hospital.

Woefully, Ondie stood outside the nursery peering though the glass, much like she did when she studied the aquarium in Dr. Mathis's office. But these weren't fish. These were babies, and among them was Dexter and Serita's child, the living, breathing manifestation of her heartache. Seeing little Reese took her back to Maya's birth and it made her pain all the more profound. Tears instantaneously flowed from her eyes and down her cheeks. She wiped them away, and when she turned to leave, she came face-to-face with Dexter.

"Ondie."

"Hello, Dexter."

"What are you doing here?"

"Is there a law against me coming to see my niece? She's beautiful. You must be so proud. You and my sister finally did it."

Dexter's apprehension was evident. "So you heard?"

"You don't have to worry; I'm not going to freak out. I'm almost as sane as you are."

"We were gonna wait until after Reese was born, but things were happening so fast. I needed to do things different this time."

"What are you talking about? What things?"

"Serita and me . . . we . . ."

"Ondie!"

They turned to see Ruth and Kenny headed toward them.

"I didn't know you were coming," Kenny stammered.

"Are you kidding? I wouldn't have wanted to miss this blessed event."

"Are you all right?"

"Couldn't be better. Since I can't be a mother, being an aunt is just as good. The Lord gives, and the Lord takes away. I read that, just recently in fact."

"Do you want to come and get some coffee with me?"

"No, Mama. Dexter was just about to tell me something about him and Serita."

Ruth cleared her throat and twisted up her face.

"This is bad, right? Mama, you could never play poker."

"Ondie."

"Just tell me; what things did you want to do different this time, Dexter? Hmmm, let me guess; you actually want to marry Serita, and you two want to live happily ever after." Ondie looked at Dexter and then to her mother and laughed. "Oh no, you didn't. This is unreal. You're already married, aren't you?" Ondie pressed her fingertips to her eyelids as more tears gushed to the surface. "Fuck!"

Ruth reached out for her and she pulled away.

"I wasn't good enough. Maya wasn't good enough. You just don't know when to quit, do you? How many more times are you going to twist the knife in my back before you pull it out?"

"Ondie, we didn't do this to hurt you."

"Really? Because it feels differently from where I'm standing. It's not a fairy tale. You're my brother-in-law now. How very Shakespearean." Ondie shook her head and walked away.

# 32

"Happy birthday to you. Happy birthday to you. Happy birthday, dear Maya. Happy birthday to you."

Ondie sat and rewatched the videotape of Maya's first birthday, rewinding, pausing, and fast-forwarding through the looking glass of a happier time.

"Blow out the candle, sweetie," Ondie encouraged.

Maya was much too content to sample the frosting from her fingers.

Dexter picked her up. "Let's do it together." Maya filled her cheeks with air, emulating Dexter. "One—two—three."

Ruth clapped and Kenny cheered from behind the camera.

Ondie was jarred by a knock at the door. She paused the tape and got up from the sofa and went to the window. She could see the tail end of Paul's Lexus. She checked herself in the mirror on the wall just inside the door before letting him in.

"I tried calling first but it rang straight to your voice mail."

"I turned my phone off."

Paul stepped inside and noted the frozen scene of Ondie, Maya, and Dexter on the television screen. "I called your mother when I couldn't get in touch with you and she told me what happened."

"Good ol' Mama. She can always be counted on to tell my business."

"She's concerned about you; so am I."

"So you braved the rush hour to drive out here and check on me?"

"Is that so terrible?"

"Well, as you can see, I'm doing just fine."

He glanced back at the television. "Reliving the past instead of taking hold of your future?"

"I'm just trying to deal with things the best way I know how."

"Is this the best way?"

"You deal with your shit your way, and leave me to deal with mine."

"Can I talk to you?"

"Oh, now you want to talk. It's been almost two weeks and here you are. Why?"

"Because I missed you. I didn't want things to end between us like they did. I don't want them to end at all. Believe it or not I was extremely busy that day you showed up in my office out of the blue. I know I could have handled this a lot better and kept in contact with you, but that's how I get when I'm under a deadline. Work is a singular focus. I suppose that's why my marriage ultimately fell apart and cut me off from my sons. I did try to call, but you didn't call me back. Ondrea, I'm here with my hat in my hands asking for you to please forgive me. Balance is not my strong suit."

"Funny, it's not mine, either."

They laughed and tension fell away.

"Are you hungry? Would you like to go get dinner?" Ondie asked.

"No. I don't want anything."

"Anything?"

Paul moved in closer to her. "That's what I missed. That smile. Those eyes."

He touched her cheek and pulled her into a kiss. She responded in kind. They continued to kiss and undress each other until they ended up in her bedroom.

Ondie pulled back the comforter and lay down and waited for Paul to join her. He was in no hurry. He slowly massaged and kissed her feet, legs, and thighs until he made his way to a familiar place. Ondie moaned in ecstasy as his lips and fingers probed her vagina. Leaving his nimble digits in place, he kissed a path up her stomach and sucked greedily on each breast. Ondie arched her back and trembled as orgasm racked her body. Paul quickly sheathed his erection, pushed her legs open, and slid down between them. She panted as he entered, and became enraptured by his primal tempo. Paul steadied himself on his knees and took pleasure watching her expressive surrender. He grabbed her thighs and hoisted her legs up so that he could lie deeper in her. After a time his heavy staccato breathing gave way to a toe-curling, palpitating climax.

"Shit," he spat as tremors surged through him. Ondie's body quaked, too, as another wave of bliss washed over her.

"Now, what was that you were saying about dinner?" Ondie teased. "I think I can eat now."

"You want to order in, or shall we go out?"

"Well, I don't have a taste for pizza or Chinese food."

"Out it is."

Paul rolled out of bed and started for the bathroom. He noticed a small jar on the bureau and picked it up and smiled.

"It's the sand you brought me back from Jamaica."

"So I see."

He put the jar down, jumped back into bed, and kissed her. "I want to take you there—soon. We could both use a vacation."

"I would love that."

"How about we go grab some jerk chicken or some oxtails? Then afterward we come back here and sweat off the calories."

"Yah, mon!"

Ondie sat quietly and pensively as they traveled to a Jamaican restaurant in Decatur. She was consumed with thoughts of taking hold of her future and not allowing her disorder to define her any longer.

Paul reached over and took her hand. She looked at him and smiled.

"What are you so quiet about?" he asked.

"I was thinking I should probably call Mama and let her know that I'm all right, and about what I want to do with myself."

"Ondrea, you can be and do whatever it is you want to do; just believe it. You're stronger than you think you are."

"Thank you."

"For what?"

"For being here."

"Your happiness has very little to do with me. The power is inside you."

"You sound a lot like Dr. Mathis."

"Then he's a very smart man. But I've got something that he doesn't."

"What's that?"

"You."

# 33

"Hello! Anybody home?"

"In here."

Ondie found Ruth seated at the table when she walked in. She threw her arms around her and gave her a loving squeeze.

"Well, look who's all smiles. Things must be going well between you and Mr. Jamaica."

Ondie went to the refrigerator and poured herself a glass of juice and joined Ruth at the table. "We're having fun."

"Fun? Is that what they call it these days?"

"I have a feeling that's what they called it in your day, too."

"Don't be smart."

"I'm just teasing, Mama."

"I'm glad that you're all right. Whatever *fun* you're having, you keep right on having it."

"So, what are you doing?"

"I'm making out a grocery list for Thanksgiving. Trying to see how much food we're going to need. I've invited Anthony. I was surprised that his mother wanted him to come. Can you believe it will be Kenny's first Thanksgiving with his son?"

"You're incredible, you know that?"

"As a matter of fact I do." Ruth chuckled.

"I'm assuming Serita and Dexter are going to be here, too?"

Ruth pulled off her eyeglasses and stopped writing. "Yes, and I'm hoping that you and Paul will be here."

"I'm not sure that any of us are ready to be in the same room with each other, let alone share a meal."

"You won't know until you try. I know for a fact that your sister misses you."

"Did she tell you that?"

"Yes, she did. She went home from the hospital yesterday. Maybe you can call her, or better yet, go by and see her."

"You want me to go to her house? Where she lives with Dexter, her husband, and their new baby? Are you serious?"

"Okay, so maybe going to her house is not such a good idea, but what if I call her and ask her to come here?"

"No, Mama. It's never going to work."

Inadequate rest and guilt had been eating away at Serita for days. She cried as she stood over Reese and watched her sleep, realizing how fleeting, even unfair, life could be. In many ways she felt that she didn't deserve Dexter or this beautiful baby girl; she was despondent.

"Hey, I made you a sandwich," Dexter said as he came up behind her.

She wiped her face. "I'm not hungry."

"You should eat something. You didn't eat anything this morning. You don't wanna waste away on me, do you?"

"I said I'm not hungry, okay!"

"Serita, I can see that something is wrong. What is it? Talk to me."

She threw herself in Dexter's arms and wept. "Everything is wrong."

"Baby, you're just tired. Why don't you try and lie down?"

She shook her head.

"Come on. I'll take care of Reese while you take a nap." He gently pulled her away from the bassinet and made a big show of the fact that he'd gotten a new mattress set while she was in the hospital. She smiled wryly, kicked off her shoes, and climbed into bed.

"You lie here for an hour or so, and when you wake up I'm sure you'll feel a lot better."

Dexter left the room, pulled the door to, and went downstairs. He sat on the arm of the sofa and considered calling Dr. Brunner, but opted to call Ruth instead.

"Hi, Ruth, it's Dexter."

"Hi, is anything wrong?"

"I'm not sure. It's Serita. She's not sleeping. I can't get her to eat anything and she keeps crying."

"Do you want me to come over there?"

"No, you don't have to do that. I finally got her to lie

down. I just don't know what else to do. I don't even know why I called you."

"I'm sure it's just her hormones. She just got home. After you have a baby your estrogen levels are off and you feel out of sorts for a while. Dr. Brunner gave her something for that, didn't she?"

"Yeah, I think so."

"Give her some time. She'll be back to normal before you know it."

Dexter glanced over his shoulder and found Serita standing at the bottom of the stairs glaring at him. "Ruth, I've gotta go. I'll call you later."

He hung up the phone and turned to Serita. "I thought you were lying down."

"Why were you on the phone with my mother?"

"Because I was worried about you."

"So why not talk to me? Why call her? What are you going to do next? Run home to Vivian?"

"Baby, what's wrong with you?"

"Nothing, I'm sorry. I'm just tired. Have you seen those pills I got from Dr. Brunner?"

"I put them upstairs on the dresser with your other stuff."

"Okay, I'm just gonna get a glass of water."

Before going into the kitchen she walked over to Dexter and kissed him. "I love you."

"I love you, too."

Ondie went back to the refrigerator for another glass of juice and leaned against the counter. "What did Dexter want?"

"He called to ask me what I thought he should do about Serita."

"What does that mean?"

Ruth got up to return the cordless phone to its wall mounted cradle. "He said she wasn't eating, and she was crying a lot. It's probably just some postpartum stress. I had it. You had it, too."

"Oh yeah, I guess he wouldn't know about that since he wasn't around to see it. Poor Dexter, he'll get a first-hand education now."

"Ondie."

Ondie smirked. "I'm serious, Mama. He can't very well turn his back on his wife, can he? He'd really be an asshole then."

"Maybe I should go over there."

"What for? There won't be anything you can do. Why don't you and I go to the grocery store together?"

Ruth looked at her list and tossed it on the table. "I'm not sure that all this is going to be necessary now. With you and Serita at odds, there may not be a whole lot to be thankful for."

As she acknowledged that she might be enjoying this moment just a bit too much, Ondie's sneer dissipated and she acquiesced. "Okay, Mama, if I could suck it up for your wedding, I can do the same for Thanksgiving. As long as Serita is willing to meet me halfway, there's no reason we can't try and be civil. I'll even come over early and help you cook."

Ruth embraced her. "That's all I ask, baby."

# 34

It took some doing, but Ruth was finally able to convince Serita to come for Thanksgiving. She assured her that she had nothing to fear from Ondie. Ruth also extended an olive branch to Bumper and Vivian. Vivian wanted to come for no other reason than to see their granddaughter; she declined because of Bumper's obstinance.

"Orvillo Henry Campbell, why can't we go to Atlanta to see Dexter and our grandbaby?"

Bumper ignored her and tried in vain to hide behind the morning newspaper. After thirty-two years of marriage he knew when his wife called him by his full given name she was really ticked. That coupled with the fact that her fair complexion turned almost crimson was enough of an indicator that he would be wise to make plans to sleep on the sofa if he didn't intend to let her have her way.

She snatched the newspaper down from his face. "You hear me talkin' to you, man? There ain't no reason we can't go and be with our son and his family for Thanksgiving dinner."

"Dexter is our family. We don't owe nothin' to them Reids."

"He married that girl, Bumper. They have a child together. And like it or not, that makes us all connected."

"Then why don't you go? You flew up there like a bat out of hell when she had the baby."

"You know how much me going by myself hurt your son. He was really disappointed that you weren't there. How would it look if I went up there for Thanksgiving without you?"

"Look, Vivian, you know me. I don't pull no punches, and I don't deal with no bull. I can't sit at a table with them people and act like everything is all right. I don't like the fact that Dexter is still mixed up with that family and I'm not gonna pretend that I do."

"He's your son."

"I know that. I love him. But I'm not gonna smile like I approve of what he's doin'."

"You don't have to approve, Orvillo. He's a grown man. Why don't you do the Christian thing and support your flesh and blood? You accepted Ondie and Maya. Why can't you accept Serita and Reese?"

"I accepted Maya, I never hid the fact that I wasn't happy that Dexter didn't marry Ondie. He knew it, too. That's why he snuck off and married that other one."

"Please, Bumper. For me."

Bumper looked into her eyes and recalled why he'd married her in the first place. He knew that if he didn't concede, he'd never hear the end of it. "All right, call and tell 'em we're comin'."

Vivian threw her arms around her husband and gave him a big kiss. "Oh, baby, thank you!"

"But I'm tellin' you right now, Vivian, if Kenny Reid starts in there's gonna be hell to pay."

The Reid household was once again bustling with energy. Ruth had been up since five in the morning cooking, cleaning, and making sure that everything was just so. Ondie showed up around nine as did Frank's wife, Maxine, and their thirty-year-old daughter. Thankfully, Maxine's daughter was much more of an asset in the kitchen.

A sumptuous cornucopia of aromas from the baked ham, fried turkey, and chicken danced a mouthwatering, nose-tickling waltz with potato salad, corn bread dressing, baked macaroni and cheese, turnip greens, and an enviable display of cakes and pies. It was a feast to rival any other of its kind.

The men were already fully involved in their football mating marathon by noon as more guests descended on the house. Dexter and Serita, along with the baby, came in with Vivian and a wary Bumper, who despite his misgivings soon found himself aligned with Kenny in a game pitting the Dallas Cowboys against the New York Jets.

"Who knew that Tony Romo could be such a peacemaker?" Ruth joked.

Reese started to tire of being passed around like a football herself and started to fuss. Serita took her upstairs to feed her and put her down for a nap. Though it wasn't blatantly obvious, everyone kept an eye on Ondie to make sure that their uneasy détente would remain intact.

For Ruth's sake, Ondie was cordial to both Serita and Dexter. But to make certain she could live up to her end of the bargain she made sure to be wherever they weren't. Still, it was difficult not to feel the least bit resentful. This time last year Maya was there running around laughing and getting into things; now the family focused on a new grandchild. Sensitive to how she must be feeling, Ruth made sure to ask if she was all right every now and again. She assured her that she was.

An extra table had been added in the dining room to accommodate everyone. Dexter naturally took his place next to Serita, flanked by his parents. Paul made sure that everyone, especially Dexter, knew how he felt about Ondie. It made her feel good to know that he was there to support her.

"I'd just like to say somethin' before we ask the blessing," Kenny said as he stood up. "This year has not been one of the best for our family, but we still have a lot to be thankful for. I'm grateful that Ruth has opened up her heart and our home to my son, Anthony. We lost our precious Maya, but God has seen fit to give us Reese. Not that she is a replacement for what we lost, but He has His reasons for doin' everything He does."

Ondie glared across the table at Serita as Kenny spoke. Whatever the intent, his little *God has a plan* speech wasn't working.

When he sat back down he asked Ruth's brother, Frank, to bless the table. Everyone joined hands and Frank prayed. Following a collective "Amen" the feasting began.

As bowls and platters emptied, Ruth went to the kitchen to refill them. Ondie got up to help.

"I think things are going pretty well, don't you, Ondie?"

"Yes. Everyone seems to be on their best behavior."

"That little Anthony sure can eat, can't he?"

"Just like Daddy."

Grease spilled on the counter and Ruth sopped it up with a couple of the dish towels she had. "I'm going to need some clean towels. I thought I had them in this drawer."

"I'll go get some more."

"I did the laundry yesterday. You should find clean towels upstairs in the linen closet."

"Okay, I'll be right back."

Ondie slipped out of the kitchen, through the dining room, and up the stairs while everyone continued laughing and outtalking one another. She went to the linen closet and found a few towels. On her way back downstairs she heard Reese fussing from Serita's old room. She pushed the door open and went inside. The tiny infant was surrounded by a fortress of pillows. Ondie reluctantly leaned over and picked her up. Her eyes instantly filled with emotion as the baby grabbed on to her finger.

"You're strong, aren't you? And pretty, too. You look a lot like Maya did when she was born. You would have loved your little cousin. I'm sorry you'll never get the chance to know her."

Ruth came out of the kitchen and set down a refilled bowl of greens and more dinner rolls. "Can I get anybody anything? Is everybody all right?"

Serita looked around. "Mama, where's Ondie?"

Ruth's eyes cut to the kitchen door and then to Ondie's empty chair. Serita jumped up from the table and bolted up the stairs. Dexter, Ruth, Vivian, Kenny, and Paul followed.

"What are you doing? Put her down," Serita shrieked, charging into the room.

"I'm not hurting her, Serita. She was crying and I picked her up."

Ruth stepped into the room and Ondie looked up to see the others in the doorway. "Oh my God, you all think I came up here to do something to this baby?"

"Give her to me," Serita demanded. "I don't want you around her."

Ondie was stunned. "What? Do you honestly think that I was going to do something to her?"

Dexter pushed into the room and went to Serita's side.

"What is this? Are you all gangin' up on me?" Ondie said.

"Give me my baby, Ondie."

Ondie shook her head in disbelief and handed Reese to Serita. "So much for our little truce. You think that just because you killed my baby I would want to do anything to yours. Well, to hell with you."

Ondie stormed out of the room and knocked into Vivian and Kenny as she did so. Paul ran after her. She went to the front closet and grabbed her coat and purse.

"Paul, take me home."

Paul got his coat and started toward the door. Ruth came bounding down the stairs to stop them. "Ondie, wait."

"I tried, Mama. That's all I can do. I'm not going to stay here and be accused of something so ridiculous as to try and hurt that baby."

"Ondie, I'm sure Serita didn't mean it."

"Then why are you pleading her case?"

Ondie glanced up at the landing to see Serita holding the baby surrounded by Dexter and Vivian; the perfect little family unit.

She opened the door and slammed it behind her. Ruth was heartbroken.

"I didn't do anything," Ondie cried. "I just picked her up. I wouldn't have hurt her. I couldn't."

Paul kept his eyes on the road as he motored away from the subdivision, but he reached out and took Ondie's hand. "It's all right."

"I can get with the fact that she thought I might try something, you know. I'm not going to lie to you and say that thought didn't cross my mind when she was pregnant. But I swear to you, it wasn't like that."

"I know, Ondrea. I know."

"You didn't see the look in her eyes, Dexter. I'm just glad I stopped her before anything happened."

"Serita, come on. You can't seriously think that Ondie would hurt the baby, do you?"

"She still blames me for Maya! You heard her. She would do anything to get back at me!"

"Serita, you're being irrational."

"Are you on her side?"

"No, baby. But I know Ondie."

"If you know her so well why did you want to take full custody of Maya? You had to be afraid of what she might do. Tell me I'm lyin'?"

"Serita, that was a long time ago."

"She's not going to get another chance. I'm not going to let her take my baby away from me."

Ruth sat on the edge of her bed applying lotion to her hands and feet after a bath. How was she going to fix this issue with her daughters? Was a permanent solution even possible? One thing was for sure, there would be no family Christmas.

Kenny walked into the bedroom, kicked off his shoes, and kissed her on the cheek. "You okay, Ruthie?"

"How can I be? This dinner was a disaster."

"It didn't start out that way. Serita and Ondie actually looked like they were tryin'."

"Were you in the same house I was?"

"Okay, it got a little rough."

"A little?"

"All I'm sayin' is once this postpartum foolishness runs its course things will get back to normal."

"Normal?"

"As normal as they can be for this family."

"Did you get Anthony settled?"

"Yeah, he's sleeping in the other room. Why don't you go with me tomorrow when I drive him back to Macon?"

"I don't think so. I can just hear him now telling those people about his father's crazy family."

"Ruthie."

"You don't think that woman pumps him for information every time he goes back home?"

"Would it matter if she did?"

Ruth shook her head. "No, I guess it doesn't. My main concern is my girls. Ondie was so hurt by what Serita said."

"Well, you gotta admit Serita has good reason to be scared."

"Scared of her sister?"

Kenny continued to undress. "Baby, it wasn't too long ago that Ondie went after them, remember? Dexter ended up in the hospital. God only knows what would have happened if Ondie would have gotten to Serita."

"Kenny, she's been okay lately."

"But you know as well as I do that it wouldn't take much to set her off again. Lil' Reese reminding her of Maya; that can't be good for anybody."

"Yeah, well, your predinner speech certainly didn't help."

"You're not blamin' me for this, are you? I was just pointin' out what we had to be grateful for."

"You may not have started the fire, but you added some gasoline."

Kenny scoffed and went into the bathroom to take a shower. Ruth picked up the phone to call Ondie. "I just wanted to make sure you were okay."

"I'm all right, Mama. I just know to steer clear from now on."

For Ruth it was a bitter pill to swallow, but until Serita came around it might all be for the best.

# 35

Christmas trees were starting to pop up all over the city. Colorful lights that seemed almost magical gave many people a spring in their steps as they continued the overindulgences that Thanksgiving customarily ushered in. Everywhere you looked you were imbued with the spirit of the season, but there was no such wonderment for Ondie Reid.

Ondie sped into the driveway of Ruth's house and parked right behind Serita's SUV. She jumped out of her car, slammed the door, and hurried inside. She found Ruth and Kenny playing with the baby in the living room.

Ruth turned her attention away from the baby and looked up at her. "Ondie, what is it?"

"Where's Serita?"

"She's upstairs. What's wrong?"

Ondie pulled an official-looking document out of her purse and waved it in front of their faces. "This is what's wrong, Mama!"

Kenny stood up and went to her. "What is that?"

Ondie handed it to him and he shook his head, sighed, and rubbed his face.

"Kenny?"

"It's a restraining order," he said in dismay.

Ruth held on to the baby and stood up as Serita came down the stairs. Ondie turned sharply and charged toward her. Kenny reached out to hold her back.

"Serita, what the hell do you think you're doing?" Kenny yelled.

"I had to protect myself and my baby."

"Are you out of your mind? A restraining order? Do you have any idea what this must look like to the courts to think that I pose a threat to you?"

"You do."

"I don't!"

The uproar caused Reese to cry out. Ruth tried to calm her, but she cried as if reacting to the vibe in the room.

"I don't want you anywhere near my baby," Serita defended.

"Oh, Serita, no," Ruth pleaded. "Hasn't this family been through enough?"

Ondie pulled away from Kenny. "You are unbelievable!"

Reese would not stop crying. Ruth started up the stairs.

"Give her to me," Serita demanded.

"No," Ruth countered. "I'm going to take her and put her down and when I get back we are all going to sit down and talk about this."

Serita scoffed. "I don't have anything to say."

"Then you'll listen!"

Ondie started to the door. "I'm not hanging around for some stupid-ass family conference. I'm outta here."

Kenny blocked her. "Your mother said we need to talk and that's what we're gonna do. Now sit down. You, too, Serita."

Ondie huffed and rolled her eyes, but didn't defy Kenny's directive. Serita anxiously sat on the edge of the sofa. Ten minutes was an eternity as they waited for Ruth to return. The air was thick and suffocating.

Serita wanted to climb out of her skin as Ondie stared daggers at her. She got up, walked over to the fireplace, and leaned on the mantel.

"Why did you do this?" Ondie asked.

Serita didn't answer. She turned when she heard Ruth on the stairs.

"All right, Reese is finally asleep and we're going to hash this out," Ruth said.

Kenny sat up on the sofa and rested his elbows on his thighs. "I just wanna know if Dexter put you up to this."

Serita shook her head.

"Does he even know about it?" Ruth asked.

Serita shot Ondie a side glance. "We talked about it. But it was my idea."

"How could you do this to your sister?"

"Did anybody once ask her how she could have done what she did to me?"

"*She* is still in the room," Ondie protested. "And *she* did what she did because of what you did."

"Maya's death was an accident. How many times am I going to have to say that before you accept it for what it was?"

"I am never going to accept that my baby is gone, do you understand me? What about Dexter, was he an accident, too?"

"You weren't even with him. When the hell are you going to let that go, Ondie? He didn't want you then. He doesn't want you now."

Ruth moved toward Serita.

"No, Mama. Ondie tried to kill us. Despite what Dexter says, I know she pushed him down those stairs on purpose. I know she would have tried to kill me, too. Hell yes, I took out a restraining order. Can you blame me? Ondie will not get the chance to harm my daughter!"

"Serita, stop," Ruth injected. "You know as well as anyone that Ondie was in a lot of pain. She could never have hurt you."

"You weren't there, Mama, just like you weren't there when she grabbed those scissors and came after me when we were kids, and a whole lot of other stuff. I'm sick and tired of everybody excusing Ondie's behavior. When is somebody going to be on my side? What if she'd killed Dexter, or me? Then what would you be saying about how much pain she was in?"

Reese woke up crying.

"Can I go now? I'd like to take my daughter home."

Ruth followed Serita upstairs to help her get the baby's things together. "Serita, have you spoken with Dr. Brunner?"

"What for?"

"Dexter told me that you haven't been sleeping. I know what it's like to feel overwhelmed after giving birth, but you're not alone. You've got me, and your father, and Dexter to help you get through this."

"I'm not crazy, Mama."

"I'm not saying that you are. But I think with everything that's been going on you may be suffering some postpartum depression."

"I'm not depressed. I just don't want Ondie around Reese, that's all."

"Do you remember after the baby shower how you told me you missed your sister?"

"Yeah, well, I guess I made a mistake."

Angrily Ondie paced the floor of Paul's loft as she recounted the details of the court order. "I can't go within a hundred feet of my sister or her baby, can you believe that? After everything she's done to me. I can't even go to my own mother's house if she's there. What kind of shit is that? She's afraid of me. She thinks I'm going to try to take her daughter away from her; of all the nerve."

Paul sat speechless staring at the document in his hand. There wasn't going to be anything he could say to make her feel any better, and he didn't want to make matters worse.

"I'm not going to let her dictate who I can see and where I can go. If I want to go to my mother's house, then I'm going to do it. I don't give a damn about a restraining order. Maybe I should just take one out against her and see how she likes that."

"Ondrea."

"What?"

"You're going to wear a hole in my rug if you don't calm down."

Ondie stopped and sat next to Paul in his overstuffed chair. "What am I going to do?"

"I know you don't want to hear this, but you're going to have to honor the court order, or you may end up in jail."

"You're right, I don't want to hear it. But I'll tell you something, she's not going to get away with this."

"I don't like to hear you talking like this."

"Don't worry, Paul. I'm not going to do anything stupid or illegal. But I'm not going to take this lying down, either."

Dexter drove up to the town house and saw Serita's SUV parked out front. In the past couple of weeks her behavior and her moods were becoming more unpredictable. He wasn't sure what to do, nor was he prepared to deal with any surprises. "C'mon, Dex, man. You can't be afraid to go in your own house." He inhaled and opened the door.

Serita was busy frying pork chops when he entered. *A good sign,* he thought. He wrapped his arms around her waist and kissed and nuzzled her neck. "Hey, baby."

She wiped her hands on a towel and turned to face him. They shared a passionate kiss.

"What was that for?" he asked.

"Can't I be glad to see my husband?"

"Absolutely." He smiled and they kissed again.

Serita squirmed uncomfortably as she felt his nature begin to rise. "Dexter, I'm not ready for that."

"Okay, no problem." He moped into the living room to find Reese awake in her playpen. He picked her up, kissed her, and held her close. He then observed Serita through the portal that separated the dining area from the kitchen. When she looked back at him, he averted his gaze.

Serita came out of the kitchen and sat on the ottoman facing him. "I made an appointment with Dr. Brunner. The medicine she gave me doesn't seem to help much, so I want to see if she can give me something else."

"When do you see her?"

"Tomorrow afternoon."

"Do you want me to take off so I can go with you?"

"No, I can handle it."

"Are you taking Reese to Ruth's?"

"No. I'm taking her with me."

Dexter nodded.

"There's something else you should know," Serita continued. "I took out a restraining order against Ondie."

Dexter's jaws tightened. He couldn't say anything.

"I felt it was the best thing to do under the circumstances. I just didn't want her coming after Reese. Since she still holds me responsible for Maya's death, there's no telling what she might do."

"According to Ruth, Ondie is back on her medication and she's doing a whole lot better."

"She was supposed to be on her meds when she pushed you down the stairs, remember? The fact is we don't know if those meds are really doing her any good, do we? Do you want to take that kind of chance with Reese's life?"

"Don't you think a restraining order is a little extreme?"

"No. I would do anything I had to do to protect Reese. And if you ever doubt what Ondie is capable of, look at that scar on your forehead, or the surgery scar on your chest. Think about how it would be if our daughter had to grow up without you. Remember how you felt when you saw Maya lying in that casket. Think about mourning another dead baby—our dead baby—then tell me I'm overreacting."

# 36

Serita closed her eyes, inhaling and exhaling slowly, as a nurse checked her blood pressure and other vitals and documented her chart. There was no denying that she'd been listless and irritable, and the look she caught in Dexter's eyes of late let her know she needed to get herself together. His attempts at intimacy were met with resistance. When he tried to hold her in bed at night she found herself pulling away; T-shirts and pajama bottoms weren't the only thing that separated them.

"Okay, sorry to have kept you waiting," Dr. Brunner said as she breezed in. "I checked on Reese and she looks great. You're doing a good job."

"I don't feel like I am."

Dr. Brunner's brow furrowed and she put her hands into the pockets of her lab jacket. "What are you feeling?"

"Honestly? Tired. Useless. Pathetic."

"The Paxil isn't working?"

"Not really."

"Okay, let me get a look at you."

Serita lay back on the table while Dr. Brunner slipped on a pair of latex gloves to examine her.

"Are you in any pain or discomfort?"

"I'm just not sleeping very much."

"Well, I can give you something a little stronger, but I'm also going to recommend you talk to someone."

"I don't need to talk to anybody. I just need a couple of good nights' sleep and I'll be fine."

"Serita, it's obvious that you're having a problem, and that's nothing to be ashamed of. Lots of new mothers go through some of the same things you're going through."

Serita teared up. "I don't want to be like this. I can't lose control."

"It's all right," Dr. Brunner assured her. "It's not a sign of weakness for you to ask for help."

Ondie tried not to think about what Serita had done. She rationalized that if the situation was reversed, she could easily have done the same thing. With Christmas Eve approaching, she decided for the family's sake, and despite the order, that she would try and talk to her sister.

She slowed down as she drove up the street where Serita and Dexter lived. Dexter's Jeep was gone, but she could see that Serita was there. At the last minute she lost her nerve and circled the block. Would Serita really have her arrested? Neither Paul nor Dr. Mathis thought it was a good idea. They both encouraged her to stay away from Serita, believing that the whole thing would blow over in time, but Ondie was impatient.

Not giving any thought to how it must look, she rounded the block for the third time before finally stopping. She could see Serita peeping out through the vertical blinds at the window. Inexplicably her heart raced. She sat and let the car idle. Just as she was about to turn off the ignition her phone rang and spooked her. It was Paul.

"Hello."

"Ondrea, are you all right?"

"Yeah, I'm fine."

"Are we still on for dinner tonight?"

"Of course."

"Cool. I'll see you around eight."

"I'll be ready."

Ondie exhaled and discarded her plan to talk to Serita. She pulled back out onto the street and headed home to prepare dinner for Paul.

"She was here," Serita said. She was looking out of the window when Dexter walked into the room.

"Who?"

"Ondie, she was sitting outside the house about an hour ago."

"Is that all?"

"Is that all? Dexter, she's not supposed to come within a hundred feet of me or the baby. She was violating the restraining order."

"Serita, calm down."

"Don't tell me to calm down. She had no reason to be here unless she came to cause trouble."

"Okay, I'll go over to her house and I'll talk to her."

"No, promise me you'll stay away from her."

"Serita."

"Promise me."

Dexter sighed. "All right."

"She won't be back. I called the police. It's the only way she's going to take this seriously."

The doorbell rang just as Ondie and Paul were about to sit down to dinner. Ondie looked out and saw a policeman at her door and another standing in her driveway. "Can I help you?"

"Ondrea Reid?"

"Yes, that's me."

"Ma'am, are you aware that there is a restraining order against you to keep away from Serita Campbell and her baby?"

"Yes, I am."

"We had a complaint that you were seen in Mrs. Campbell's neighborhood earlier this evening. You wanna explain that?"

Paul stepped up behind Ondie and cut into the conversation. "When was Ms. Reid alleged to be in Mrs. Campbell's neighborhood?"

The beefy Nordic-looking officer gave Paul the once-over. "Who are you?"

"My name is Paul St. James." He whipped out his wallet to offer proof. "Ms. Reid and I are seeing each other. I'm also an attorney."

The officer looked at his notes. "Mrs. Campbell states that she saw Ms. Reid outside her house around six o'clock."

"That's not possible," Paul interjected. "I've been with Ms. Reid since five."

"Is that true, ma'am?"

Ondie shifted her eyes between Paul and the officer. "Yes. I was nowhere near my sister's house at six o'clock."

"Apparently Mrs. Campbell was mistaken," Paul snapped. "Now, if there's nothing else, Ms. Reid and I were just about to have dinner."

The officer hesitated a few seconds longer and then apologized for bothering them. Ondic watched him return to his partner and they looked back at her and exchanged words before getting into their cruiser and driving off.

"Why did you lie for me?" she asked, closing the door. "If he wanted to, he could probably find out that you weren't here at five. All he has to do is check your office."

"I worked from home today. Why did you go to your sister's house?"

"Because I thought I could talk some sense into her. I just want to put all this behind me and move on with my life."

Paul shook his head. "Well, you see the results of your actions, don't you?"

"Yeah, I should have listened to you."

Paul pulled Ondie into him and kissed her forehead. "I can't imagine what this must be doing to you or your family, but it's going to be all right."

"There is no way you can guarantee that, no matter how many times you say it."

# 37

If there was any good to come out of all this it would be that Ondie and Paul were growing closer. Memories of how she once felt about Dexter were just that—memories. She looked forward to what the new year held for her and Paul; perhaps love would not be out of the question after all.

She'd been shopping all day in order to buy something festive for an evening on the town. Paul was taking her to the Sambuca Jazz Café, and somewhere in the back of her mind she had thoughts that tonight just might be the night that their relationship would go to another level.

Paul found it surprising that as an Atlanta native she'd never gone to a premiere spot like Sambuca's, but there were a great many things that she'd yet to experience.

It was just after five on Saturday evening. In order to affect a mood while she dressed, she put a Wynton Marsalis CD on the stereo, turned the lights down low, and lit a couple of fragrant iridescent oil candle lamps.

She then slid into her garden tub and let the warm water of lavender and vanilla wash her cares away.

Several minutes into her soaking she was surprised by a loud pounding at the door. She sat up in the tub and listened thinking that whoever it was would go away, but the pounding continued. Could it be Paul? Had she miscalculated the amount of time she had to get ready?

Ondie got out of the tub and toweled off. She then grabbed her robe and slid her feet into her slippers. One glance through the sheers and she knew that it wasn't Paul.

"Open the door. I know you're in there. I saw your car in the garage."

Ondie hesitated wondering why Serita was there. "What do you want?"

"You know damn well what I want. Open the door!"

Despite a feeling of foreboding, Ondie opened the door. Serita entered so forcefully it caused Ondie to stumble backward and lose a slipper.

"Where is she?"

"Who?"

"Don't act like you don't know. Where's Reese?"

"How the hell should I know? I haven't seen Reese since we were last at Mama's house."

"You're lying!"

"I don't have a reason to lie. If she's not with you maybe she's with your husband."

Serita was not being put off. She tore through the house screaming the baby's name.

Ondie chased after her and snatched her arm to

stop her tirade. "What the hell is the matter with you? She's not here!"

Serita shoved Ondie and she tumbled into a table and knocked over one of the oil lamps. Ondie recovered and chased Serita to the back of the house. The oil from the candle flowed into a stack of magazines and they caught fire.

"Serita, what is wrong with you?"

"You took my baby and I want her back!"

"Are you insane?"

"No, sister, you already got that covered!"

As Serita started into Ondie's bedroom Ondie took hold of her again, but without the proper footing Serita was able to shake her loose. Meanwhile the oil spilled onto an area rug underneath the table. The errant flames increased and quickly burned through the rug, igniting an electric cord that ran to a lamp.

"If you don't get out of here right now I'm calling the police."

"Call them! Then you can tell them what you did to my baby."

"Damn it, for the last time—"

They were interrupted by the piercing shrill of the smoke detector. Ondie darted out into the hallway to see the flames running havoc over the carpet and on the sofa, shooting up toward the ceiling. The room filled with thick pungent smoke and the heat beat them back and blocked any possible escape.

"Oh my God! We gotta get out of here."

Ondie dashed back into her bedroom and dialed 911. She then threw open the window and pushed out the screen.

"We gotta save Reese!" Serita said.

"I told you, Reese isn't here!" Ondie grabbed a pair of jeans and a sweatshirt from a chair in the corner of the room and pulled them on. She then picked up her cell phone and stuffed it into her pocket.

Serita stood dazed and confused. Ondie shook her. "Look, I don't know what the hell is going on with you, but you better climb out this window right now or I'm going to leave you in here!"

Serita registered no response.

"Damn it, are you listening to me?" Ondie climbed up in the window. "Are you coming or not?"

Serita snapped to and climbed onto a chair and out the window. Neighbors gathered along the street to gawk as fire engines roared up to the house and immediately went to work.

In the midst of other houses that twinkled with holiday cheer, the horrifying blaze was surreal. Ondie cried helplessly looking at the devastation.

The fire was knocked down within minutes, but the long-term damage would not be so easily forgotten. Thankfully it was limited to the living room and a confined area of the dining room. Insurance would restore much of the house, but precious keepsakes would be lost forever.

Paul called to let Ondie know that he was on his way and she tearfully told him what had happened. She then called Ruth and Kenny.

Paramedics checked them out and arson investigators poked around. Paul sped up the street and had to stop halfway because of the emergency vehicles and local television news crews. He jumped out of his car and ran to Ondie. "What happened?"

Ondie shook her head and looked at Serita, who was leaning on her SUV in the driveway.

"What's she doing here?"

"I don't know. It's crazy. There were candles burning and I was taking a bath, and then this—this nightmare."

Paul took off his suit jacket and wrapped her in it.

"Ondie!"

She and Paul turned to see Ruth and Kenny running up the sidewalk pushing through the crowd.

Kenny pulled Ondie into his broad chest. "Are you all right?"

"No," she sobbed.

Ruth spotted Serita shivering in the driveway and instinctively knew that this catastrophe had something to do with her being there. "Serita?"

"I thought she had Reese."

"Why would you think that?"

"I was asleep and when I woke up she was gone—I panicked."

"So you thought your sister took her?"

"Yes, what else was I supposed to think? She's been stalking us for days."

"Have you spoken to Dexter?"

"I was disoriented. I couldn't think."

Ruth took her phone from her purse and called Dexter. She was disturbed by what he had to say. A chill ran through her.

"Ruth, what is it?" Kenny asked.

"Serita said she came here because she thought

Ondie had Reese. I just talked to Dexter. He doesn't have her, either. He doesn't know where she is."

Ruth's call put Dexter on alert. He and Serita lived in Smyrna, not very far away from Ondie's Marietta home. He was there within fifteen minutes. After he identified himself to police, they let him through.

A lump formed in his throat when he looked at what remained of the house. He didn't know quite what to make of it all. Why was Serita there? And the even bigger question, where was Reese?

"Serita?"

She grabbed him and held on tightly, but he wanted answers and pushed her away.

"Where's the baby?"

"I thought she was here."

Dexter was perplexed. He looked at Ruth and Kenny and then to Ondie as if they had the answers. He then grasped both sides of Serita's face. "Where is Reese?"

"I don't know. I don't know."

"What the hell do you mean, you don't know?"

Kenny tried to pull him off her.

"Get off me, man! My baby girl is missing. She's only a month old. She didn't fuckin' get up and walk away!"

Serita wrung her hands. "I took a couple of pills and I fell asleep. When I woke up she was gone."

Ruth closed her eyes and clutched her chest, afraid to give voice to what she thought had taken place.

The commotion drew the attention of a police officer and he walked over to where they gathered on the lawn. The same officer had come to Ondie's door a few days earlier.

He went over the details of Serita's statement and

reintroduced the restraining order against Ondie. Paul was quick to point out that Ondie did not go to Serita—Serita came to her. Again Ondie denied having anything to do with Reese's disappearance and she was becoming unnerved by the unspoken indictment she felt was on everyone's lips.

"Like I've already told you, I got up this morning. I went to get my hair done, and then I went to the mall. When I left the mall I came home and took a bath."

"Is there anyone that can substantiate that?"

"You can call the stylist at my mother's salon. I was there until two o'clock."

"What about the mall?"

"This is ridiculous. I don't know who saw me there. You can talk to the people at Macy's. I could show you my charge card receipt if you want, that is if it hasn't been burnt up. Look around, Officer, I'm the victim. My house is ruined."

"Did you go to your sister's house today?"

"No, damn it! I was nowhere near Serita's house." Ondie looked into Kenny's and Ruth's faces and then to Dexter and Paul. "You believe me, don't you, Paul?"

"Officer, it's pretty clear that there's no baby here. And Ms. Reid has been devastated by this tragedy. It's late and it's cold, and unless you have evidence to the contrary, there is no reason to treat her as if she's guilty of something."

"I didn't realize you were a defense attorney, Mr. St. James."

"I didn't realize one was required."

The officer smirked and turned his attention to

Serita. "Mrs. Campbell, are you sure you don't know what happened to your baby?"

"You think I did something to her, don't you? Well, I didn't!"

"Serita, calm down," Kenny injected. "Nobody is pointing a finger at you."

"But it's okay to accuse me?" Ondie snapped.

"That's not what I'm sayin', Ondie."

"Then what are you saying, Daddy? Reese is gone and I'm the only one who had a reason to hurt her?"

"Ondie, don't get yourself worked up," Ruth cautioned.

"Don't get worked up?" Ondie screamed. "My house is gone! And you all are standing here looking at me like I did something wrong!"

Serita charged Ondie. "You killed her to get back at me, didn't you? Didn't you?"

"Get away from me!"

Dexter and Kenny subdued Serita and she passed out.

The officer wasn't sure what to believe, but he knew it was going to take some doing to get it all sorted out, and there didn't seem to be enough proof to charge anyone with a crime.

As Serita was being carted off to the hospital, he called in a report. There was no time to waste if there was any hope of uncovering the truth. The officer and his partner headed to the Smyrna town house with Dexter in tow. It was after ten o'clock as they canvassed the neighborhood. The house next door to them stood empty, another of the neighbors had been at work earlier that day, while one who lived directly across the street was out of town. There didn't seem to be any clues offered in the town house, either. A break-in was quickly ruled out and nothing appeared out of place. A one-month-old baby was out there somewhere. If no one had her, then they would have to conclude that she was dead.

It took over two hours for the arson squad to complete their investigation. They located the source of the fire and officially ruled that the candle oil was the principal accelerant. It was after midnight before Ondie was escorted back into the house to sift through ashes and check for anything that might be salvageable. The living room was a complete loss. The interior of the house was singed with soot, and the sickening smell of burnt rubber and wires filled their nostrils. Ondie's sensory recall shook her to the core and reminded her of all the times she feared a fire that wasn't there; now it was all too real.

Fatigued and realizing that there wasn't much she would accomplish at that hour, she decided to wait until daylight and come back. Before leaving for the hospital, Ruth insisted that Ondie go to her house. To keep Paul from having to drive back into Midtown, she invited him, too.

A neighbor helped Paul board up the gaping hole that used to be the front window of the house, and his wife offered them hot coffee. Once they secured the rest of it as best they could, Ondie and Paul thanked them and went on to Ruth's.

As a new day dawned, they all knew more than anything else that this was not going to be a very merry Christmas for any of them.

# 38

Ondie awoke after only an hour of restless sleep. Paul lay next to her snoring softly, undisturbed. She eased out of bed, slipped into her jeans, and tiptoed quietly down the stairs. She was enveloped by the comfort of her mother's home, but unquestionably shaken and saddened as well.

The smell of coffee brewing from the kitchen almost made things right again, but nothing was as it should be. Ondie found Ruth sitting in the darkness of the living room illuminated by the glow of the television.

"Mama?"

Ruth turned to Ondie, her countenance filled with sorrow. It was apparent that she hadn't been to bed at all. Ondie sat next to her on the sofa, held her hand, and laid her head on her shoulder.

"I didn't hear you and Daddy come in."

"We got back from the hospital about three. Where's Paul?"

"Out like a light. Mama, you look so tired. You should try to get some sleep."

"I can't. I was watching the news hoping to hear anything that would help us find Reese." Ruth's voice was husky with exhaustion and strain.

"There's still no word?"

"Nothing."

"What about Serita?"

"She was hysterical and incoherent when we got her to the hospital. They had to sedate her. Ondie, I want you to know that I never thought for one second that you did anything to that baby."

Ondie rose from Ruth's shoulder. "I know, Mama."

"No, I really need to say this and you need to hear it. I know that you've had your problems, and God knows that you and Serita haven't been close lately—"

"That's an understatement."

Ruth grimaced.

"Sorry."

"You fought hard to keep your illness from affecting Maya. In my heart I know that you could never have hurt her any more than you would have hurt Reese."

Tears streamed down Ondie's face. Ruth wiped them away.

"I didn't see it," Ruth admitted. "I thought your sister had been spared this nightmare, but being postpartum had to trigger something in her that none of us knew was there."

"Do you think Serita . . ."

"I don't know," Ruth cried. "I've been praying that she couldn't have done something this awful, but I just don't know. Somehow I always thought that she was the strong one. Now I realize that I failed her just as much as I have you."

"No, Mama, don't say that. You didn't fail. You did the best you could. You couldn't save us any more than you could have saved your mother. We have to learn to save ourselves."

Dexter's head bobbed and he jerked awake. He rubbed the crust of sleep and tears from his eyes, yawned, and stood up to stretch. He sluggishly moved to the window and watched the sun coming up, promising a new day with no intention of delivering him from the misery of the previous one.

He turned to see that Serita still hadn't stirred. She looked so tranquil. He felt conflicted, angry, and culpable. Why hadn't he seen what had been right in front of his face? He'd witnessed it before with Ondie. Practically every day after Maya was born he was concerned for her safety. Bumper used to tell him that he needed to man up and take custody of Maya before Ondie did something to her. Fate was cruel; Ondie was not the one to fear. Still, he didn't want to let his heart believe what the police suspected.

Dexter's eyes filled with tears. He reflected to another time when he had had to make tough decisions regarding his future. Ondie was pregnant and they were a month away from being married, but whether divine intervention or not, he walked away. He thought about his father's scathing caveat when he told him that he and Serita were married, and it made him weak. *"What is it with you and these Reid girls? They stuff can't be that good. I'm tellin' you, boy, you gon' rue the day you got mixed up with that family. Didn't you have sense enough to learn your lesson dealin' with Ondie?"*

Dexter twisted the gold band on his finger and thought about his vows; *in sickness and health.* He was sure that he couldn't walk through the darkness with Ondie; was he man enough to honor his pledge to Serita *till death*?

# 39

"Hey, it's Serita. I'm not available. You know what to do when you hear the beep."

"Girl, where are you? It's Tonja. This is probably the tenth message I've left. You need to call me back. I'm not kidding."

The tall slender woman hung up the phone and combed her fingers through her shoulder-length dreadlocks. She sighed in disgust and flipped on the television news, and the shocking report of the fire at Ondie's house the night before caught her off guard. She sat in stunned silence and listened.

"Good morning, it's Monday, December twenty-fourth. We begin with the developing story of a fire that occurred last night at this Cobb County residence. Channel Two has just learned that although the fire is being called an accident, it appears to have begun over a fight between two sisters concerning this missing one-month-old baby girl. It is not known where the child is at this time, but Smyrna and Cobb County police are working with the GBI and a Levi's Call has been initiated. Anyone with information concerning the whereabouts of this missing baby girl is asked to call the numbers you see here on your screen. If you have any . . ."

"Oh, shit!"

Tonja flipped off the television and picked up her telephone.

"Hey, it's Serita. I'm not available. You—"

"Damn it!"

The woman paced frantically, wiping her clammy hands on her jeans while scanning the numbers in her cell phone. "Dexter, it's Tonja."

Serita's closed eyes twitched rapidly as the events that had led to her altercation with Ondie spooled through her subconscious.

"I'm so tired. I just need to lie down for a couple of minutes."

Just as Serita had closed her eyes Reese cried out. "No," Serita moaned. "What now?" She dragged herself out of bed and languidly walked over to the crib. She stared down at the tiny creature, beet red from exertion. "Reese, what is it? I've fed you, and changed you, what else do you want?"

Serita threw back her head. "Will you please shut up!" The baby's protest continued. Serita then leaned into the crib and picked her up. Reese's body shook as her cries intensified. Serita held her to her breast and rocked her. "Shhhhhh! It's all right. Mommy's here. I didn't mean to yell at you. Please, just stop crying."

Serita sat down on the bed and opened her shirt,

but Reese refused. "I don't know what you want. I wish Dexter was here. He'd know what to do."

Just as she was about to call Ruth, the doorbell rang. Serita held on to Reese and made her way downstairs.

"Tonja."

"What in the world? I could hear Reese screaming all the way to the street."

"I don't know what to do. I'm exhausted. I just want to lie down, but Reese won't stop crying."

Tonja closed the door and removed her jacket and gloves. "Let me see her."

Serita passed the baby to her friend and she soon settled down.

"Aw, you're a good girl for Auntie Tonja, aren't you?"

"How did you do that?"

"I don't know. I guess I got the touch."

Serita fell on the sofa. "Can you teach me? I'm a horrible mother."

"No, you're not. But you look like shit. I came by to see if you wanted to get out for breakfast."

"I can't. I just really want to sleep, that's all."

"Okay, tell you what. I'm not scheduled to fly today or tomorrow. Why don't I take Reese off your hands for a little while? That way you can get a few hours of sleep, and when you get up you can come and get her."

"You would do that for me?"

"Of course. But I expect full babysitting service when I have mine. And you better have bought me one hell of a Christmas present." The woman laughed. Serita was simply relieved. "Come on; let's get some of her things together."

After Tonja left the town house with Reese, Serita

went back upstairs to bed. Not remembering that she'd already taken one of the prescribed pills to help her sleep, she took two more.

Serita gasped and her eyes sprang open to find Ruth sitting at her bedside. "Mama!"

"Are you all right?"

She grabbed Ruth's hand. "I remember. I know what happened to Reese."

"I know, baby. Dexter called me. He went over to Tonja's to pick her up."

Tears instantly filled Serita's eyes. "How could I forget my baby? How could I do something like this?"

"Everything's going to be all right, Serita. Just lie back."

"No, I want to see Dexter. I want to see Reese."

"Dexter will be back soon enough. You just calm yourself and rest."

"What kind of mother am I?"

Ruth shook her head and pressed her fingertips to her eyes to hold back the tears that lined her lids.

Once they heard about what had happened with Reese, and believing the worst, Bumper and Vivian wasted no time making the trek back to Atlanta. With Dexter on the verge of mental and physical collapse, Vivian insisted that he rest before returning to the hospital to deal with Serita.

Bumper could see that his son was in a great deal of pain and was amazingly sympathetic. When Dexter was ready, it was he who volunteered to drive him back to the hospital while Vivian stayed at the town house and kept an eye on Reese.

Both Ruth and Kenny sat vigil at Serita's bedside as they waited for news of their granddaughter. Ruth was wired on caffeine, having only had a short nap herself. When Dexter arrived they were waiting outside the hospital room. Kenny was not too pleased to see Bumper, and the feeling was mutual.

"Dexter, how's Reese?"

"She's okay, Ruth. My mom is watching her."

"Thank God. I'm so glad this is over."

Dexter shook his head. "No, it's not over."

"What do you mean by that?" Kenny asked.

"Serita needs help. I think we all can agree on that. I can't let her near Reese until she gets it."

Ruth covered her mouth with her hands.

Kenny piped up. "You can't keep that baby away from that girl. It would kill her."

"Kenny, we just spent the last several hours thinkin' that Reese might be dead. This time we got lucky. What about the next time?"

"There's not gonna be a next time."

"You can't guarantee it, and I won't take that chance."

Tears filled Ruth's eyes. "What are you saying?"

"I think she needs some kind of treatment before she can come home."

"No," Ruth sighed.

"Are you talkin' about lockin' her up?" Kenny yelled. He was past enraged at this point.

"If that's what it takes."

"You son of a bitch!"

Bumper leaped at Kenny and attempted to swing on him. Dexter intervened and pulled him back.

"Dad, I can handle this."

"I ain't gonna stand here and let this sorry-ass nigga' talk to you any kind of way."

"I'm gon' speak my mind," Kenny objected.

"It don't matter what you think. Dexter is the girl's husband. It's his decision how things should be."

"You need to stay out of this, Campbell!"

"I'm all the way in it. This affects my family just as much as it does yours."

"Dexter, please don't do this," Ruth pleaded.

"Ruth, I don't see any other way. Serita has got to talk to somebody."

"But she would die if you took Reese away from her."

"I'm not takin' Reese away. I just want my wife to get help. You can understand that, can't you?"

"I'm not gonna let you do this to my baby girl," Kenny balked.

"Let me? Kenny, you don't have a say in this, not this time. Serita is my wife and I need to do what's best for my family!"

Dexter pushed through them and went in to see Serita. All Ruth could think about was her mother and father and the day her mother went away and never came back.

Serita's big brown eyes lit up when Dexter entered. Ruth, Kenny, and Bumper filed in behind him.

"Did you find her?" Serita asked.

Dexter nodded.

"Are you mad at me? I didn't mean to do it. I just forgot and got mixed up. I—I took way too many of those damn pills, and I wasn't thinking straight."

Dexter pulled a chair up to Serita's bed and took her hand. His eye's misted. "You know I love you, right?"

"Yes."

"I want what's best for you and Reese."

"I know that, baby. And when I get home I promise that I'm going to be the best wife and mother you've ever seen."

Dexter choked. "Serita."

The door to the room flew open and a ruddy, lanky man, with a British accent, dressed in scrubs and a lab coat, hustled in. "Hello, everyone. I'm Dr. Morse, staff psychiatrist. And you must be Serita?"

"Psychiatrist? Dexter, what's going on?"

"You're her husband?"

"Yes."

The doctor shook Dexter's hand. "We spoke on the phone."

"These are Serita's parents, Ruth and Kenny Reid. And this is my father."

"Nice to meet you all. Now, Mr. Campbell, as we discussed, I'm just here primarily for a psych consult and to evaluate your wife and offer a diagnosis as to what the course of treatment should be. I brought these forms for you to sign."

Serita tensed up. "What?"

Dexter took the pen and clipboard and stared at them. Tears ran down his cheeks and splashed on the paper. He inhaled and quickly signed.

"After I spoke with you I tried to reach Dr. Brunner," Dr. Morse said, "but her answering service said that she was out of town for the holiday. I left a message for her to call me back. But while I'm waiting to speak to her in regard to your wife's medical history, we'll have a nice little chat. Perhaps we can get to the root of the problem."

"Dexter?"

Unable to speak, Dexter leaned in and kissed Serita on the forehead. He then turned and rushed out of the room. Bumper followed.

"Dexter!" Serita tried to get out of the bed and go after him, but the doctor held on to her. A nurse entered to offer assistance.

"Mama, what's going on?"

Ruth pulled Serita into an embrace and sobbed. "It's going to be all right."

"No, I wanna go home. I wanna see my baby! Daddy!"

"That's enough of this shit," Kenny shouted. "I'm takin' my baby outta here."

Kenny took hold of Serita and Dr. Morse reached out to block him.

"Mr. Reid, I understand that you're upset, but there is a lot more at stake here than you realize."

"You don't know a damn thing about it!"

"I talked to your son-in-law, and I've spoken to the police. I also consulted briefly with my colleague, Lewis Mathis. Mr. Campbell told me that your eldest daughter is a patient of his. Now, I know you don't want to have to deal with this, today of all days, but the sooner we try, the better off everyone will be."

"Why can't she just come home with us until after Christmas?" Kenny cried.

"Mr. Reid, this is Mr. Campbell's decision."

Kenny flushed with rage. He charged out of the room to find Dexter. He didn't have to look far. Dexter was down the hall in the waiting area.

"You asshole!" Kenny yelled, scaring away the few other people that were there. He yanked Dexter by the scruff of his neck and slammed him into the wall. "I told you what I would do to you if you hurt Serita."

Dexter kneed Kenny in the stomach. He released Dexter, doubled over, and fell to the floor. Bumper walked in with two cups of coffee just as Kenny pulled himself up into a chair.

He sat coughing and crying. "How can you do this? She's my little girl."

Serita's gut-wrenching appeal to go home could be heard up the corridor as Ruth opened the door to leave. She fell back against the wall overcome with despair. Kenny found her there, and together they consoled each other and then left the hospital.

Bumper tried to give Dexter the coffee, but he was too upset to take it. Bumper set both cups down on a table and put his arm around his son. "I know none of this can be easy for you. You've had some hard choices to make, but you stood up and you did it. I'm proud of you, son."

Dexter buried his face in Bumper's chest and wept.

# 40

Ondie folded her cell phone shut, slowly sat on the edge of her bed, and pulled off her work gloves.

Paul bounded into the room. "I sifted through the rubble and found a few more pictures, but I don't think you'll want them, they're pretty much destroyed." He tossed the pictures aside and knelt down in front of her. "Ondrea, are you all right?"

"That was Mama on the phone; they found Reese."

"Is she . . ."

"No. She was with a friend of Serita's."

"That's great news, right? Why do you look so sad?"

"They're keeping Serita in the hospital for a psych evaluation."

"Well, under the circumstances isn't that for the best?"

"Mama thinks that Serita may have this disorder."

Paul got off his haunches and sat next to Ondie. "Do you want to go see her?"

Ondie shook her head. "I don't know what good it would do." She stood up and went to her closet. "Most everything smells like smoke. It's all going to need to be cleaned. I should be grateful that the fire didn't spread back here."

"We'll take care of it."

She turned toward the bureau and picked up the jar of sand, held it close to her, and closed her eyes.

"What are you doing?"

"Wishing I was anywhere else but here right now."

Paul went to her and put his arms around her waist. "Someday you will be."

It was a silent night, but not all was calm. Dexter perched on a chair in the waiting room with his elbows on his knees and his face buried in his hands.

"Dexter."

He looked up and saw Ondie standing in front of him and dried his tears. "I didn't expect to see you here."

"I wasn't sure I wanted to come. I just looked in on Serita. She was asleep and I didn't want to disturb her."

Dexter exhaled slowly and sat back, but didn't make cyc contact with Ondie. "I was praying. Can you believe it? I haven't done that for a very long time. When I was growing up I did that a lot; went to church and everything. You know Vivian; she wasn't gonna have it any other way in her house."

"Do you think He heard you?"

"Who?"

"God."

"Who knows?"

Ondie sat in a chair next to him and reluctantly reached out and touched his hand. He glanced at her and she pulled back.

"We've gone through a lot this year," she said.

He scoffed. "We've gone through hell."

"I never told you that I was sorry for what I did to you."

"You didn't do anything to me, remember? I tripped and fell."

Ondie smirked and pulled at her ear. Dexter took her hand.

"Believe it or not, Ondie, I care a lot about you. I hope one day you will find the happiness that you deserve."

"I hope the same for you, too; and for my sister and the baby."

He laughed. "You know what all this has taught me?"

"You mean other than the fact that you married the wrong sister?"

Dexter looked at her and shook his head.

"I was teasing. It was a bad joke. Sorry."

"No, I've learned that karma's a bitch!"

# 41

"You look good. Dare I say happy?"

"Things have gotten a lot better. The renovations at the house are complete and I'm in a really good place for once."

"I like the sound of that."

"Me, too. I got up this morning and looked in the mirror and she wasn't there."

"She?"

"The beast that I couldn't control."

"How do you feel about that?"

"It's strange and it's wonderful at the same time. It took long enough, don't you think?"

Dr. Mathis stroked his beard and smiled. "It takes as long as it takes."

"You have been there with me practically every step of the way; through college, losing Dexter, having Maya and losing Maya, and finding my way out of all of it."

"You did all the hard work."

"I don't think I could have done it without you."

Ondie pressed her fingertips against the bridge of her nose. "It's been a long winter, but seasons change."

"Speaking of change, how is your relationship with your sister these days?"

"It's never going to be what it was. Although, looking back, I doubt if it was ever what it should have been. I haven't seen her since she was in the hospital. I just didn't know what I'd say to her."

"Has she tried to contact you?"

Ondie shook her head. "No. And I'm okay with that for now. I just want to put some distance between me and all this ugliness, and I guess she and Dexter are doing the same thing."

"How does that make you feel? Dexter and Serita, I mean?"

"I don't think it makes me feel one way or another. Whatever I felt for Dexter died with Maya." She got up from the chair and went to the window. There it was, the same pandemonium and inexhaustible construction delays she'd seen from this very spot for what seemed the millionth time. "I'll miss you, Doctor, but I will not miss this."

"When you get back, I want a full report."

"Absolutely. Who else am I going to talk to?"

The warm clear turquoise waters of the Caribbean washed up against the coral that stretched along miles of beach blanketed with silky soft white powdered sand. It was the off-season in Negril. Gardens filled with tropical coconut palms, fruit trees, and an assortment of blooming flowers and orchids attracted more than butterflies and hummingbirds.

Ondie lounged seductively shaded by a wide-brimmed straw hat. Her two-piece white bikini accentuated her bronzed skin that glistened under the sultry rays of the welcoming island sun.

"For you, madame."

She lifted the brim of the hat and pulled off her sunglasses. Paul towered over her. His muscular torso and thighs were enough to make Michelangelo's *David* take note. He stooped down beside her and handed her a tall pineapple drink in a bamboo-styled container. "Don't worry, its nonalcoholic."

"I wasn't worried." She smiled.

"To infinite tomorrows."

They toasted and drank. Paul then took her drink and set them aside.

"What are you doing?"

"Give me a moment."

He removed the chain around his neck and put it around hers. "Fe mi heart and soul is fe you."

Ondie's eyes misted. "I don't guess I need you to interpret that, do I?"

They embraced and kissed. She abruptly pulled away.

"What is it?"

"I've got something I need to do."

She reached inside her bag and extracted the glass jar that held the sand he'd brought to her a thousand miseries ago.

"What are you going to do with that?"

"You'll see."

Ondie took off her hat, got up, and ran out to the shoreline. She stood and reflected on the past year and everything she'd been through, and all she'd lost. But this paradise far away from the shackles of her previous existence represented a whole new beginning. She twisted the lid off the jar and dumped the sand back onto the shore from whence it came. "To mi fucha, and let go of di darkness."